STORM

Justice

Pamela Cowan

Running Horse

125 S 1st Avenue #401
Hillsboro, Or 97123
503-810-1817

In partnership with Windtree Press

Windtree
Press

818 SW 3rd Avenue, #221-2218
Portland, OR 97204-2405
855-649-0821

DEDICATION

This book is dedicated to those who have worked with victims and/or offenders and have seen too much, heard too much and know too much.

ACKNOWLEDGMENTS

I would like to thank my husband and best friend, Jim, for being the amazing person he is. I'd also like to thank Jeanne, who counts being locked in the trunk of a car and driven down a bumpy road as only one of the fun experiences that comes with being the daughter of a thriller writer.

Also, I would like to thank the members of the Northwest Independent Writers Association, especially Tonya Macalino and Brad Wheeler, who, by keeping the bar high, force me to do my best; the Klamath Writers Guild; Becoming Fiction and all my other writer friends. Through all of our shared experiences—you are my tribe.

Finally, for their technical assistance and words of wisdom (those that are not so wise are mine and mine alone), I want to thank Sheriff's Deputy Jason Leinenbach, Washington County, OR Sheriff's Office; Probation Officer Sheila Clark-White, Washington County, OR Probation & Parole; and Administrative Specialist Araceli Sandoval, Health & Human Services, Washington County, Oregon as well as my long-suffering editors: Charla Billick, Jacqueline Hopkins-Walton, Annie Long and of course, the amazingly kind and brilliant Cathy Speight. I am in your debt.

CHAPTER ONE

IT WAS DARK, just the other side of two a.m., as they drove down Evergreen and turned into the industrial complex. Howard had his keys out and ready before Storm had a chance to back the dark-green Honda into the slot nearest the doors marked Traynor Chemical.

The keys clattered in Howard's hand, making Storm wonder if he was nervous. She didn't like him being nervous—didn't like having a partner at all—but she had little choice. Storm had the determination and strategy, but Howard had the upper-body strength.

Storm watched Howard get out of the car, open the back door, and reach in to remove a gym bag. The dome light gave her erratic glimpses of him: short brown hair, starched gray collar, the back of a large, red-knuckled hand. After he slammed the door, Howard moved quickly toward the building.

Storm climbed out of the car, shut the door softly, and stretched her back. The street light cast a spidery shadow of her tall figure across the asphalt.

It wasn't as dark as she would have liked, but it was quiet. The only sounds were the occasional car going by on the other side of a sheltering row of evergreens, the shrill peeping of tree frogs, and the steady hum of the lights.

Howard returned and opened the trunk, releasing a whiff of oil once spilled on the trunk liner, and the stronger stench of sweat.

Mr. Everett was awake and beginning to struggle. It wouldn't do him any good. Storm had zip-tied his wrists in front of him and wound duct tape from his wrists to his elbows. She'd stuffed a wad of paper towels in his mouth and pulled a pillowcase over his head, winding tape around it so he couldn't talk or see. If he tried to make a sound, he'd start to swallow the paper towels and then he'd vomit—and then he'd die.

Grabbing Mr. Everett's shirt, Howard half lifted, half dragged him out of the trunk.

"Let's grab all your crap, why don't we," Howard said. He reached back into the trunk and took out a bag, similar to the one he'd already carried into the building, and swung its strap over the man's shoulder. "There we go," Howard said encouragingly.

Storm shut the trunk and, taking one of the man's upper arms, helped lead him into the building. He staggered, his shoes scuffing the sidewalk.

Sometimes it felt like she was supporting all his weight, then he'd shift, and she'd only feel the light touch of her hand on his arm. He tried to get away once by backing up, dragging Storm along for a second, and knocking her purse from her shoulder until Howard overpowered him. Storm him not to try it again and poked him in the ribs with the point of her knife. A good inch of the tip went in. He jerked away, making a squawking sound. Storm wiped the tip on his white shirt and held her purse away from the slowly widening blood stain.

There were four rules: no weapons, no trophies, no connections, no bodies. If they followed the four rules, they might be caught, but they'd never be convicted.

They took Mr. Everett into the building and down the long hall to the kill room. The room's designer had never meant for that to be its function; in fact, just the opposite. The room, an oversized shower to be used in case of a chemical spill or splash, was supposed to save people from harm. The irony was lost on Howard but not on Storm. She stepped into the room anyway.

The rectangular room was about eight feet wide by sixteen feet long, with two doorless entries opposite each other at the near end. Along each long wall, a row of five shower nozzles jutted out of the smooth concrete surface. Each was connected to a flexible hose which could be removed to focus the water. At the far end of the room, an ADA-compliant handrail was bolted into the concrete. In the ceiling, a maze of pipes carried water and other liquids in, out, and through the building.

Storm watched as Howard reached into the pocket of his windbreaker and pulled out a dog collar, one of those nasty looking pinch collars she'd occasionally seen worn by pit bulls or Dobermans. He slipped the collar over Mr.

Everett's head and around his neck. Next, he snapped on a heavy leather leash he had taken from his gym bag.

Everyday objects—items that wouldn't look out of place lying on the seat of a car—were the tools Storm thought they should use. Even her 'knife' was only a letter opener.

Howard tossed the leash over a pipe in the ceiling and pulled. The chain slipped through the metal circle on the collar and tightened around Mr. Everett's neck, bringing him to his toes. While Mr. Everett squealed ineffectually through his gag, Howard walked to the opposite end of the shower room to a built-in cabinet. From it, he extracted two plastic-wrapped sets of overalls, complete with booties and gloves.

He tossed a set to Storm. She caught them and kept going, taking the pack and her purse out of the room and into a back hallway to keep them out of harm's way.

She poked a finger into the plastic wrapping and tore it away, then donned the protective gear. When she stepped back into the room, she found Howard similarly dressed. He reached to unwind the duct tape so that he could remove the floral pillowcase over Mr. Everett's head. He ripped the tape away and stepped aside as their prisoner, gagging and coughing, spit out a wad of paper towels.

Storm waited, pulling nervously at the cuffs of her sleeves, until the coughing fit was over. When Mr. Everett made eye contact, she spoke his name softly.

She knew speaking in a near whisper would force him to be quiet and concentrate to hear her. Not that she was worried about noise—the building was soundproof. The desire for his silence and attention was about teaching him respect for others, a lesson Mr. Everett sorely needed to learn, though it was a little too late in coming.

Storm finally allowed her carefully controlled outrage to rise to the surface, making her hands shake just as much as Howard's had earlier. She hissed at him from between clenched teeth. "You have been found guilty of unforgiveable crimes. You have been judged and you have been condemned. You have nothing to say that anyone wants to hear, and you are now going to die in a way that befits your crimes."

"I know you," said Mr. Gavin Lester Everett. "I know you. You're . . ."

Storm waited for it. For the sudden realization as he registered her features and remembered. Ensuring that they saw her so that later they would recognize her was an additional difficulty. It required planning, changes to her schedule, and added a level of complexity that wasn't necessary—but it was so worthwhile.

He didn't disappoint. His eyes widened, his jaw dropped, and he said, "You were in the office with . . . you're a . . . you bitch. What do you think you're doing? I'll—"

"You will do nothing. On the other hand . . ." Storm nodded, giving the go-ahead. Howard's eagerness was disturbing, but also comforting. This wouldn't take long. Once again, Storm marveled at how very ordinary Howard seemed. He was tall and broad-shouldered, but other than that he was nondescript; he had brown hair, brown eyes, average looks, an average car, and an average job. Only when he began to work did one see the deeper person, the dangerous stranger with a hunger for hurting.

He used a box knife to cut off Mr. Everett's pants. He'd already carefully cut away his shirt with none of that violent, shirt-tearing, button-popping, sloppy bullshit seen on television. When he'd finished, Howard stood back to admire his work. Mr. Everett, his arms still duct-taped, stretched tall, eyes wide, now wore nothing except a pair of green boxers, gray socks, and black shoes. Storm thought he looked as defenseless and scared as a man could.

She reached into her purse and removed a small, battery-powered curling iron. It was handy for trips or even at the office—perfect for 'a quick pick-up when the humidity made your curls droop,' or so said the advertising. She only cared about the part that said it got hot instantly.

"There were thirty-seven cigarette burns on your son," she said. "We would be happy to use a cigarette on you, but it would be a mistake to introduce an open flame in a building where chemicals are kept. The sprinkler system is very sensitive, so Howard tells me. We've had to be a bit creative." Storm flicked the curling iron on. "Have you ever felt a burn? Have you ever wondered what thirty-seven of them would feel like?" she asked.

"You wouldn't dare. I'll have you arrested. I'll tell everyone what you did."

"You won't be telling anyone anything. The only thing you will be—"

"Storm, are you talking to someone?" asked Howard.

She looked at him and shook her head. "Of course not." They never spoke to the garbage. It wasn't a rule, more a suggestion, like in that pirate movie with Johnny Depp, but it was a good one. She touched the metal curling rod with her forefinger. "Ouch. You'd better take this," she said, giving it to Howard handle first.

"Thank you," he said, and he turned to Mr. Everett with a brilliant smile.

The first burn was on Mr. Everett's neck. *You'd think he was a little baby the way he's shrieking,* thought Storm. Why, the iron wasn't even fully hot and only left a red mark, much like a hickey. The second and third burns were on his collar bones. The left one was pink, the one on the right more of a burgundy shade. Mr. Everett didn't yell quite as much with those, but he did struggle to move away and ended up choking.

Howard waited for him to recover and settle down before dragging the iron down the middle of his chest, again more teasing than cruel. The next two burns though, were pretty fierce. Even Storm sucked in a little air and bit her lips as Mr. Everett's nipples blistered and turned black. After that, there were little touches here and there—such small burns Howard refused to count them toward the planned thirty-seven.

"It's his own fault if he won't stand still," Howard growled. Storm could tell by the rough snarl of his voice and the way his eyes had narrowed that he was growing annoyed with Mr. Everett's constant twisting and turning.

She could tell Howard was beyond annoyed and downright angry when he jerked Mr. Everett's boxers down, grabbed his scrotum and pulled it aside to thrust the hot iron into the space between his balls and his leg, holding it there. When Howard jerked it away, sweat and tears ran down Mr. Everett's face, and urine dribbled down his legs.

"He was bad," Mr. Everett sobbed. "He didn't listen."

"He was five when they took him away the first time," Storm said. "How bad can a five-year-old be? But you got him back, didn't you? You got him back two more times, and each time he was bad, very, very bad."

Mr. Everett screamed, shouted, but Storm was no longer listening. She held the picture of Mr. Everett's son in her head, and the image had its own beat, a thrumming sound that drowned out any noise.

Thirty-seven burns take a long time to accomplish. By the time he was done, Howard was using his sleeve to wipe sweat from his forehead, and Mr. Everett was hanging half-conscious from his chain-link noose.

Storm turned off the iron and laid it on the concrete to cool. It gave off a smell like old barbecue.

Storm turned on the cold-water faucet closest to Mr. Everett, took the handheld shower nozzle, and directed the stream at him. He sputtered, jerked back, and rose on his toes, breathing hard and crying. She washed the tears and snot off his face.

He tried to spread his legs so that the cool water would soothe the burns between them and on his scrotum and penis. Howard laughed at how he jumped around following the water, so easily directed—a marionette whose strings were a release from pain. Storm let him have several minutes of this, moving the water from burn to burn, letting him feel the pain ease.

"I'm sorry," Mr. Everett blubbered. "Sorry I done that to Andy. Got fucked up sometimes, drugs and shit, wasn't really me."

"I'm sure your son was sorry, too," said Storm. "Did that stop you?"

Howard had gone to the hallway to retrieve something from his bag. As he returned he raised his hand to show them a homemade whip made from several strands of clothesline. Braided along its length were heavy metal nuts and washers whose edges he'd sanded thin as a blade.

Storm said, "Give me a minute," and hurried to the far end of the room, out of the splatter zone. This was how Howard took his pay. She knew it was beyond the punishment she would have inflicted, but she needed Howard, and he needed this. To alleviate her guilt, to punish herself, Storm stood witness to every moment of brutality.

The whip came down on Mr. Everett's red and quivering flesh. Each slash of the whip sent droplets of blood spray against the walls. He danced in his confined circle, exposing his back, his front, then his sides. Blood ran in rivulets from the gashes. Howard moved from legs to buttocks to torso. He left the head and face for last, knowing that once he gave in to the impulse to erase that face, it would be over very quickly.

He didn't wait long.

Half an hour later, one of Mr. Everett's eyes had been whipped into a mush that dripped from a half-empty socket. His upper lip was torn in half, exposing broken teeth. His bottom lip was a swollen lump covered in blood and saliva, and still he persisted in living. He didn't move much, just the occasional twitch and groan, but it was frustrating, infuriating.

Finally, becoming more worried about the passing of

time than how messy she might get, Storm decided to step in. She took the whip from Howard's tired hands, brought it around Mr. Everett's ankles and jerked his feet out from under him. He dangled, his breath cut off, his face going from red to blotchy to bluish gray until finally he stopped moving. She held his legs up a few moments longer to be sure.

Panting, Howard leaned against the handrail, his hard-on evident. "What do you say, huh beautiful?" he asked, looking down at himself and giving her a thin smile.

Storm shook her head. "I told you before. I'm married, and even if I weren't, I would still never get involved with you. Do what you need to do, but leave me out of it. I'm going to get the cart. And hurry up. We've spent too much time here already."

Howard nodded and reached in the pocket of his coveralls for a fresh pair of gloves.

The torture and killing necessary for Howard's sexual release was knowledge Storm thought might be useful for controlling him. Losing even a shred of her control over him at any point would have been very dangerous. He was a stone-cold killer, a real sociopath. What if he decided he no longer wanted a partner? Well, at the worst, he would torture her slowly to death. A fate she'd observed him deliver twice. At best, he would end their relationship. She had to avoid that as well. The truth was, she needed him. He was a means to an end, a path to justice.

Storm went through the back door of the shower into the hall. The lights, on at half power to save energy, made everything dim and conveyed a sense of peace, even sleepiness. She stepped into a women's restroom, using her elbow to switch on the light. There was a row of stalls and a counter with three sinks and soap dispensers. A pretty silk orchid, a bottle of lily-scented lotion, and a box of Kleenex were arranged in one corner. The ordinariness, the pretty little touches, bothered her in a way she couldn't explain.

Stepping up to the counter, she stared at her reflection in the mirror. The harsh white light highlighted the streaks of auburn in her dark-brown hair, made her olive skin seem sallow, and cast deep shadows around her brown eyes.

She didn't see any blood but took a tissue, and dabbed her face, and then carefully slid it over her hair, still pinned into a tight chignon. She checked the tissue and found it spotless, except for a small amount of beige residue from her makeup. She dropped the tissue into the first stall toilet and flushed it away.

Taking her time, in no hurry to interrupt Howard, she walked to the copy center and took one of the cars used for hauling out recycling.

By the time she returned, Howard was lowering Mr. Everett to the floor. With no further conversation, Storm helped him load everything into the cart: Mr. Everett, his clothes, the whip, and the curling iron. Howard took the cash from Mr. Everett's wallet and tossed the wallet on the pile. After one final look around, Howard pushed the cart out of the room and down the back hallway, his destination the incinerator in the room at the end.

The building was leased to a company that manufactured acids used in the creation of computer chips. By-products were destroyed in a special incinerator called a thermal oxidizer. The oxidizer was basically a series of large barrels, the first big enough to hold two men if they hunched a bit.

The first barrel used intense heat to incinerate anything placed inside it and then fans pulled the gases formed through various passageways and filters, finally releasing supposedly harmless water vapor into the atmosphere.

This was usually done at night so that the billowing clouds of white smoke didn't bother anyone, particularly those pesky, environmentally conscious anyones.

As soon as Howard left with the loaded cart, Storm took a bottle of cleaning solution from a storage cabinet. Using the blast of the shower hoses and scrubbing at the worst of the stains with a small towel, she was done in no time.

Carefully, she removed her overalls and booties and rolled them up around the towel. Howard returned, shoving the now-empty cart under a shower head. After he washed down the cart, he dried it with a towel from his pack. Removing his outer garments and adding them to hers, he picked up the bundle.

With Storm pushing the cart they headed back down the hall.

After returning the cart, they went on to the incinerator room. Howard had placed Mr. Everett's body, curled in a fetal position, inside the oxidizer. Their tools had been thrown in with him. Howard stepped forward and placed the rest on top of the pile and then stripped off his gloves and added them. "I get it all?" he asked, taking a slow look around the room.

Storm pulled off her gloves and stooped to place them into the incinerator. "I think you did," she told him. "I don't think we forgot anything."

"Cool."

She stood up straight and took a step back. Howard gave her a smile as he slammed the heavy metal door, turned a dial, held down a button, and flipped a switch. With a throaty hum, the incinerator came to life.

This, for Storm, was the worst part. She had to leave not knowing whether the incinerator had done its job. There was no glass to allow her to see inside, and she couldn't open the machine again until it had cooled off—far too long to hang around. Storm simply had to take it on faith that it was functioning correctly. Faith. That was something she didn't have in great supply.

"Let's check the floors on our way out," she said.

"Of course," said Howard. "How come you always have to remind me of everything?"

"Just trying to be careful," she said.

"Yeah, I guess, huh?" They stopped at the door to the shower room. It looked damp, but would be dry by morning. The smell of disinfectant was strong, but it always was, and using the familiar cleaner wouldn't raise any alarms.

Storm sighed audibly. It was over. If someone were to enter the building unexpectedly and catch them there, they'd sheepishly apologize and confess they were using the building for a romantic liaison. Embarrassing, but not life in prison, or worse.

They walked out to the car. The quiet, the relative darkness, and the cool air made the night feel strange, the way it sometimes did after going to a movie on a sunny afternoon and leaving in the dark.

Only Howard's car was in the parking lot. The cars going by on the road were infrequent and ghostlike, a whir of sound, a splash of light, and then gone.

Howard reached into the backseat and removed the leather belt he'd left there. As he settled the belt, with its night stick, flashlight, and bundle of keys around his narrow hips, light played across the silver badge pinned to his shirt.

It read Traynor Chemical and beneath that: Security.

CHAPTER
TWO

HER HEADLIGHTS SWEPT across the house as she pulled into the driveway and parked in front of the garage door. To her right, she could see the bone-white vinyl fence bordering her front lawn and the roses that clung to it. The light and shadows made the last of the season's dark-red blossoms look like bloated clots of blood. She shook off the gloomy image, knowing it was simply her mood, the aftermath of the killing, and that it would soon pass.

One of her rules was that she didn't take trophies, but she found she wanted to remember the men they'd killed. It was a way of paying respect. She didn't think the two men they'd dealt with deserved to live, but she didn't think they deserved to die unremembered. Taking a moment, she recited their names and a little something to help remember their crimes. "Jeffrey Franklin Malino, dogs. Gavin Lester Everett, burns." There, now she would never forget them.

She left the windows open and switched off the engine. The smell of roses was heavy in the air. Closing her eyes she focused on the scent, allowing her body to relax as her mind filled with the concept of being home with nothing ahead but dinner and spending time with her family. No more blood or bones. No more screams. As the soft night breeze washed against her flushed cheeks, she felt herself sink into the warm leather seat. She felt the throb of her pulse slow and the knotted tension in her forehead ease. She had survived, would continue to survive and fulfill the promises she'd made.

The cooling engine made a ticking sound. Tick. Tick. Tick. It made her think of clocks and time, and suddenly, she was no longer drifting; she was right there, right in the here and now. And in that now, she was a busy, married, working mom with a very long to-do list.

And one of the things on the list was dealing with Tom, her husband. No doubt he'd be angry with her again. He hated it when she was late, and that night she was later than usual. *No, don't think about that yet*, she told herself. *Relax, smell the roses, and feel the wind*. How nice it would have been to let everything float away on the breeze. Forget Tom's anger, Howard's lust, the past, the present, all of it.

"I'm home," she announced. After dropping her bag on the table in the entry, she moved through the living room and into the kitchen.

Dressed in jeans, red tennis shoes, and her favorite Seattle Seahawks T-shirt, Storm's daughter, Lindsey, was still young enough at seven to think that a parent's arrival was exciting. She leapt from her chair at the table, where she'd been coloring, to give her mom a hug and download a day's worth of information.

"Mom, guess what? My teacher said we're going to have a substitute next week because she's going away to have a baby, and the new teacher has a bearded dragon lizard and she's bringing it to class. And guess what else? Grandma called and maybe she's coming to visit but not until winter but that's not long, right? And guess what else?"

"Hold on, Sugar Pop. Where's your dad?"

"He's in giving Joel a bath. We had pahster, and he got sauce all over his hair and everything. It was sooo gross. How come you call me Sugar Pop?"

"Pasta," Storm corrected automatically, amused by the passion and energy of her eldest and by the question about her nickname, a story she'd told at least a dozen times. "I call you Sugar Pop because, when I was going to have you, all I wanted to eat was Sugar Pop cereal. Sugar Pops for breakfast. Sugar Pops for lunch."

"Sugar Pops for dinner," they both chimed in.

"So that's why you are my Sugar Pop," explained Storm.

"But my name is really Lindsey, right, Mom?"

"Yep. Lindsey Sugar Pop Mackenzie."

Joel skidded through the kitchen, his father in stocking feet, stomping close behind.

"I'm the towel monster and I'm going to get you," her husband, Tom, yelled.

Joel dashed past his mother and sister, headed for the living room and the usual confrontation on the couch, where the towel monster would finish drying his hair, and then stuff him into his pajama tops. It was a nightly routine, and mom and daughter ignored it, turning their attention to a school assignment that required the deft use of coloring crayons.

After a few moments, victim and monster returned to the kitchen. "Hello, wife," said Tom.

Storm saw Tom was still in his office clothes and must have cooked in them. Pasta stains dotted the front of his shirt, and water from Joel's bath had plastered the rest to his slightly tubby stomach. His shaggy blond hair was in disarray, and a light sheen of sweat across his forehead spoke of his need to hit the gym a bit more often. Well, she hadn't fallen in love with his body; she fell for his sense of humor and the way it was reflected in his twinkling green eyes.

"Hello, hubby," she replied. "I see you've cleverly cornered the child again. Smiling, she reached down to smooth a lock of damp hair out of Joel's eyes. He hugged her leg by way of greeting and climbed into the chair next to his sister to see what she was doing.

"Yeah, it was tough," Tom said. "Kid's getting too fast for the old man. They're both getting too big. Guess we should stop feeding them."

Storm smiled. "Ah yes, food. I assume you guys have had dinner already." It was a statement, not a question. Her eyes swept across the piles of dirty dishes and pots and pans covering every surface.

"Saved you some in the microwave. Figured you'd be home late. What's this . . . the second time this week and it's only Wednesday?"

Storm threw him a stern look, and he nodded, his lips turning up in a phony smile. He had promised not to argue in front of the children. Sometimes she had to remind him of that. Usually, a look was all it took. His expression said fine, but they'd discuss it later.

She loved her family. Her kids were great. She was still crazy about her husband, but she hated always having to explain where she'd been and with whom. Coming up with excuses to explain the time spent staking out her targets was proving more and more difficult. She'd have to give it some thought. Maybe invent some sort of club that she'd like to attend and he'd never venture near—maybe a woman's book club or something to do with knitting. She smiled softly.

Absently, she took her daughter's ponytail out of the elastic band, ran her fingers through the fine strands of blond hair, the color identical to Tom's, and redid it so that it was centered correctly. "I'll tidy up the kitchen and heat up the dinner you made. It smells great."

"Do you mind if I catch some TV?"

"Of course not." Her thoughts moved on to important issues such as what she'd prepare for the kids' lunches, where she'd put that permission slip for Lindsey's field trip, and how she would find her next target.

Storm rinsed the last of the soapy dishes, wiped down the counter tops, prepared a crustless PB&J sandwich, half a banana, three Nilla Wafers, and a carton of juice for

Lindsey's lunch. She found, signed, and slid the field-trip permission slip into Lindsey's backpack, which she hung on its hook by the front door. She laid out clothes for both kids, remembering at the last minute that she had promised to take a change of clothes for Joel to his day care. She read *Damien and the Dragon Kite* to Joel and made sure he was asleep before checking on Lindsey, whom she caught reading under her covers. It was just her average weekday evening.

After a final look around to be sure everything was in place and ready for the next day, she rewarded herself. She heated the plastic-wrapped plate of spaghetti Tom left for her in the microwave, poured a glass of wine, and settled down to enjoy a late dinner.

Tom entered the kitchen. The television in the family room was still playing in the background; the sounds of screeching tires and sirens were a clue that he'd been watching one of his cop dramas. "Finally getting something to eat? You must be starving." He stood behind her and gently rubbed her shoulders. "Rough day?"

She sighed, sat up straighter, enjoying the feel of his fingers digging into muscles she hadn't realized were tense. "Yeah. These late trainings are going to kill me. But we can't have all the staff gone during work hours, you know?"

"I know. I don't mean to give you a bad time about it. We miss you is all—me and the kids. Maybe we should go away somewhere. Have you all to ourselves."

"That sounds great," she enthused, though inside she cringed, knowing she'd already taken most of her vacation days in the pursuit of her most recent target. Maybe she could arrange some unpaid leave or pretend she was ill and take some of her sick time.

Tom's hands left her shoulders, sliding down her arms and up again. His fingers slipped to her neck, softly moving across the tender skin. He took the comb from her hair, and it fell loose around her shoulders. "Why don't you hurry up with that," he said, with a catch in his voice.

Storm took one last bite of spaghetti, emptied the glass of red wine, and leaned back into the luxury of his hands moving across her skin. She felt his strong fingers slip through her hair, gently pulling on the strands. A welcome chill slid down her back.

"Let me up," she said hoarsely. He stepped back, to pull out her chair. She stood, half-turned, and he kissed her, his body moving into hers so she could feel his need. She moaned against him, wanting him just as much. He took her hand and led her down the hall toward the front of the house and their bedroom. When they stepped into the room, he switched on the light. She turned it back off.

"Honey," he said.

"No." It was an old argument, which she never lost. The light stayed off.

They moved toward the bed, and as soon as she felt it against the back of her knees, she let herself fall, soft and boneless, onto the comforter. Unable to see her, his hands fumbled and then found her narrow hips and slid to the zipper in front of her slacks. He unzipped her pants and pulled her shirt loose, unbuttoning it from bottom to top.

"Stormy, Stormy," he whispered, using the pet name only he was allowed to use, his voice soft as a caress. He continued undressing her until she lay naked, vulnerable, waiting, and then removed his own clothes.

Kneeling between her legs, he leaned forward and kissed the inside of her left knee. His tongue flicked out to trace circles across the soft skin of her thigh. He licked unhurriedly, moving up her leg. She gasped, tense and waiting, but he teased her, moving to kiss her right knee and working his way slowly up that leg. Finally, he kissed her mound, nuzzled her, and slid his hands upward until they reached her breasts. He curled his fingers around them and squeezed.

Storm panted and rolled her hips toward him. His thumbs found her rock-hard nipples, rubbed across them just as he wrapped his tongue around her sensitive and tingling center, bringing a spasm of pleasure. She reached down and dug her fingers in his hair, pulling his warm mouth tightly against her.

He let go of her breasts and moved his hands to her legs, pushing them farther apart. His tongue traced circles and flicked against her. Her hips jerked forward as the surge broke, and the waves of an unexpected orgasm forced an exhalation and a strange broken noise from her throat.

From that place, she descended reluctantly. Her breathing slowed. The momentary respite from her thoughts, fears, and needs ending far too quickly.

Unwanted images flashed through her mind. Once again, she saw the face of Mr. Everett, recalled the sound of Howard's dreadful whip as it sliced through the air and met flesh. Had it been just a few hours ago? She shuddered and tried to push the thoughts away.

Tom helped. His warm hands slid up her stomach; his mouth followed, leaving a trail of kisses, and his teeth nipped at her skin lightly, almost, but not quite hurting. When his hands found her breasts, her nipples were hard again, her body impatient and hungry for more.

"I want you," she moaned, unnecessarily. Scooting back, she slid her hands across his arms and tugged him toward her. Climbing onto the bed, he placed his knees between her legs. His arms held the majority of his weight as he lowered himself onto her. She rocked her hips, reaching for him. He responded to her invitation and slid hard and fast into her tight wet warmth.

"God, you feel good," he said, his voice ragged. He took her wrists and pinned them above her head, then rolled over, taking her with him, never losing the connection between them. Pulling her wrists free of his hands, she sat up, astride him, and began to move, grinding her hips, taking him in as deeply as she could. Her hands were splayed across his chest. His hands clutched her waist and moved to her thighs.

He rose to meet her, twisting, and then thrusting hard, hesitating for one long moment, and then repeating the movement. Their rhythm grew faster and faster, their breathing shallow and quick. His strong fingers dug into her skin, and she felt it: that breathless place, that quiet waiting moment. She threw back her head, squeezed her eyes shut and let the sensations overwhelm every thought.

As the tension in her body grew, she tightened around his shaft. He groaned but kept up the rhythm she craved. Sweat slid down her back, slicked her thighs, and still she went on. She took shallow panting breaths. Then her breathing stopped altogether. Her entire being focused on the physical sensation. The pulsing orgasm came from her toes, drew from her fingers, rushed to the center of her being, and she fell. That was what it was like: a sudden, devastating, crashing free-fall.

Tom groaned again and dug his fingers into her thighs as he pulled her down, harder and harder, until he came deep inside her.

He breathed out slowly and unclenched his fingers. She would have bruises. Storm didn't mind. There was a wide grin on his face as he slid his hands up to surround her waist to pull her down on top of him. She jerked back as if stung, rolled off and away from him to the edge of the bed. "Baby, baby, I'm sorry," he said. "I didn't mean to."

"It's okay," she told him. "It's fine." But it wasn't fine. Sometimes sex made her emotional, blunted her anger, and tore away her defenses. Stinging hot tears gathered behind her eyes. After a moment, her silent choking sobs shook the bed. He wrapped the sheet around her and then his arms, making certain he didn't touch the scars.

It was a long time before he knew about the scars. At first he'd thought she was simply shy or possibly frigid. What a mistake that was. She was anything but frigid, as long as he didn't touch or see her scars. She had allowed him to look once.

"I want you to be sure you know what you're getting," she told him. It was the day he asked her to marry him. They'd taken a long weekend and rented a vacation house in Rockaway Beach on Oregon's north coast. He was surprised she'd accepted his invitation.

During the first twelve months of dating, he'd never managed to get past second base. He was hoping for sex when she agreed to go away with him but rented a two-bedroom, just in case he'd misread the signals. If he had and she intended to keep him waiting until marriage—if that was what she wanted—well . . . that's how it would be.

He'd surprised her over dinner with a special lobster—a ring garishly tied to one claw. She laughed until she cried, but refused to give him an answer.

That night, she came out of the bathroom, her hair still wet from the shower, wrapped in the robe she'd bought for the occasion. She turned, dropping the robe. His eyes had followed its descent from her shoulders to the floor, where it formed a puddle of red Chinese silk at her feet. His eyes traveled upward from her slim ankles to her rounded calves, her firm thighs and buttocks and—the shock of it.

He was relieved she had turned away, hadn't seen the look of repugnance that must have crossed his face, nor the morbid interest that had kept him from looking away.

Across most of her back was a tracery of raised flesh that was too white, surrounded by gouges of flesh that were too pink. The border of this tangle of tortured flesh was an uneven and unnatural series of blocks. The edge of skin grafts, he realized, that had been applied to replace the flesh burned from her back. The scars extended from buttocks to shoulder blades and across the back of her right arm, nearly to her wrist.

She bent down, gathered the robe around herself, held it closed with one hand, and turned to face him, a tentative smile on her lips. The bravery in that smile took whatever he had kept of his heart. He begged her to marry him.

She said, 'Yes.'

A decade later, Storm put her head against Tom's shoulder and let the tears, and the images, come. She thought about earlier in the day, about Mr. Everett, but it wasn't his pain or the brutality of his end that filled her eyes with tears. It was the picture of his son. She had stared at that boy's photograph until it burned into her memory as deeply as any of the scars in her flesh.

There had been nothing uncommon about that face. He had freckles, untidy brown hair, and ears a little too big for his head. It was his smile and his eyes that had drawn her. His dark eyes so filled with the anticipation of pain that they made a mockery of the small, hopeful smile he wore.

Taking a deep breath, Storm rolled forward and kissed Tom's chest. "Look what you do to me," she whispered in his ear. "Do you make all the women cry?"

"Always," he told her. "Unfortunately, I also tend to make them run away. Better?" he asked.

"Better. I think I'll get a shower."

"You sure? I believe there might be a round two," he said, a smile in his voice.

"Now you're just bragging. We'll see how you feel when I get back."

"You sure you don't want to 'feel' how I feel right now?"

Despite the dark, Storm knew Tom was waggling his eyebrows.

"Animal. I also have to go shut off the television before it wakes up the kids."

"Oops."

"Yeah. Oops. Now behave until I get back." Storm pulled on her old, white, terry-cloth robe and padded barefoot down the hall to the family room, the flickering television lighting her way. On her return, as she headed for her shower, she was greeted by the sonorous sound of Tom's snores. She would have loved to wake him up and tease him about round two, but she was a mess, untidy, emotional, and exhausted.

Better get some sleep. Tomorrow is a new day, a fresh start, another chance to fix all the things wrong with the world.

CHAPTER
THREE

THOUGH STORM WOKE with a slight headache and puffy eyes, she was well rested and deeply calm. Sometimes a good cry was not such a bad thing, or maybe it was the sex. With a wry smile, she reached over and shut off the alarm, giving Tom a little more precious sleep. She slipped out of bed without waking him and quietly made her way to the bathroom.

Early morning was Storm's favorite time of day. She loved getting up at five a.m. while everything was still peaceful and perfect. She followed the same routine every day: a splash of cold water on her face; pull her hair back into a ponytail; dress in black spandex shorts, a long-sleeved T-shirt covered by a short-sleeved T-shirt, her newest pair of Nike cross trainers, and head out to the street. If it was raining, she would pull on a hat, slipping her ponytail through the hole above the band.

Only on rare snowy days, when the sidewalks were covered in dangerously slippery ice, did she miss her run. There was never enough rain, no matter how torrential the downpour, to keep her inside.

History taught her that there was something she needed from her morning run, something that fed her soul and made it possible for her to face another day with unruffled calm. At five, street lights still sent wide ovals of light across the sidewalks, porch lights cast their own weak yellow light across lawns, and sometimes a security light would sense motion and snap a harsh white spotlight on as she passed by.

That morning, her path took her from light to dark and back again, sidewalks sparkling as if imbedded with tiny diamonds, shadows holding mysterious shapes. She heard dogs barking in the distance, the lonely sound of a train. She smelled wood smoke and the wonderful scent of flowers that was probably someone's scented dryer sheets.

As she ran, she could hear her own breathing, feel the burn in her thighs and calves, the tiny ache in her lower back and the smooth looseness of her muscles and joints working, propelling her forward. Her thoughts, dark memories, ugly deeds—they were always there. But when she ran, she left them far behind in the dark, just more mysterious shapes not worth exploring.

She thought about the day ahead. As soon as she got back she'd make sure Tom was up, bully and beg the kids to get up, get dressed, eat breakfast, finish their fruit and juice, and brush their teeth.

Tom, not much of a morning person, would probably sip his coffee and stare at his family with a bleary-eyed look of total incomprehension. His normally cheerful disposition would kick in around the time he got up to pour his second cup. By the time the kids were gathering their bags, there was usually a good deal of silliness as the three climbed into Tom's car. Sometimes, Tom would still be in his pajamas, a cup of coffee in his hand, his sockless feet shoved into an old pair of Adidas sneakers he kept by the front door.

Storm thought about how lucky she was Tom worked from home. The task of delivering the kids to their schools and other activities had fallen to him.

On school days, she would watch from the window as he strapped the kids into their seats before taking them to their respective daycare and elementary schools. When they waved goodbye, a wave of fear would hit, a sense of foreboding that she was seeing them for the last time. She would smile through the fear and wave harder, not willing to share her myriad of silly worries, determined that fear would not be a legacy she would pass on.

Panting, her feet flying across the pavement, Storm thought of her need for control. As soon as the car carrying her family was out of sight, that need would overcome her, and she would prepare for the day in her own carefully orchestrated way.

First, she would visit her closet. Tom had his own on the other side of the room. Hers was a small walk-in, its contents carefully segregated, with home and work clothes on different walls.

She had exactly ten work outfits, long-sleeved, button-front shirts in a multitude of solid colors, which she paired with black slacks. Her work shoes were black with square toes and chunky stacked heels that took her from a tall five eight to a very tall five ten.

After selecting a blouse and a pair of pants, she would choose a bra and panties, a silky camisole, and a pair of knee-high nylon socks, carrying everything to the bathroom. After locking the door, she would shower, fix her hair and makeup, and dress.

Usually, she wore her hair up for work, twisted into a neat chignon, held in place with a tortoiseshell comb that complimented her reddish highlights.

She always rubbed scented lotion into her skin and wore a floral-scented deodorant but didn't wear perfume, which gave her a headache.

Instead of foundation, she dusted her face with tinted mineral powder and swept on a bronzer and some peach blush. She would apply two tones of earth brown on her eyelids and draw espresso-brown liner across the top and bottom lashes, not bothering with mascara, as her lashes were dark and long enough to suit her. She would wear berry-scented lip gloss, reapplying it several times a day. Her look was professional but not girly, neat but not obsessive.

Dirty laundry would be placed in the hamper and the damp towel hung to dry. She would make sure everything was in place and tidy before returning to the master bedroom.

She owned ten silver necklaces, some beaded and

some with small pendants. All could be worn with either one of the three pairs of earrings she owned: one set of small hoops, one medium, one set of posts with a quarter carat inset diamond.

Sometimes she wore a tennis bracelet with matched sapphires. She depended on her cell phone to tell her the the time.

Because there were no special meetings scheduled for the day, she would select a simple silver chain and the medium hoop earrings. Finally, she'd slip into one of her five pairs of work shoes.

Standing in front of the full-length mirror, she'd hold up a hand-mirror and make certain the blouse she wore was not too sheer, that the camisole hid any sign of the mottled flesh on her back, that the cuffs of her blouse were buttoned at her wrists.

For twenty years, since the accident when she was thirteen, Storm had tried to conceal her scars. For the most part, she had been successful.

CHAPTER
FOUR

THURSDAY MORNING, Storm settled into work with the anticipation of meeting more than the usual number of clients. New policies had been implemented requiring additional 'face time' with her clients, while at the same time, budget cuts had resulted in larger caseloads. There wasn't a thing she could do about it but try to wade through as many meetings as she could in the eight hours, that followed, nine if she skipped lunch.

She pulled all the files for the clients with whom she'd scheduled appointments that day. Each of the files was divided into several sections containing: court orders, general conditions of probation, a list of fines and fees, presentencing investigation notes and chronos—a narrative written each time there was an interaction with a client—an action plan, police reports, criminal history, and copies of the client's pay stubs.

After scanning the files to familiarize herself with them, Storm sat back waiting for the phone to ring. She didn't have to wait long. At 8:05 a.m., the receptionist called to tell her that her first appointment had arrived.

Taking a sip of the latte she allowed herself on mornings she expected to be difficult, she headed down the hallway. After five years of walking that hall, she didn't really notice the rose-pink carpet or the beige walls hung with ugly examples of modern art.

She opened the door into the reception area, taking in the scuffed white walls, blue vinyl chairs and corkboards filled with posters for recovery centers and anonymous addiction meetings and said, "Eldon Shatterly?" Three men turned to look at her. One, a chubby blond who looked about seventeen, stood up.

Giving him a thin smile and a nod, she said, "Hi, I'm Storm McKenzie, your probation officer. Would you follow me, please?"

Her first appointment of the day suffered from having been in the wrong place at the wrong time. Eldon, who had no other offenses, not even a parking ticket, had accepted a ride from two almost-strangers he'd met during his first semester of college.

"They wanted to stop and buy some beer at Murphy's, you know, one of those stores at gas stations," Eldon explained. "I was about to get out and start walking. They were acting weird, laughing about nothing, really. I figured they must be stoned, but it was raining like anything, and I had a tear in my backpack and didn't want my books to get wet. Anyway, they were in the store a long time, and I heard some big bangs, two of them, and they ran out and jumped in the car, and we took off real fast. I don't even think they remembered I was there. There were these cop cars and lights coming out of everywhere. The car slid sideways into a ditch, and they jumped out and ran, but I just stayed there."

Storm looked down at the open file on her desk. "And after that, the police pulled you out of the car, and you learned that your friends had robbed the store and shot at the clerk?"

"Yeah, but they weren't really my friends. Plus, they didn't shoot the guy, just sort of at him, so—"

"So you didn't get charged with accessory to murder. You were lucky."

"I guess," said Eldon, his tone conveying he believed the opposite.

Storm sighed. He probably had a point. Luck—good or bad—was, like most things, a matter of perspective. "Well, it looks like you've been meeting the requirements of your probation. Your fines and fees are paid on time, and you've complied with everything the court ordered. I expect I'll be able to close your file in two months."

"Okay," said Eldon, with nothing in his voice or manner to indicate he was happy about that, either. Storm wondered if he realized how often she had to extend probation periods for clients, who, for one reason or other, didn't fulfill their court-ordered sanctions or got behind with their fees. Maybe having a client who didn't know the probation system all that well was a good thing. Maybe this would really be the one and only time he'd be involved with it. She hoped so.

"Let me walk you back to the lobby," she said. Traversing the same corridor, she said goodbye to Eldon and ushered in her next client.

The morning went much the same way until a little before noon, when one of Storm's coworkers, Nicky, stood in the doorway and said, "Want to do lunch?"

"Sure. My last client didn't show, so I can even go now if you want."

"Cool. Let's go get sushi."

"Works for me." Storm grabbed her raincoat and purse.

The probation department was on the third floor of the courthouse. There were twenty-four probation officers and four main teams, or units, that dealt with drug and property offenders, sex offenders, domestic violence, or parole and mental health. Storm was on the drug and property team, so most of her clients had been charged with using, manufacturing, or selling drugs, or with property crimes such as burglary, theft, arson, vandalism or shoplifting.

Nicky was new to both the job and the team, so Storm had been elected to show her around. From there, a sort of mentoring relationship had formed that was now moving toward a real friendship.

"So, what's Jackson done now?" Storm asked as they stepped quickly down the back courthouse steps. The sky was gray with storm clouds, and a light mist surrounded them.

"Jackson?" Nicky laughed. "Do I complain about him that much?"

"No more than anyone complains about an ex-boyfriend."

"Right," said Nicky, doubtfully. "Hold on a sec." She gathered up her long white-blond hair, twisted it atop her head, and pulled on a knit hat she drew from her coat pocket. "Okay, good to go."

They moved out from under the shelter of the giant sycamores lining the sidewalks around the courthouse just as the skies let loose and huge drops of icy rain fell. Storm pulled the hood of her raincoat over her head, and the two women ran across the road to the Japanese restaurant on the corner.

After running through the thunderous downpour, stepping into a warm, quiet atmosphere filled with delicious scents of cooking was a welcome change. Soft lighting gleamed across dozens of bottles of sake on shelves lining the walls. Lute music from hidden speakers and the cascade of water across stones from a fountain just inside the foyer added to the ambience.

They hung their dripping coats on hooks by the front door and followed the hostess to a table. Immediately, hot tea and soup appeared. "This is what heaven must feel like," said Nicky.

"Mmm," agreed Storm, sipping her jasmine tea. The restaurant was busy, with diners seated at each of the tables of heavily lacquered raw wood. Their conversations seemed hushed. The pounding rain sliding down the windows created an atmosphere of isolation and calm, as if they were cut off from the world.

"So what did you want to talk about if it isn't Jackson?" asked Storm.

"Can't I just want to have lunch with a friend?"

"No, you're far too cheap for that," said Storm.

"Frugal. The word you want is frugal," corrected Nicky, smiling. She took off her knit hat and combed her fingers through her hair.

Not for the first time did Storm realize what an odd couple they were. Nicky was short and curvy and loved to wear anything pastel with lace and ruffles. She had blue-gray eyes and wore her blond hair in loose waves around her shoulders.

Storm was tall and covered her boyish build with tailored clothing in somber tones. She had dark eyes and hair she wore pulled back in an almost severe style. Their personalities were different too. Storm was reserved; Nicky was flamboyant.

As if to demonstrate, Nicky leaned forward and let go with a series of sentences at high speed. "I'm so glad you could do lunch. I just have to vent. I have a new client. Someone I . . . well, I don't want to say I don't want her on my caseload. I can handle her, it's just . . ."

Storm listened silently, a half-smile on her lips. The miso soup was delicious, with chunks of tofu and bits of carrot and onion floating in the fishy broth, steam rising to tickle her nose as she took small sips.

"Have you ever had a client you wanted to kill?" Nicky asked bluntly.

Storm almost spit out her soup. She inhaled instead, and that was almost worse. She choked and sputtered.

"Are you okay?" asked Nicky. "Do you want something

to drink?"

Storm shook her head, coughed hard, and was finally able to draw a breath. Why do people always offer you a drink, she wondered, when you already had what felt like a lung full of liquid? Taking another deep breath, Storm waved Nicky off.

"I'm fine. I'm good. My soup just went down the wrong way, I guess."

Uncomfortably aware that others in the restaurant were looking at her, Storm was eager to lose their attention.

She took a small sip of tea. When she didn't choke or cough, she refocused on Nicky. She leaned in and whispered, "So, what do you mean, kill a client?"

"Oh gosh." Now it was Nicky's turn to look embarrassed. "I didn't mean literally. Or at least probably not literally," she corrected herself, smiling to make it a joke. "Did you hear about the Helena Smith case?"

"Helena Smith? Oh sure. Isn't she the nutcase who was living in her car? The one who kept her kid on a mattress under the car 'cause her boyfriends didn't want to hear it crying?"

"Yeah, that's the one. And the kid didn't know how to walk or talk or anything when Child Welfare found him, even though he was almost three. I don't want to tell you all the things that were wrong with him physically."

"Thanks. I hear enough stories every day."

"Yeah, well, you can put this one in your top ten. I just don't get it. I don't get why she didn't put her kid up for adoption if she didn't want to take care of him. Food stamps, maybe? Anyway, I don't understand how this . . .

this evil bitch can be out walking around. She should be in a deep dark hole in the basement of a prison somewhere or better yet, in a deep dark hole in the ground."

"I take it she's not locked up, or dead?"

"Far from it. Somehow she got off on an insanity plea, even though the insanity was drug-induced and the drugs were self-administered. They put her in the state hospital in Salem for a while, but once she straightened herself out, they released her, and now she's on probation."

"And now she's yours," Storm said.

"Yes. Lucky me. Now she's mine. Got an appointment with her this week, and I don't want to set eyes on her. I've seen things in her file, and . . . all I want to do is find her and put an end to h—"

The server interrupted with Storm's sashimi and tempura vegetables and Nicky's chicken yakisoba. The conversation stopped, and Nicky, perhaps regretting her unprofessional rant or the dark desire she'd revealed, shifted the topic to Jackson, her troublesome ex.

Storm smiled, nodded, and asked all the right questions, all the while gleefully considering whether she might have found a new partner, a better partner than Howard. Someone whose urges she would neither have to control nor fear.

It was a prospect she'd have to examine more closely. She'd have to be careful though, take her time and be very, very sure before taking Nicky into her confidence.

* * *

Though the rain had slowed, the sky was even darker by the time Storm returned to her office. If she hurried, she might be able to sneak out a tad early and spend some time with Tom and the kids.

At a little after one, the phone rang. "You've got two guys here saying they have appointments," said Carrie, the receptionist. "A Rick Ramirez and a Howard Kline. Did you overbook?"

For a moment Storm was unable to speak. What was Howard doing there? He knew better than to go to the office unless it was urgent. Had something happened?

"Storm?"

"Sorry, Carrie. Checking my schedule. Yeah, I did double book, didn't expect Rick to show. Tell him I have to change his appointment, push it back half an hour. I'll come up and get Mr. Kline."

"Okay."

Storm pushed open the door to the reception area. Though he was seated with his back to the door, she recognized Howard immediately. She looked across the room, making eye contact with Rick Ramirez and gave him what she hoped was an apologetic smile.

"Howard Kline?" she said.

Howard stood up and moved toward her as she held the door open for him. "Please follow me." She led him farther into the building and to her office.

Storm indicated the chairs in front of her desk, matching gray metal chairs with woven gray-and-blue upholstery. Behind her faux-woodgrain desk was her chair, dark blue, ergonomically designed and able to swivel. If the difference in chairs was meant to give her a psychological advantage, a sense of control or of superiority, it failed miserably.

Taking a seat, she stared across the desk at Howard.

He said nothing; he just looked around her office with an air of fascination.

"What is it you want?"

"Haven't been in here a while. That a new plant?" He was looking at a philodendron, its vines covered with glossy green leaves hanging down the sides of a tall file cabinet.

"Yes. Why are you here?"

"Calm down. No big deal. Hey, nice picture. He had spotted a picture frame on her desk to the left of her monitor. He picked it up, turning it so he could see it more clearly. It was a picture taken at the last county fair: Tom and Storm, Joel and Lindsey holding four large cones of pink cotton candy, posed in front of a wash of neon lights.

Storm loved the picture of her family. They looked so normal, so nearly Norman Rockwell happy and perfect. It annoyed her that Howard was looking at it, touching it. It seemed pushy, even rude. His nervous, twitchy movements were contagious. She wished he'd sit still.

Reaching across the desk, she took the picture frame and set it firmly back in its place, this time making sure it was turned so that only she could see the photograph.

"Last time, Howard. Why are you here? You don't have an appointment."

"Yeah, I know. I was going to call, but I thought it would be easier to just come in. I need a trip permit to leave Oregon, that's all. I want to run up to Washington. I got a line on a job up there, better job than this security thing, though it does have its perks," he said.

Storm hated the look on his face. It was the kind of look she imagined a blackmailer would wear as he handed over a copy of the evidence. She was probably imagining it. She forced herself to relax.

"A trip permit, huh? That shouldn't be a problem."

"Didn't think it would be," Howard said. Again the smirk and the tone bothered Storm, making her stomach feel cold and achy, like it was filled with chips of ice. She wondered, for about the hundredth time, whether this partnership was such a good idea.

As if realizing he'd pushed things too far, Howard's attitude changed from demanding to apologetic. "I'm sorry I didn't call. This job just came up real sudden, and I didn't want to risk losing it."

"What sort of job is it?" Storm asked, leaning forward, her elbows on the edge of the desk, her chin resting on the back of her clasped hands.

"Manufacturing, assembly line," he said, his brown eyes lighting up. "Boeing," he added, naming the aerospace and defense corporation.

"That sounds great." Storm didn't really mean it. Directing Howard's pathology so that he was taking part in the justice killings was one thing. Letting him loose in Seattle was something else entirely. Besides, they had been in it together from the start. Despite her concerns, just what would she do if he left?

"Yeah, they have a program where they hire felons. Could be a whole new start," he continued. "Plus, it's not that far away, you know. I would still be able to get down here . . . from time to time."

"I see," she said, nodding to show she understood that he'd just promised to continue helping her. She wasn't quite so sure he'd be able to follow through on that promise. If he got a job in Washington, if he left her jurisdiction, why would he bother to return? She had nothing she could use to hold him—at least, nothing that wouldn't reveal her own guilt. Once he transferred, he'd be gone from her life. She was sure of it. Well, she decided, as he rambled on about the possible new job, there was no sense in worrying. He didn't have the job yet.

She stood up and turned to the file drawers behind her desk. She slid open a drawer, ran her forefinger across a row of tabs, found what she was looking for, and removed a document. Turning back to her desk, she sat down and placed the form in front of her on the desk. "When and where is this interview?"

Howard smiled like Christmas morning and gave her the details. She filled out the trip pass, signed it, and handed it over. "Good luck. I'll walk you out."

"Thanks. Thanks for the pass and for the luck," he said. Storm wondered how someone who seemed so normal and who could act so pleasant could have developed such a need to inflict pain. Aware that she would probably never know the answer, she mentally shrugged and led him back to the reception area. "Rick," she said to her client. "Sorry you had to wait. Could you come with me now?"

Storm strode down the hallway, halfway to her office with Mr. Ramirez. She didn't see Howard tear the pass in half and toss it into a trash can.

CHAPTER

FIVE

"MOM!"

"What now, Lindsey?" Storm asked, sending an exasperated look at Tom, who was driving and apparently unwilling to enter the fray.

"Joel is changing the channel again."

"Joel, your sister is watching a movie. Why can't you settle down and watch it, too?"

"Dunno," said Joel, with an exaggerated shrug.

The salesperson who had enthused about the portable DVD player, claiming it would eliminate fighting between siblings, was either misinformed or lying. The thing created more, not less, conflict.

They had come as a pair mounted behind the front seats so the kids could each control what they watched. Within the first week, Joel's player had stopped working. Since sticky fingers were all over it, like fingerprints at a crime scene. Storm didn't think the warranty would still be valid.

"Please try to behave. We're almost there, and you're getting your dad all rattled."

Tom, driving at his usual grandfatherly speed and whistling silently between his teeth, looked as rattled as a drowsy well-fed pup. Storm wondered if he was able to remain so calm because she was a stress sponge, absorbing all the tension and leaving him free to drift worry-free through a cotton-soft world with no sharp edges.

"Are we there? Are we there?" demanded Joel as the car slowed and pulled off the road and into the gravel parking lot.

"We're here," said Tom. "Everybody out."

Within moments the entire McKenzie family had piled out of the van. The kids charged toward the open gate set in the short cyclone fence that circled the park.

Tom and Storm paused to survey the area. "How'd you find this place?" Tom asked.

"Someone at the office told me about it. Said it would be a good place to bring the kids, let them burn off some energy. Nice, huh?"

"Very."

It was a cool, clear Saturday afternoon. The sky was the soft color of blue chalk. Just inside the fence surrounding the park was a row of maples, their leaves beginning to turn from green to red and yellow. A few had already fallen and now tumbled across the grass as a cool breeze gusted across the field, carrying the smell of burning leaves with it.

"Watch for puddles," Storm called. The playground equipment stood in a far corner of the park, and the kids were heading straight for it. Shrubs blocked the view, so she couldn't tell how muddy the ground was under the monkey bars or swing sets.

Storm supposed it didn't really matter. The kids would have a great time no matter how wet or muddy they got. She might have ended up with dirty car mats, but that was a small price to pay for their fun, especially considering she had a completely selfish reason for bringing them, and it had nothing to do with play.

Two blocks away was the current home of Helena Smith, no doubt somewhat better than an abandoned car parked under a bridge. True, Helena had not been Storm's next target, but sometimes you had to be open to change.

That Thursday, upon returning to the office after her lunch with Nicky, Storm had logged into the database and quickly found all she needed to know about Ms. Smith. Though released, the court determined she would not regain custody of her son. That was something, at least.

Storm read the entire file and learned Ms. Smith's son was living in a foster home specializing in the care of high-needs children. He had made some progress, was now able to sit up by himself, and no longer screamed when someone entered the room.

After hearing Nicky's rant against the criminal justice system in regard to the woman, and after reading her file and considering her parenting skills, Storm had decided

Ms. Smith deserved to move to the top of the list.

As she strolled through the park, Storm shuddered, thinking about Ms. Smith's child and the life he had lived on a filthy mattress under a rusting pile of cold metal. She rubbed her arms as if the chill was from the cold.

Tom had moved ahead and was now helping Joel up the stairs of the slide. She watched her sweet son careen down, yelling at top volume, landing on both feet with a thump. He quickly raced back to the stairs so Dad could help him up for another turn.

She imagined him as a baby, trapped under a maze of corroded metal, cold, hungry, his skin covered in urine burns and bed sores. Anger began to grow, a soft glow, an ember, but it was there. It would be there when she needed to call on it.

Pushing the dark thoughts away, Storm dragged herself out of her vivid imaginings and back to the here and now.

Lindsey had found a swing and was studiously pushing herself back and forth, her concentration focused entirely on her goal. She had always been the more serious of the two children. The one Storm felt needed her least. It was funny how two children from the same parents could be so different.

Tom laughed, the sound starting an old familiar ache in her heart. She wished she could laugh like that, join them in play so fully and effortlessly.

Lindsey and Joel would be like him. She was sure of it. Despite Lindsey's serious nature, she would be open to happiness and to laughter. Storm took no credit for that. It was Tom, the good parent, the son of good parents. That was something worth passing on. Much better than the inheritance she'd received.

Walking up to watch her family play, Lindsey came upon a trio of picnic benches. Finding the soaked wood too damp to sit on, she leaned her hip against one and stood quietly, feeling the warmth of the sun across her shoulders.

The motion of Lindsey's swing was hypnotic. It should have been lulling, but Storm couldn't relax. The smell of something burning grew stronger—not just leaves anymore, something like insulation, plastic.

Unexpectedly, she wanted to go home, escape this place that was nothing more than a means to an end for her, an end her family would never understand or condone. How could they? They had no idea what was out there, of the cruelty and the evil of people. Even Tom, who was older than she, had no idea. She hoped he never would.

What if she just forgot why she had gone there, let herself pretend it was really just to let the kids play? She could do that. She didn't have to make a wrong turn on the way home, drive slowly until she spotted the house, confident no one would look twice at a family cruising past in a ten-year-old SUV with a 'Friends of Oregon Zoo' sticker in the window.

They left fifteen minutes later, both kids pretending reluctance, but also a little chilled and damp. Neither of them argued much as they settled into their seats.

"That was nice," said Tom, after they'd buckled the kids in. He took Storm's hand and kissed her fingers. "Cold," he said, blowing warm air against her finger tips.

"Mmm," she agreed. "But you're colder and you look sleepy. "Mind if I drive?"

"Of course not," he said, handing over the keys. "Anything else on the agenda?" He climbed into the passenger seat and buckled his seatbelt.

"What do you mean?" she asked nervously.

"You know, pick up a movie and maybe some fried chicken."

"Your night to cook," she said, relieved. "Of course we'll eat out."

"Hey, you make that sound like a common occurrence."

Storm just rolled her eyes and started the car.

"Did you ever stop to think this is not a bad thing?" he continued. "Have you ever really tasted my cooking?"

"You are a perfectly fine cook," she told him. "You can pretend otherwise all you want. But I'm not going to argue about going out. It means I won't have to do dishes."

"Hey, I think you took a wrong turn," Tom pointed out helpfully. "You were supposed to go left coming out of the parking lot."

"Oh, really? Well, since we're heading this way anyway, might as well go down a few blocks. Never been in this part of town. Maybe there's another park or, who knows, maybe a store that sells Oregon Ducks stuff." Tom was a huge fan and collector of University of Oregon football team memorabilia.

"Now you're just teasing me," he said.

Storm drove slowly past the mid-century ranch-style homes painted in predictably pastel shades.

The house was off-white, with faded green trim, the address above the door hand-painted in thick black letters. A ragged hedge bordered the garage side, a six-foot wooden fence the other. As she drove by, Storm wondered if Howard would use the hedge or the fence to shield their approach.

Or maybe Howard wouldn't be using either. Maybe she didn't need him for this. The idea seemed to lift something from her—the weight of worry, she supposed, or some unnamed dread.

Ever since Howard's unexpected visit to get the travel permit, she'd been thinking about him and their partnership, weighing the pros and cons. He was an element in her planning she could not totally control, and that was worrisome.

She'd even pulled his file and reread every word, trying to find some clue to help her control his actions. There wasn't much: born in Sacramento, California, April 9, 1977, thirty-six years old, three arrests for disorderly conduct, two convictions. The first got him an overnight in county, the second a resisting arrest that earned him thirty days, a course in anger management and a year of probation. That time, he'd had the bad judgment to punch the police officer who was trying to restrain him.

His issue seemed to be a lack of impulse control. That was a trait she found dangerous in a partner. Maybe his moving to Seattle wasn't such a bad idea, but could she go it alone? That was the question. Maybe Helena Smith held the answer.

* * *

"That was fun, Mommy," said Joel, as they settled around the table for some chicken from a drive-through near their house.

"I think we should go again," agreed Lindsey.

"I'm glad you liked it," said Storm. "I'm sure we can go back, and there are parks and playgrounds in lots of other places we haven't seen yet. Maybe we can visit them too."

"Mmnumum," said Joel, trying to talk around a mouthful of mashed potatoes.

"Okay, we'll talk about it later. For now, we eat!" Tom emphasized his words by grabbing a drumstick, waving it around, and taking a huge bite.

Storm shook her head, but her smile took away any sense of disapproval. Again she was utterly amazed at Tom's skill as a parent by his seemingly endless patience and sense of humor.

There were times when she felt she should tell him the truth about herself. It might have helped him understand why she acted so strangely sometimes, made him more sympathetic. It wasn't that he wasn't always kind, but she knew there were days, especially her bad days, when he wondered what was going on in her head. Sometimes he even asked.

"Why are you so sad today? It feels like you're not here, like you're somewhere else."

"I just want to be left alone," she would say. "I have a headache." It was one of her little white lies. Usually it worked. Sometimes it left him looking lost. It was at these times she most wanted to blurt out the truth about her childhood.

Of course, she would never do that. To do so would be to take away the entire fiction she had created about the sad way she'd lost her parents in a car accident. Or the wonderful life she'd had after her loving aunt had adopted and raised her.

At least the story about her aunt was partly true. She had been a wonderful woman, loving and kind. The lie was that she died at the start of Storm's first year of college, the victim of a heart attack.

She had built a column of lies on a mountain of ash and she knew how tenuous it was. Storm hated the lies, but worse, she hated the thought of being viewed as even more of a freak, even less normal.

"You should eat some of those green beans," she said to Joel. "Lindsey, don't poke your finger in your brother's potatoes. Tom, should I heat up some of that apple pie for dessert?"

Normal was good.

CHAPTER

SIX

AT THREE A.M., Helena Smith's street was dark and draped in fog. Storm drove past the house, turned right, and parked at the curb. On both sides, generic houses stood in unremarkable rows. Parked in their driveways and along the street, a few cars huddled like giant, sleeping, metal dogs.

She sat quietly, looking back and forth from windshield to rearview mirror, searching for any movement. Using her thumb and first finger she tugged at the edge of her jacket's sleeves, slowly working her way around the left sleeve and then the right.

There was no wind, nothing to stir the branches of the

hawthorn trees lining the street. Even the fog hung where it was, a dense mist that obscured the houses and made everything dim and otherworldly.

Earlier, in her garage, she had opened the trunk of her car and unzipped the red duffle bag she kept there. It held road flares and markers, jumper cables, a small canvas zipper bag of tools, a quart of oil, a mini first-aid kit, a folded wool blanket for kneeling on, and most importantly, a bundle of zip ties and a roll of silver duct tape. She had put the tape and a handful of zip ties in one pocket of her dark-green Columbia windbreaker. The other pocket held a stun gun and a slim tube of pepper spray.

Storm was certain Helena was in. She had called the home number listed in the database, and a woman had answered with a tentative hello. "Wrong number," Storm had mumbled, before hanging up the payphone.

Now her biggest concerns were how to gain entry into the house and how to learn if Helena was alone. Storm wasn't too worried about overpowering her. The woman was about five feet tall and thin as an ironing board.

The only way to figure out how to get into the house was to get out of the car. Storm had removed the overhead light bulb so she could open the door at night without its telltale glow. Still, the sound of the door opening seemed loud enough to draw the attention of everyone in the nearby houses.

Adjusting her sleeves one final time, she took a deep breath, got out of the car, and shut the door softly behind her. Her jaw ached, and she realized she was gritting her teeth.

She'd never been this tentative, this nervous before.

Of course, Howard had always been there. He'd been the one to approach their targets, confront, and subdue them. It was only after they were down that she stepped in, making sure they were bound correctly and couldn't break free during their transport to the kill room.

Storm straightened her shoulders, walked across a small island of patchy grass to the sidewalk, and strode purposefully toward the corner. Turning down Helena's street, Storm's breath quickened. In her dark spandex and running shoes she looked like a runner taking a break. She stopped in front of Helena's house, bent forward with her hands resting just above her knees and pretended to be trying to catch her breath.

There were no lights on in the house, not even a porch light. The barest touch of reflected light from a distant street lamp lined the sharp edges of the roofline, showed her the railroad ties separating driveway from lawn, and glinted from the dark window panes.

There was no sound except for the infrequent shushing noise of tires as cars moved past on the main road a block away.

Storm walked with all the confidence she could muster straight up the driveway as if she belonged there. She tiptoed uneasily past the dark picture window to the front door. The curtains didn't stir, and she kept moving, reached the front door, grasped the door knob, and turned it slowly. It moved a short way and stopped. She tried the other direction. Same result. The door was locked. She'd have to try the back door or look for an unlatched window.

She retraced her steps, again crossing nervously in front of the picture window, feeling exposed. As she moved along the garage door, planning to go around the side of the house and look for a way into the backyard, she noticed the garage door was askew. The darker-than-dark shadow at its base was much wider on one side.

Storm felt along the bottom edge of the door until she found the garage door handle. Wrapping her hand around the narrow metal band, she pulled. Abruptly, with a sound like thunder, the door rolled up several feet. Storm froze, her hand clenched around the handle, keeping the door from moving any farther.

Holding her breath, every sense alert for sound, light, motion of any sort, Storm stood for several long seconds. After two full minutes had passed, she carefully loosened her death grip on the garage door handle, testing to see what would happen. The door stayed where it was, leaving an opening of over three feet.

Ducking low, Storm slipped under the door and into the garage. It was even darker inside than the street, but her eyes quickly adjusted. She was in a two-car garage, a wide space that seemed to echo its emptiness.

She could make out the gloomy form of a rickety row of shelves along one wall and a gleam of white near the back. Pulling a small flashlight from her pocket, she played the narrow beam across the space.

The wooden shelves held nothing but two jars of dried paint. At the back, in the far corner, was a hot-water heater and next to it, a washer and dryer. A small pile of laundry was heaped on the top of the dryer, an open bottle of liquid detergent next to them. They were the only sign that someone was living in the house.

Overhead was a row of cobweb-covered fluorescent

lights and empty rafters. To the right, a wall of unpainted sheetrock and a door.

Storm moved cautiously toward the door, slowly sliding each foot across the smooth concrete floor, wary of tripping across something in the thin erratic light. She found the doorknob, and wrapped her hand around it, took a deep breath, and turned. Expecting the same sensation of resistance she'd felt on trying the front door, she was surprised when the knob turned easily.

She clicked off the flashlight and turned the door handle again, this time slowly pushing the door open a crack. The mingled scents of tuna fish and lemon-scented furniture polish met her.

When nothing happened, she opened the door wider and stepped up the single step. She was inside. Looking around, she could barely make out the contents of the room. A gray-on-gray gloominess draped each piece of furniture. Afraid to chance the light, she felt her way across the linoleum.

A refrigerator hummed, and there was the ticking of a clock. Aware she was taking a lot of time to cross the room, Storm wrapped her fist around the lens of the flashlight and turned it on. When she opened her fingers slightly the feeble pink light enabled her to make out the edge of a table and three chairs just in time to avoid bumping into them.

Now she could see what she'd suspected. She was in a dining room, and just ahead was the kitchen. To her right was a carpeted living room. She could make out a brick fireplace and the ticking clock sitting on on end of the mantle.

Closest to her was the back of a couch and facing it, under the picture window, what looked like a pair of lawn chairs. Moving into the living room, she saw a short dark hallway to the left. Storm realized she was sweating, and a tick had started in her left eyelid, the twitching an annoyance she didn't need.

She moved down the hallway. The first door on the right was small and louvered; she assumed it was a coat closet, but as she stepped past, she heard the sound of a furnace kicking on. Though it was only a subdued click, the unexpected sound made her jump.

Wiping her sweaty palms on her pants, she moved farther down the hallway. The next door was on the left and stood open. The flashlight's glow showed her a small bathroom with worn fern-patterned wallpaper, and the standard white tub, sink, and toilet. The worn linoleum was gold with a Mediterranean pattern popular in the 1970s.

The next room, also on the left, was bare but for a couple of empty cardboard boxes that looked as if they'd been tossed haphazardly inside. On a normal day, Storm would have been hard-pressed not to rearrange them into a tidier pattern.

Across from the empty room, and the only one left to check, had to be Helena Smith's bedroom.

Storm reached into her pocket and pulled out the stun gun. It switched on with an audible snap, and again she froze, afraid she'd awakened the night's target. After a few breathless seconds, she moved forward, reached for the doorknob, and opened the door.

There were no curtains on the window and enough ambient light from the street to reveal a double bed, a nightstand, and a small dresser. The bed looked neatly made and completely empty. Surprised, Storm decided to take a closer look.

She had taken two steps when she realized something had changed. A sound—a dull, pounding noise—filled her ears. For a split second, her intense focus on the bed and the bedroom kept her from moving, from recognizing that the sound came not from the bedroom, but from the hallway behind her. She swung around, stun gun in hand, but it was too late. A woman's body crashed into her, shoving her into the room, knocking the weapon from her hand. Storm tumbled backward, falling first onto the edge of the bed, and slid to the floor awkwardly, one leg tucked beneath her.

A bony knee ground into her thigh. Storm reacted to the pain and shoved her forearm into her attacker's face, pushing her back. Free of the woman's weight, Storm was able to squirm away, almost out of reach.

As she struggled to her feet, a hand caught her hair, nails tore into the skin of her scalp, and she was pulled backward. At first she fought against it, but then she let herself fall back. Her elbow landed hard on some part of the woman's anatomy, and she was free. Rolling away, she spotted the stun gun, grabbed it, and held it to a pajama-clad thigh.

There was a high-pitched shout, but rather than being stunned by the powerful electric shock, the woman seemed galvanized. She jerked away and ran, her bare feet making the same light pounding sound as she ran down the hallway, this time in the opposite direction, with Storm close behind.

"Help!" the woman screamed. "Help!"

Storm lunged, trying to catch the back of the woman's pajama top, but she was too slow. She jerked her hand back just in time to avoid her fingers being slammed in the bathroom door.

"Help! Somebody help! She's trying to kill me!"

Storm rattled the door handle, but the door was locked. Frustrated, she kicked the door. The screams grew louder.

"Help! Help! Help!"

"Shut up!" Storm shouted. "Helena Smith. Shut the fuck up, or I'll shoot you through the door."

The yelling stopped as if she'd flipped a switch.

"Who are you? What do you want?" the woman whispered. "Tim isn't here. He owe you money or something? I don't have no money and he's in jail. You ain't getting money from me. You might as well leave."

"Shut up," Storm repeated. She stepped away from the door and paced the length of the hallway. What if the neighbors had heard all the yelling and called the police? How much time did she have? What should she do? Had the woman seen her?

"Damn. Damn. Damn," she repeated as she paced, running one hand through her disheveled hair, the other still wrapped tightly around the apparently worthless stun gun. She found a switch on the wall and flipped it up. Two lights in the hallway ceiling came on. The light helped make the night seem both more and less real.

Think, she commanded herself. If the police showed up, what would she tell them? *I was driving around and heard someone yelling. I came in to see what was going on and found a woman in the bathroom?* Yeah, that would never work, and even if it did, it would only work until Ms. Helena Smith saw her and realized who she was.

A week ago, Storm had checked Nicky's appointment calendar and then made sure she was around at the right time to 'bump' into Helena. Of course, no introduction had been made, but Storm had seen her picture in the paper. Plus, the stiff way Nicky was holding herself was a tip-off.

She made sure Helena got a good look at her. The world was a small place, but not that small. The coincidence of her just driving by . . .

"You still out there?" a plaintive voice asked.

"I'm here. You just be quiet a minute." Storm walked to the living room, peeked through the curtains. Nothing seemed to have changed. She didn't see lights on in any of the nearby houses.

She pulled out her cell phone and found his number, carefully listed as a mobile number under her doctor's name.

"Howard," she said as soon as she heard his voice. "I need you."

She told him what she'd done and where she was. She was afraid he would say, no, he couldn't come. It would be a way to punish her for acting alone.

"Keep her quiet. I'll be there in fifteen minutes," he said.

She hung up and went back to stand near the bathroom door. After a few moments, Helena Smith asked, "You going to let me out of here?"

"Soon," she lied. "I have to see if you're telling the truth about Tim. I've got some friends checking on your story."

See if he's really in jail."

"I knew this had to be about him. That man is trouble. Hell, all of them are."

"Quiet,"

"Yeah, I'll be quiet, but I ain't stayin' in here all night, you hear me?"

"I hear you. You do what I say or you'll wish you had."

"I don't even think you got a gun," was the unexpected response. "I didn't see a gun, just that shock thing. I thought they would hurt worse, since I'm not very big. I seen them on YouTube. Some guys were shocking each other on their tongues and their dicks, and they didn't hardly jump. I figured it was because they were big guys. Or maybe they just had a cheap one, you know, not like the cop's Tasers. You can't buy those, I think."

"Yeah, maybe they were cheap ones," Storm agreed. This was no time to give a lesson on the difference between a Taser and a stun gun. "Only this one is a cop's Taser," she lied. "I just didn't push the button right or something. So unless you want me to try it again, shut the hell up!"

"So, are you a cop?" Helena Smith asked.

Storm didn't answer. She wanted the conversation to end. You didn't talk to the garbage. She didn't want to think of Ms. Helena Smith as a person. Her child was a person. The Helena Smiths of the world weren't people; they were monsters, an evil that had to be removed.

Storm thought about the file and the description of Ms. Smith's son. Though she had no picture this time, she didn't need one to imagine the urine burns, bedsores, and toes, missing because of frost bite.

She let herself slip into that state of empathy she felt

for all the victims and imagined the starvation, the thirst, and the unending loneliness. From empathy for the victim grew anger for the abuser. From anger grew the strength to see the mission through.

As always, these thoughts made Storm aware of the tight pull of the skin across her back and arm. She thought of her younger self, not with the love and nurturing her therapists tried to convince her was the way to heal her inner child, but with contempt, even shame.

She had been a coward at thirteen—obedient and fearful. She deserved what she got. But Helena Smith's child had been too young to fight back. He didn't deserve it. He deserved justice. He deserved her angry best.

"So, are you a cop?" Helena Smith asked again.

"You know what I am," Storm said softly, not wanting to raise her voice and invite Helena Smith to do the same.

"Did you say something?" the woman asked.

Storm ignored her. When she continued to ask questions, she continued to ignore her.

A few minutes later, she heard footsteps on the front walk and a light tap at the door. She practically ran to unlock it. But realizing it might not have been Howard, she slowed down and peeked cautiously around the side of the curtain.

"Thank heaven it's you," she whispered, opening the door only wide enough for him to slip inside. Nervously, she told him, "She's got some boyfriend named Tim, and she thinks we're here for him. She was screaming so loud a little while ago, I was afraid someone would call the cops."

"Seriously?" Howard asked with a wry smile. "People don't call the cops in this neighborhood."

"That's what I was hoping," she said. "Can you help me deal with this? I need to get her out to Evergreen."

"What the hell were you going to do with her, all by yourself?"

"I was going to make it look like an accident. Like she fell in the shower."

"Leave a body? Break your own rule?" Howard asked incredulously.

"I was going to be really careful. I didn't have a choice. You're the only one with access to the incinerator."

"Damn right. Which is why I should have been with you on this. What were you thinking, trying to pull this off alone?"

Feeling like a chastised child, Storm said, "Your new job." The half-lie she'd concocted rolled off her tongue effortlessly. "I figured if you moved to Seattle, I'd be on my own, so I might as well get out there and prove I can handle it without you."

This was the moment she'd dreaded. She didn't want Howard to guess she wanted to break up the partnership. She couldn't risk his anger.

If he thought she had gone out on her own because he had threatened to leave, well, that was one thing. He couldn't blame her. But if he thought she wanted him gone . . . if he had even an inkling she'd considered how to get him arrested and out of the way. . . the repercussions were too awful to contemplate.

She'd seen what Howard did for fun when he was calm. Storm didn't want to imagine what he'd do when angry.

Howard stared at her for a moment, brow wrinkled as

if he was trying to decide on a response. Finally, in a patronizing tone that made her want to slap his face, he said, "You sure didn't prove you could go it alone now, did you?"

Storm flushed but squelched her instinct to argue with him. This was not the time or place. Besides, he was right and she knew it. "I guess not," she agreed. "I thought she was sleeping in her room. She must have been on the couch and heard me walk in. She's not completely stupid, though if she was really smart, she would have run instead of jumping me.

"So, if it makes you feel better, no, I didn't prove I could go it alone. I have no idea how to get her out of that bathroom. Hell, I'm just lucky there's no window in there."

"You sure about that?"

Storm thought a moment. "I looked inside earlier, but no, I'm not sure."

"Damn," he exclaimed. "Where is she?"

Storm pointed to the bathroom door. "She locked herself in."

"Hey, you in there," Howard called, grabbing the doorknob and rattling the door. "Come out."

There was a loud thud followed by another.

"At least she's still in there. Move back," he said. Storm backed down the hall, keeping her eyes on Howard. Using all his weight, he rammed his shoulder against the door, down low near the lock. It broke open with a tearing splintering sound. He staggered forward into the bathroom. Storm ran in behind him and saw Ms. Helena Smith holding the heavy ceramic top of the toilet tank. A dent in the wall showed where she'd tried to break through.

"What the hell were you trying to do? Break into the next room?" asked Howard. The woman swung the toilet lid at him. Howard grabbed it, tossed it into the bathtub, and punched her in the face. She went down in a heap, falling forward, almost into his arms. He stepped back, raised his hands, and crashed to the floor. "You got it?" Howard asked.

"Yeah," said Storm. Taking zip ties from her pocket, she knelt and tied the woman's wrists and ankles. As she finished, Helena regained consciousness and drew in a deep breath. Before she could scream, Howard stepped forward and kicked her, the toe of his boot driving into her ribs. She gave a low gasp of pain.

Not seeing a washcloth, Storm ripped a corner from a threadbare towel and stuffed it in the woman's mouth. She tore several pieces of duct tape off the roll and used them to hold the gag in place.

Howard knelt beside Helena Smith and used his thumb to roughly wipe away the tears trickling down her cheeks. "Guess you finally figured out we aren't here for your boyfriend, right?" He patted her shoulder and stood up. "Seems like you've got it all tied up," he said, smiling at the bad pun. "That about all the help you need?"

Again, Storm was annoyed by the smug look, and again, there was nothing she could do about it.

"No," she reluctantly admitted. "I still need you to get her out to Evergreen and take care of the rest. It's getting late, and people will start showing up for work. Don't your facilities people get there early?"

Howard looked at his watch. "A little more than an

hour. I'd better hurry. One thing, though."

"Yeah?" she asked impatiently.

"My payment."

Storm lifted an eyebrow and cocked her head as she tried to understand this new demand. "What payment?"

"Well, there won't be time to play," he said, indicating his watch, "and I did get woke from a sound sleep to come out and help you. Seems I should get a little something."

"Like what?"

"Like a kiss."

"You have got to be kidding?" Disbelief and annoyance tightened her voice.

"Not kidding," Howard said, and this time there was no smile, just a look, from far inside his eyes. Storm had seen that look before, just as Howard drew back his whip.

"Fine," she said, putting her hands on her hips and pursing her lips. She was making his demand seem like a minor inconvenience, a joke.

He moved across the bathroom and into the hallway. His hands wrapped around her upper arms and he pulled her forward with surprising gentleness. She lifted her face and narrowed her eyes. He moved in, his lips finding hers. A shiver ran down her spine and she trembled. He moaned, misunderstanding the cause. Her emotion was not passion. It was fear.

This was a man who could, if annoyed, kill her without hesitation or remorse. Repulsed by his tongue sliding between her lips, she thought of closing her mouth tight against him, maybe even biting him. Instead, she closed her eyes tightly, relaxed her lips, and let his questing tongue inside. She even let the tip of her tongue touch his so that the kiss would feel genuine.

Finally, the kiss ended. He stroked the back of her head, just once, with an unexpectedly light touch. "Get her stuff. I'll wrap her in a blanket, and we'll put her in the trunk." He sounded like a man offering to help prepare for a picnic.

Storm nodded and hurried to complete her task, collecting the woman's personal belongings, her makeup, toothbrush, clothes and purse, and any pictures she could find, all of which would be incinerated with her.

The other two abusers they'd targeted and killed had been on probation. They were drowning in fines and fees and facing court dates and further sanctions. When they disappeared, the first thing everyone thought was that they'd skipped. If she and Howard were careful, everyone would believe the same about Ms. Helena Smith.

While Storm shoved the last of the clothes into one of the cardboard boxes in the spare room, Howard carried the night's target into the bedroom like a bride and dropped her on the bed. "You might not want to watch this."

"You going to do it now?"

"Less trouble and faster. You're right, we don't have much time."

"Okay, but let me tell her why."

"Go ahead," he nodded.

Storm stood at the foot of the bed and stared into the woman's eyes, which glistened with tears. "Helena Smith," she said. Her voice was clear and strong as she made the pronouncement. "You have been found guilty of unforgiveable crimes. You neglected your son to the point of torture. You have been judged. You have been condemned, and now you are going to die in a way that does not even begin to befit your crimes. Howard?"

Helena Smith tried desperately to roll away from Howard's reaching hands. She drew her knees up and kicked at him. Storm watched as he batted her feet aside and landed a punch to her chest that left her wheezing and weak. He flipped her onto her stomach, slammed a knee into her back, and reached for her head. With a sudden jerk and a wet crunch like the snap of a stalk of celery, he broke her neck.

Storm swallowed the bile rising in her throat. The room turned a dull gray, all the edges losing their sharpness. A roar filled her ears. She reached behind her for the wall and turned, resting her cheek against the cool surface.

The sudden and unalterable fact of death was overwhelming her. Storm clung to reality as a crazed vision, something she imagined as a wall of roiling black and gray storm clouds filled her thoughts. She fought to stay conscious by pressing her face against the wall until her cheek ached and the pain and the 'thereness' grew. In what seemed like forever, but was only seconds, she was able to take a deep breath and straighten her knees.

When she recovered enough to speak, she asked, "Where's your car?"

"Driveway." He dug in his pocket and tossed her the keys. He was subdued, the smirk gone, hunger abated. "You okay?" he asked.

She nodded. "I'm good. I'll be right back.

Storm found he had backed his car into the driveway. She opened the trunk then returned to the house to get the duffel and hold the door for Howard so he could carry the blanket-wrapped body outside. Strangely, she was no longer nervous about being seen.

She placed the duffel next to the body and closed the trunk.

"I'm going to put everything in the oxidizer and poof, it's all over," he promised.

"You still have to check. Make sure everything is clean," she cautioned.

"I will."

"What about the smoke?"

"It's still damned early. No one will see it."

"Good."

"Storm?" he said.

"Yeah?"

"No more going out on your own."

She shook her head.

"Say it," he demanded.

"No more going out on my own. Hell, Howard, I didn't get anything right. She didn't even recognize me."

Howard reached out and squeezed her arm and gave her a smile she couldn't read. Then he climbed into his car and drove away.

She would have to do something about him. That kiss was just the beginning, a bizarre first-date expectation that was bound to grow. Remembering his mouth on hers made her shudder. Storm rubbed at her arm where his fingertips had dug in and hoped there'd be no bruises.

Mentally, she ran through the list: Jeffrey Franklin Malino, dogs; Gavin Lester Everett, burns, and Helena Smith, car. There were three now, but Storm knew she would never forget their names.

For a moment, she drifted in a daze, her mind momentarily shutting off as if exhausted and unable to process more. Then, suddenly, as if a switch had been flipped, she shook it off and rushed to her car, in a hurry to reach the sanity and safety of home.

CHAPTER

SEVEN

A WEEK AFTER the disastrous night at Helena Smith's, Storm sat in her office, enjoying a rare moment of quiet. The days had gone by in a whirlwind of work: clients to interview, narratives to write, appearances in court, trainings, and home visits. It was an unending loop. New clients came in, old ones left.

She hoped the clients she saw gained something from their work with her—not just a fear of punishment and having to answer for breaking the law, but that they could survive without and do well without resorting to committing crimes. She wanted to teach them how to find a job and keep it. Show them they could find help with their addictions. Help them cope with their anger in a world that had not been overly kind. Maybe she should have been a social worker.

There had been more than the normal number of court appearances that week, and she'd made more than the usual number of home visits. Her caseload, which had already been staggering, had recently increased. Even so, there had been a few precious periods of quiet times when no one was making demands.

During those rare breaks, Storm had cleaned her office, rearranging files and retyping numbers and notes. It was her habit to scrawl on bits of paper and sticky notes. She was consciously focusing her energy and pointedly not looking for the next target. She needed a break and to put some welcome distance between herself and Howard.

During one of those rare moments of inaction, sitting in her extremely neat office, she stared idly into the middle distance and let her mind fill with scenes from that night.

The woman's near escape had rattled her. What if there had been a window in that bathroom? What if Helena Smith had escaped and accused her of attempted murder? What if Helena had managed to overpower her, hurt, or even kill her? What would Lindsey and Joel have done without a mom? Or Tom, without a wife?

Maybe it was time to stop this entirely. Not just quit using Howard, but quit.

She'd never set out to be some sort of avenger. The first one—the man who had used his pit bulls to discipline his children—that one had been unplanned, completely spontaneous. She'd been unable to live with the idea that the man who'd let his dogs disfigure his daughter's face and tear off his son's ear was walking around free. She didn't care if the arresting officers had made a mistake. Hell, if she'd seen what they'd seen, she'd have made a mistake, too. She'd have killed the bastard right then and there.

Luckily, the universe had given her a better option, one she had a chance of walking away from, free and unsuspected.

Howard had been in her office for his usual meeting with her. They had talked about the community service hours he had left. He'd complained about the impact on his job and how was he supposed to pay his fines if he was always missing work. She'd only half listened. It was a complaint she'd heard many times before.

He'd switched topics, sharing the conversation he'd heard between two young lawyers discussing the man who used his dogs on his own kids.

Howard had said, "Too bad they can't send that guy to prison. You know how much prisoners love child abusers."

Storm had, for a moment, forgotten the nature of their relationship and agreed with him. They spoke about the horror of both the crime and the injustice of the man walking away with little more than a slap on the wrist.

Howard had hinted at the dark things he'd do, the justice he'd seek, if only he'd known where the man lived. Storm had slid her fingers across the surface of her keyboard, thinking, wondering.

The shared database held each parole officer's list of clients. She could view the entire database, look at any file she liked. Never sure what had emboldened her to do it, Storm opened the database. She found the address, jotted it down on a sticky note, and handed it to Howard.

Her stomach had flipped, as adrenaline rushed into her bloodstream. Her hands shook as he reached out and took the note from her. He studied it carefully and looked up at her. On that day, there was no smirk on his lips. He seemed like a man filled with righteous anger, one who craved justice. She identified with the desire.

"Come with me," he whispered urgently. "Come and stand watch."

"I can't," she said, shocked by the idea.

"It'd be a lot easier if you were there to let me know if someone was around. You know, just kept an eye out. Think about it. Think about those kids. Look at the paper again."

Storm didn't have to look at it again. The image in the newspaper would always be there: the boy, his hand over one ear, a stream of blood running down his neck, his thumb in his mouth, seeking comfort; the girl, fine blond hair, her mouth open to scream, showing baby teeth. A blood-soaked rag hid one half of her face but left far too much to the imagination.

The dogs had been put to sleep. They had savaged the children as if they were ragdolls in a game of tug-o-war, and had earned their deaths. Now it was time for their father's.

Howard had called it a justice killing, and she now thought of it the same way. She didn't feel they had committed a crime. There was no crime in putting things right, though the rest of the world might not have seen it that way. No, what they did was right and just and necessary.

They'd done some good in the world. She and Howard had eliminated three really bad people and by doing so had protected many more. No, she was not sorry about what they'd done, but she was also realistic. Luck had a tendency to run out. It was time to think about stopping.

There was a quick light rap, and Storm looked up to see the anxious Dolph Lundgren lookalike who was her supervisor knocking on the edge of the doorway. "Hey, Big Ed."

"Hey, Storm. I was wondering if you'd seen Nicky around."

"No. She took a couple days off. Went out of town."

"Oh, yeah, I forgot. Can't keep up my own schedule, much less keep track of everyone else." Big Ed, who was six foot four inches tall and nearly too wide across the shoulders to fit through the doorway, smiled apologetically. "Do you know who's covering for her?"

"I am."

"Well, that's damned handy."

"Why, what's up?"

"Nothing you need to worry about. Just wanted to give Nicky a heads-up that one of her clients has gone missing. Got a call from a detective this morning. Said it looks like she was murdered."

"Murdered?"

"Yeah. At least, that's what the sheriff's office thinks. They got a call from her boyfriend, saying she'd disappeared and the place was trashed. They went over her residence, and it looked like she'd cleaned it out, you know, like she was going somewhere."

"Uh-huh?" she said, maintaining eye contact,

encouraging him to continue.

"They found a floor safe in the bedroom. Thing had her birth certificate, social security card, some pictures from when she was a kid. No money or credit cards or anything like that, but still, who leaves without their important papers, I mean voluntarily, right?"

"Right. That does sound strange. Though I guess, maybe if she was in a hurry . . ."

"Yeah, or drunk, or stoned, or who knows what. Anyway, just wanted Nicky to know."

"Okay, I'll tell her if I see her. Oh, and Ed, what was the client's name?" Storm asked, though of course she already knew.

"Helena. Helena Smith."

Keeping her face carefully neutral, Storm scribbled the name on a sticky note. "Okay, got it. I'll let her know."

"You know, it'll probably turn out to be the boyfriend," said Big Ed. "It's always the boyfriend or the husband. He probably forgot about clearing out the safe, if he even knew about it."

"Yeah, that's probably it. I'll be sure to let her know if I see her before you do."

"Good. Okay. Thanks," said Big Ed. With a nod, he left.

Storm let out the breath she'd been holding. Damn it. She knew he was talking about Helena Smith from the start. Her heart had hammered so hard, she was sure he could hear it. Her hands were so icy, she'd had a hard time writing the name. She looked at it now, the shaky letters spelling Helena Smith, spelling out the name of the last person she would ever target.

She was done. She was scared. And she had to get in

touch with Howard. Let him know everything had changed. The other ones had gone so well. No one ever questioned that the last two targets had skipped town.

People on probation, people who had to do things they didn't want to do, knew they wouldn't do, sometimes they did skip. But the police weren't buying it this time. This time, there was enough evidence to raise suspicion.

God, who'd have thought that a drugged-out, used-up mess like Helena Smith would have had a floor safe or anything worth keeping inside one?

The phone rang and Storm answered it from habit.

"H-h-hell-o," she said, her voice breaking like strings on a violin wound too tightly.

"You okay?" Tom asked.

Storm held the phone away, coughed, gathered her thoughts.

"Tom?"

"Yeah."

"Sorry. Frog. What's up. Are the kids okay?"

"Kids are fine. Do I call that seldom?"

"No, just . . . I don't know. Just nervous, I guess." Storm forced a smile, a big believer in the idea that people could 'hear' a smile through the phone.

"I'm calling with good news, so no need to be nervous."

"What kind of good news?"

"The best. You know that job me and Rylan have been working on? The proposal for the new county building?"

"Of course. That's all you two have talked about the last few months." Rylan Durst was Tom's sometimes-partner on larger projects. They'd worked together off and on since their days sharing a dorm room.

"Hang onto your hat. We got it!" Tom practically shouted into the phone.

"That's fantastic," Storm enthused.

"I know. It's insane. Rylan just called. We have to meet with the project manager, some guy with a hard to pronounce name. You know him?"

"No," she said, feeling amused. Just because I work for the county doesn't mean I know everyone who does. I barely know half the people in the probation department."

"Sure. I just thought maybe you could help with the name."

"Sorry," she said. Storm was glad Tom's thoughts were focused on a new project. He was less likely to notice her feigned enthusiasm. The only thing she could concentrate on right then was Helena Smith and the police. Had she or Howard left anything behind? Had the house been wiped free of fingerprints?

"—doing some consulting too. So not just one of those, hand-it-over kind of jobs. Storm?"

"Yes, I heard you, Tom. That's great."

"And it means I might even see you once in a while. We could do lunch when I'm out there."

"That would be awesome. I can't wait. When will you know everything?"

"As soon as we meet with this guy, this project manager. The meeting's at one, so I'll call you right after, okay?"

"Of course okay. You'd better call as soon as you know for sure."

"But we know we got the contract."

"No, I mean for sure about lunch. I mean you buying my lunches. That's so awesome."

"This is what you see as the thing to celebrate, me buying your lunch? Not your husband's talent being recognized. Not your husband's career taking off. No. Just a free lunch?"

"Damn right," Storm said with a note of glee—or was it hysteria in her voice. She hung up.

She wanted to lower her head to her desk, close her eyes, and think. Instead, she picked up a pen and opened her daily planner with small innocent movements that anyone looking into her office would have found normal. The fact that she was simply tracing over the top of words that had already been written, that she was too anxious to even try to read, was not important. What mattered was keeping a calm demeanor and waiting until she could talk to Howard.

Storm wanted to call him, but the risk was too high. Rule number four. No connections. That wasn't just no connections to the targets, it also meant no connections between Howard and herself.

Over the last few months she had called him several times, calls made during the day that could be construed as calls to a client, until Helena Smith and the frantic one at three in the morning. How would she explain that?

Her thoughts jumbled, her emotions in chaos, Storm considered her options. She wanted to be clear on what her next steps would be before she found an out-of-the-way pay phone to call Howard. She shad to warn him.

Or did she?

CHAPTER EIGHT

AT FIFTEEN TO FIVE, knowing she needed more time to think and might have been late getting home, Storm reached for the phone to call Tom. Before she could touch it, it rang, making her jump.

"Washington County Pro—" Before she could complete the greeting, the receptionist cut in.

"You've got a client in the front office. Says he hasn't got an appointment but was hoping you could fit him in."

"What's his name, Carrie?"

"Howard Kline," she answered.

Unsure whether she was relieved or angry, Storm said she'd be right there and hung up. What the hell was

Howard up to now? Did he need another travel permit? Was he going to deliver another version of 'I told you so' about her inability to handle Helena Smith?

It didn't matter. At least she would be able to talk to him about what she'd learned from Big Ed.

"Howard," she said, standing at the door to the reception area. "Please, come with me."

Deceptively, like an obedient dog, he stood up and followed her to her office.

Howard sank into the ugly gray chair on the opposite side of her desk. He looked relaxed, even pleasant. She noticed his normally cropped short hair was growing out. His clothes were clean, with a northwest flair. If she hadn't known he was a sociopath with a penchant for torture, she'd have pegged him as a store clerk at some high-end outdoor store like REI or Cabela's.

"What brings you here today, Mr. Kline?" she asked, emphasizing the mister and trying to establish a professional distance between them.

"Brought you a present," he said. He reached into his shirt pocket and pulled out something white, the size and shape of a playing card, and placed it on her desk.

"Is this what I think it is?" she asked, looking from the card to him.

"Mag key," he said softly, casting a quick glance over his shoulder. She also looked out into the hallway. It was empty. Many of her coworkers had already left for the day.

"Just remember . . . security is there to make sure the employees make it to their cars from six in the morning until eleven at night. Give it a little more time to be sure, though. You should be good from midnight until five."

He pushed the key to the center of the desk. "There, now you got everything you need. And don't worry. No one is going to be looking for it. I liberated it from a guy who has never come in early or left late in his life. That key has been in his desk gathering dust a long time. Even if he figures out it's missing, I doubt he'd report it. I mean, they're supposed to keep their keys on them, though I doubt half of them do."

"But why?" she asked. She slid her nails under the card, and picked it up. It seemed so harmless, but she knew it was anything but. With a quick series of motions she slid open the file drawer in her desk where she kept her purse, opened the purse, dropped the key inside and slid the drawer shut.

She looked up at him and cocked her eyebrow at the familiar, annoying half-smile he wore.

"Well," he replied. "I know you promised not to go it alone again, but if you're like me . . . and you are . . . I figure you'll do what you want. So if you're going to go out there on your own, you might want a way to finish the job. Less chance I'll find my butt in a sling if I keep yours out of one, huh?"

"I guess," Storm replied. "Though I really did mean what I said. I'm not planning on doing that again. It was just an experiment. You know, in case you did move to Washington or wherever. Speaking of which, how did your job interview go? Have you heard anything?"

Howard looked at her blankly for a moment, then, "Oh, it went okay, I guess. Haven't heard yet. Probably won't, but it was worth a shot, right?

"Right." Storm got up and peered into the hall. No one

was in sight, though she could hear voices from a couple of the nearby offices. She returned to her seat, leaned forward, and in a low voice said, "Listen, something's happened. I was going to find you at work tonight to tell you. That woman—well, the police found a safe in her house. It was full of the kind of things you don't leave behind. They think her disappearance is suspicious, and they've opened an investigation. Think. Is there anything we left behind? Anything that could connect us to the house?"

The smile left Howard's face, and a look of concern replaced it. Storm was pleased to see his brow knit with concentration as he gave the problem the attention she'd hoped he would. For several long moments, he stared down at the peeling surface of her desk. Finally, he looked up.

"We wore gloves the whole time," he said in a low voice. "I didn't get hurt when I hit the door. No blood anywhere."

"That's not entirely true," she admitted.

"What?"

"She scratched me. At some point she grabbed my hair, and her nails dug into my scalp. When I got home and took a shower, I felt it stinging, and I found dried blood in my hair."

"Shit," he exclaimed. "Well, they can't scrape her nails for evidence. I put her in the oxidizer and she's vapor. But I guess some of your blood could have transferred to something. Shit."

"What are we going to do?"

He thought about it for a moment, rubbing his fingers

across his cheeks to his temples. Then he dropped his hands to his lap, shoulders slumping. "Nothing we can do. Just wait and hope."

"The good news," he continued, "is that she wasn't anyone's favorite bitch. I doubt the cops will throw many resources at figuring this one out. Plus I hear all DNA stuff isn't as easy as they make out on those CSI shows."

Storm nodded, a headache starting at the base of her skull. "I'm not great at waiting, but you're right. It's all we can do."

"You're damn right I'm right, baby," Howard cooed, falling into his predictable habit of coming on to her whenever a chance presented itself. "You just hang with me, and you know I'll take good care of you."

"Thank you, Mr. Kline," Storm responded. "Let's keep in touch."

"Yeah, let's do that, let's keep in . . .touch. I feel like you haven't thanked me for your present yet. Maybe you'd like to do that later, huh? When we get in touch."

Gritting her teeth, Storm smiled. "You're a real funny guy, Mr. Kline. Now, why don't I walk you back to the reception area?"

"That would be real nice, Ms. McKenzie," said Howard.

That afternoon, Tom called to let her know he'd picked up the kids from school and daycare and dropped them off at a different daycare, one they used for emergencies now and then. He'd be late getting home, as he was meeting with Rylan to discuss the county job. She'd picked up the kids and parked them in front of the electronic babysitter so she could get a shower.

The shower was long and hot, and she scrubbed every inch of her skin until it was bright pink. Afterward, she dressed in comfortable, gray, yoga pants and a long-sleeved black jersey with a bright-orange Oregon State Beavers logo. Barefoot and with her hair in a high ponytail, she threw herself into creating a perfect 'evening with the family.'

She made a quick dry rub and put four chicken breasts into the oven to bake. Next, she got the kids busy snapping green beans while she diced some bacon to sauté with the beans. That night was a special night for Tom, and dinner needed to be special, too.

The recipe called for almond slivers. There was a bag around somewhere. But where? She'd gone through the pantry, the bread drawer, the snack bowl. Where the hell were they? She was almost in tears. "Where are the almonds?" she asked the kids. "Did you eat the almonds?"

"No, Mom," said Lindsey, her eyes wide at her mother's unusually frantic tone.

"What almonds?" asked Joel.

"The slivered almonds. The bag of slivered almonds I bought at the store to make your father's favorite—"

"Smoke," said Joel.

Storm spun from the table to see smoke rising from the sizzling pan of bacon. She rushed to the stove and pulled the pan away. Bacon grease sloshed over the side and ignited.

She froze for a millisecond, mesmerized by the low flames dancing across the stove's red-hot burner and then turned, set the pan in the sink, took a cast iron lid from a cabinet, and calmly placed it over the burner. She left it there a moment then lifted it, releasing a puff of smoke. The fire was out.

"Wow!" shouted Joel. "That was cool."

"That was scary," argued Lindsay. "Fire is dangerous. It can burn you up. Tell him, Mom."

"Your sister's right," Storm said. "Fire is dangerous. That's why you have to learn how to control it. You have to stay calm and put the fire out."

"That's why kids don't play with matches," explained Lindsay to her brother."

"That's right too, Sugar Pop. You can't use matches until you've learned all about fire safety, but that won't be until you're a little bit older. Now, since you guys did such a great job with the beans, how about you get a special extra TV hour?"

"Woohoo!" Joel shrieked, his usual enthusiasm, and sometimes wearing energy, diverted from the kitchen to the family room.

"What about you? Don't you want to watch TV?" Storm asked her daughter, who had unexpectedly stayed behind.

Lindsay rolled her eyes. "I don't want to watch the stuff he watches, but if I don't, he whines like a baby."

"Then, how about helping me finish dinner?" asked Storm, opening the back door and waving the smoke from the room.

"Can we make a cake?"

"Cookies," Storm compromised, thinking about the roll of dough she'd tucked in the freezer after the last shopping trip and how much less messy it would be than a cake.

"Okay. Cookies." Lindsay walked into the kitchen and stared curiously at the grease-and-ash covered stovetop.

Storm shut the door, crossed the space, and bent to kiss the top of her oldest child's head. "You're growing up way too fast," she told her.

Later, Tom congratulated his family on putting together 'The best chicken, beans, mashed potato and chocolate chip cookie dinner, ever!'

He'd also appreciated the banner they hung over the table. True, it said HAPPY BIRTHDAY, which wasn't quite right, but the color and excitement it added made it work.

Storm spent the evening laughing at Tom's witticisms and trying to keep it light and airy for the kids, but by the end of the evening, her headache was raging. By the end of the night, she was rubbing her temples and rolling her head from shoulder to shoulder to work out the tension.

"Mommy doesn't seem to be feeling well," Tom told the kids.

"It was the smoke," said Lindsay.

"Smoke?"

"From the fire."

In all the excitement of preparing a special dinner to celebrate their father's news, the kids had momentarily forgotten the fire. Tom turned to Storm with a quizzical expression. "Fire?"

"Just a little grease spill. I was frying something and got distracted."

Tom's brows rose. He might not have known the entire story around Storm's childhood accident, but he knew she was not one to become distracted around a potential source of fire.

After the kids had gone to sleep, Tom found Storm in the kitchen, drying and putting away the dishes. He lent a hand, companionably quiet at first, but then he said, "Even the kids have noticed you're not yourself lately. What's going on, Stormy? You're hardly ever here, and when you are, you seem light years away."

Storm shrugged. "I don't know. Just a busy time of year, I guess. Holidays are coming up. Lots of planning to do."

"I hear you, but you know, this new project—it's huge. The money it brings in will make this a pretty good Christmas. Plus, it will allow me to bid on other bigger projects. This is a real important time for me. I hate to ask you, but can you try just a little harder to get home on time, spend more time with the kids?"

"Of course," Storm answered, sliding a spoon into the utensil drawer. I just—"

"I know, you're just tired. I get that. I do. You work hard. You keep a perfect house. You put it all on yourself, though. Me and the kids, we don't need a perfect house, and I never asked for a perfect wife."

"That's good, because you sure didn't get either one," Storm said.

"What's wrong with our house?" His tone was so plaintive, Storm's heart went out to him. Sometimes the little boy in him shone through, and she wanted to protect him, save him from the big, bad world.

"There is nothing wrong with our house. It's just not perfect. Nothing is perfect."

"Maybe not, but you're pretty damn close, so when you start grease fires, when you show up late with lame excuses, well, we notice."

"Look, maybe you're right," Storm admitted. "Maybe I

do need to be here more. I've taken advantage of having you at home. Here, hand me that."

She took the bowl he'd been drying over and over and put it in the cupboard. He took another from the rack. "I realize what this new job means, and I promise to cut back on the late nights. No more Avon, Sylvia Jewelry, or Naughty Nights parties."

"Hold on there. Don't go giving everything away. Those Naughty Nights parties now . . . we might consider an exception there."

Storm grabbed the damp sponge off the edge of the sink and threw it at him. It bounced off his shoulder and to the floor. At first, he pretended to be shocked and then wound the dish towel and snapped it at her. She turned and ran, and of course, he followed, all the way to the bedroom and a headache cure.

CHAPTER NINE

THE RESTAURANT'S pretentious furnishings, granite bar, too much wrought iron, and black-framed art-for-the-masses didn't annoy Storm as much as the prissy waitresses did.

Still, the chef was good, the tomato and basil soup hot and creamy, the grilled cheese crisp and also hot. Hot was important in the midst of November, in the middle of a week when temperatures hovered around freezing and rain threatened to turn the streets into skating rinks.

Storm sat in a booth at the restaurant across from her friend, Nicky, whose hands were wrapped possessively around a large cappuccino. She was staring as if fascinated at the pattern of a leaf drawn in froth inside her cup.

"The reason I didn't tell you I was taking time off to go away with Jackson," she said, "was because I'd done so much complaining about him, I was afraid you'd be mad."

"It's your life," replied Storm. "If you want to go and ruin it . . ."

"See what I mean?" said Nicky, with a toss of her head. Her newly shorn hair, dyed white blond except for the powder-pink ends, had been so heavily gelled that it stayed in place like a spiky helmet.

"I was just joking. Heck, I haven't even met the man. Plus, I do feel bad that you guys have broken up again."

"Hey, how did you know we broke up? I didn't tell you."

Storm laughed. "You didn't have to. Your hair told me. Every time you break it off with him, your hair gets shorter, and weirder. If you want sympathy, well, I'm very sympathetic . . . for your hair."

"It's not that weird. Is it? I mean, I can get the dye stripped out. Should I do something else?"

Storm smiled at her friend. Six weeks and nothing much had changed. Work was the same. Nicky and Jackson were still back-and-forthing. Even Tom's new job hadn't had as much impact as they'd expected.

It had been a peaceful six weeks—uneventful, boring. But boring had been wonderful, especially since she'd been expecting someone to knock on her door, cuffs in hand . . . and they hadn't.

"Not to change the subject, but—"

"To change the subject," they both chimed in.

"Yes, well, remember that client of mine Big Ed talked to you about? That woman who disappeared?" asked Nicky.

"Sure, I remember. What about her?"

"I got a call from the sheriff's office this morning. They're calling off the investigation. It won't be completely closed, of course, but they aren't going to actively pursue it anymore. They figure the boyfriend did it—if she was murdered, I mean. He's in jail now, for distributing, and will probably be in prison once he sees the judge and gets his sentencing. Might even end up on your caseload one of these days. So, as far as they're concerned, he's off the streets anyway."

"What was he distributing?" Storm asked, not even mildly interested, but trying to hide the relief that threatened to lift her from her chair and send her floating around the room. For the first time in weeks, she felt like she could take a deep breath.

"Meth. What else?" Nicky replied.

"What else," agreed Storm, with a shrug.

Storm tried to call Howard twice that afternoon to give him the news, but each time it went straight to voice mail. Either his phone was turned off or the battery was dead.

Later that afternoon, Storm called Tom. "I think I might be a little late, maybe just half an hour or so. Will you be able to pick up the kids? It looks like snow, so I need to finish some things up just in case the roads are bad tomorrow and I can't get in. Plus, I want to get some work together to do from home. Don't want to waste my vacation time."

"You're so funny, Storm. Call to tell me you'll be a few

minutes late. Forget to tell me you'll be three hours late."

"I guess my OCD is intermittent," Storm joked.

"You mean CDO?"

"What?"

"If you were really OCD you'd get it."

Storm pondered a moment. "Oh, the right order alphabetically. I'm going to hang up on you now. That was bad, even for you."

"One can only try. Anyway, don't worry about the kids. I'm only working half a day today. Dads need downtime too, you know."

"Game?" asked Storm.

"Game," Tom replied. "Ducks against—"

"Spare me the details. Just don't make a mess. Don't let Jeremy eat us out of house and home, and tell Rylan that if he smokes one of his cigars on the porch, to keep the darn doors shut."

CHAPTER

TEN

SOFT AS A KITTEN'S PAWS, fat flakes of snow patted the windshield of Storm's car. It was early for a winter storm. Although snow could fall heavily across the higher elevations, it was rare in the Portland area. Rare enough that even a dusting caused slowdowns in transportation, schools to open late or not at all, and weather guessers to rant tirelessly and with great drama on every local news station.

Shivering at the chilly touch of the upholstery and the frigid steering wheel, Storm slid the key into the ignition and turned it. The car hesitated as if complaining about having to start on such a cold night but finally, reluctantly, turned over.

It was midnight. Storm had tried to reach Howard twice more with no luck. Her OCD, or CDO as Tom had joked, would not let her rest until she spoke to him.

The burden of fear these past six weeks had been oppressive. He—no, they—hadn't deserved that. Sure, they had played a dangerous, even ugly game, a game whose rules she'd unwisely broken, but they'd also brought a little justice into the world. She felt they'd earned their luck, even if she couldn't trust it to continue.

She wanted to let Howard know they appeared to be in the clear. Since their last conversation he'd been compliant with her requests to neither call nor visit her at the office. Finding him, telling him the good news as soon as she could, seemed like something he'd earned.

Storm sat for a few minutes, letting the windows defrost and watching the snow spin in obedience to the wind. As soon as she'd shared the news with Howard, she'd head back home. A hot shower, warm pajamas, and a good book figured heavily in her daydreams. Planning to work from home meant she could sleep in, and she was looking forward to that as well.

With icy-cold fingers, Storm grabbed the steering wheel and backed the car out, thinking about Howard and how anxious he must have been and the relief he'd feel when he learned they were probably safe.

Storm parked in the empty front lot of Traynor Chemical and felt the car tremble, buffeted by a gust of wind. The storm and high winds promised in the weather report were in full effect. Though the snow had stopped falling, the conflicting breezes whipped it up and sent it dancing across the parking lot in spirals and whirls.

Clutching the far-too-thin fabric of her coat, Storm sprinted for the front door. Normally, she'd have pushed the talk button on the intercom and waited for Howard to let her in. But it was far too cold for that. She swung her purse containing the mag key across the face of the reader. The light on it went from red to green, and there was a distinct click as the door unlocked. She grabbed the handle, pulled the door open, and stepped inside.

The vestibule was much less windy but not appreciably warmer. She swung her purse again, and the second door unlocked. She pushed through and stepped gratefully into the warmth of the well-heated building.

She wasn't sure where Howard would be in the vast maze of hallways and rooms but thought she would find a phone in one of the offices and call him. She would avoid using her cell phone to call him if at all possible.

The building smelled like bleach and, oddly, curry. No doubt someone's lunch or dinner, maybe even Howard's.

She moved into the familiar hallway, the one that led to the kill room. As she walked, motion sensors flicked on the lights, so she was always moving toward shadow, leaving behind light.

If she remembered correctly, there was a phone mounted on the wall just on the other side of the showers. It had probably been put there in the event of a chemical spill so someone could call 911. *Probably installed before the time everyone had their own cell phone,* she mused.

Halfway down the hall, Storm heard a sound that made the hair on the back of her neck stand on end, her stomach clench. It was a shriek of pain, and her reaction was visceral, primal. In any culture, such a sound would have signaled danger. Storm didn't think the danger was to her, though. She charged forward. Blood pounded in her ears. A steady light ahead drew her on.

Skidding around the corner of the doorway and into the familiar shower room, Storm saw what she'd expected. A woman was standing, her body taut as she danced on tiptoe, trying to avoid being strangled by the rope that circled her neck, and was tied to an overhead pipe. She was helpless, with her arms tied behind her. She was also unable to speak; duct tape had been wrapped around her head from nose to chin. The woman stared at Storm and then looked quickly to the door opposite the one Storm had entered. Then she repeated the motion. She was trying to warn Storm of Howard's presence.

"Shit, it's you," said Howard as he stepped inside the room and leaned a sawed-off wooden baseball bat against the wall. "Heard you coming down the hall and scrambled. What are you doing here?"

Storm struggled with the question while her thoughts spun frantically. She took in the woman's expression of shock and fear. Blood was running down one of her ankles in a thin but steady stream. She smelled the copper scent of that blood and the musk of sweat and urine. Her mind reeled, and she stepped back until she was against the wall, just as her knees gave way and she slid, as if boneless, to the floor.

"What the hell?" said Howard. "You okay?"

Unable to answer, Storm wrapped her arms around her knees and put her head down. She was shaking. Not just on the outside but on the inside as well. She was trembling so hard, she thought she might come apart, her very cells vibrating to broken shards.

She hugged herself tightly and took deep, calming breaths.

Howard dropped to his knees beside her, took her hands in his. "Man, you're so cold." He rubbed her hands.

After a moment, she was able to lift her head and look him in the eye. "What are you d-doing?" she asked, so hot with anger she wondered if he could see flames dancing in her eyes.

"Just an experiment," he said. She heard the echo of her own words from six weeks earlier. "Wanted to see if I could do one on my own, and guess what—I can. Not that I want to . . ." he trailed off, as if to reassure her she would not be left out.

"You can't do that," she said, her voice growing incrementally stronger with each syllable. "You can't just kill innocent people."

"Oh hell, Storm, she's not innocent. Not by a long shot. I picked her up on 82nd in Portland. She was working a corner. It took me two minutes and twenty-five bucks to get her into my car. Plus, she's an addict. She's got pick marks all over her face, and her teeth are starting to rot. She'll be dead inside a year, anyway."

"You can't kill someone just because they're killing themselves," Storm argued.

"Sure you can," Howard said with a tight smile. "Look." He pointed.

Storm turned her head and saw that the woman was no longer fighting the noose around her neck. She had either passed out or simply given up. Whatever the reason, she had stopped fighting to stand erect, and the noose had tightened, strangling her.

Storm rolled to her hands and knees and slowly got to her feet. "Get the cart."

After the cleanup, once all signs of the murder—not a justice killing this time—had been burned or washed away, Storm turned to Howard.

"You can't do this again. We kill for a reason, to avenge the abuse of the innocent and to prevent the continuing abuse. We're supposed to be protecting people. You can't just pick people off the street."

"I hear you," Howard said. "I know that's what it's about. But how do you know what she does when she goes home at night? What if she goes home to a house full of kids who'd be better off without her drugged-out ass?"

"I don't know. But we can't kill someone on a maybe. This has to stop. Promise me you won't do this again?"

"Sure. No problem," Howard reassured her. "I told you it was just an experiment, a one-time thing."

"Do you swear?" she demanded.

Howard crossed his heart and nodded. There was no smile on his face. He seemed subdued and sincere.

Taking a deep breath, Storm consciously set the past hour behind her. She'd gone there for a reason. "I have something to tell you. I found out the police are dropping the investigation into Helena Smith's disappearance. They can't have found any blood or anything else to connect us as suspects. We were lucky . . . this time. That's another reason you can't just break the rules and do what you want. You don't want to blow this, Howard. You don't want to use up our luck."

"You sound like one of those Vegas gamblers," said Howard. "Like luck's something you find, not something you make. Like it's got a life expectancy."

"It does. A short one. We're already past ours."

"Nah, that's just superstition talkin'. You sound like my grandmother. She used to have all these weird ideas, too. Don't walk under a ladder. Never break a mirror. Sheep on the left is good luck. Stomping kittens is bad luck. None of that stuff is real. Luck is doing what you want, whenever you want, and not getting caught."

"Damn it, Howard, that's my point. We could have been caught."

"That would have been your bad luck, huh?" said Howard. "Wasn't my blood in that house."

Storm had been leaning with her back against the wall. Howard was standing in front of her, arms crossed. Now he uncrossed them and put his the palms of his hands on the wall to either side of her face. The gesture was like a lover getting ready for a kiss or a fighter trapping someone in place.

She wasn't sure what she was more afraid of: being kissed by him again or of being hit. Neither action promised to lead to a happy ending.

"Or did you plan to rat me out if you got caught?" he asked. His dark eyes drilled into hers, searching for some sort of truth she might have been hiding from him.

She shook her head but didn't try to step away or even break eye contact, afraid that in this cat-and-mouse game it was not a good idea to appear too mouse-like. "What would that get me?" she asked honestly. "You think I'd get less time if they found out I had help killing three people?" She made a scoffing sound and frowned at him. Her appearance of confidence worked, and he stepped back, dropping his arms.

"So, what now, huh?"

"What do you mean, what now?" she asked, pushing a stray strand of hair behind her ear and stepping away from the wall.

"We're home free. It's been over a month. I say it's go time," he explained.

"Have you not been listening? There is no go time. We are done."

"We can't be done."

"Why not? You don't give a damn about my reason for doing this. I thought you did, but not after this."

"Oh, give it a rest, will you? We do want the same thing, and I screwed up. Do I have to remind you that you broke the rules, too, and for the same reason? We had to prove something to ourselves. Well, we're done with that. I've already said I won't do this again. So, can we stop talking about justice and start talking about keeping your ass out of the fire?"

"I just told you, our asses, as you so nicely put it, aren't in the fire."

"I agree with half of that. My ass is just fine. But yours I'm not so sure about."

"Why?"

"Look, I was thinking. The cops got an idea now that this Hannah Smith . . ."

"Helena," she corrected.

"Don't matter," he said. "Point is, they think she didn't just disappear. They think she was killed, huh? That might get someone thinking. Maybe they look at her probation record. Maybe they cast out a little wider and look at a whole lot of probation records. They start to see a pattern. Three people have disappeared and all from your team. That's what you told me, right, that you heard about these people from your own team?"

Storm swallowed hard and reached inside her coat sleeve to tug at the cuff of her shirt sleeve. There was a loose thread. She pulled at it until it tore free, then she moved on, plucking all around the edge.

"That wouldn't be such a big deal for us," he continued. "But one thing is going to stand out. You know what it is?"

Storm wasn't sure, but she suspected what he would say next, and she wasn't disappointed.

"Four people on your team. Three people missing. Each one of your team has got someone missing except you. Your clients are all right where they should be. That seem funny to you? It might seem funny to someone."

Storm thought about it. Was he right?

"Also," Howard went on, "I sort of need this one. Your unexpected appearance ruined things for me, and you know what happened with the last one. You owe me one," he said.

"I owe you one?" Storm repeated, a sense of helplessness crawling down her spine as cold as the snow melting from the collar of her jacket.

"Damn right. In point of fact you owe me two, but I'm letting that second one go. What I do expect is, you make sure the next one is a woman—and not some heifer either. Truth is, a man can only last so long with Rosie Palm. I need some real, well, you know," he said, his cheeks unexpectedly flushed a blotchy red. "Next one has to be a woman, and I get to have some alone time with her. Make up for you ruining my fun with this one."

Storm contemplated Howard having sex with the poor woman whose body she had helped him dispose of, a body that was torn, bones broken—an innocent woman.

No, she couldn't think about that. If she dwelled on it too long she was afraid some essential part of who she was would change. Already she felt remorse, a terrible clawing guilt she could barely stand. Dark moments, deep regrets. If she succumbed to them, she might have done something stupid. She could have turned Howard in, maybe even herself. The prospect of peace through repentance appealed to her. The idea of a calm mind, untroubled by anger or a need for vengeance—was that even possible?

She couldn't afford such thoughts. Tom needed her. The kids needed her. She'd made a mistake choosing Howard for a partner. This was her punishment for that mistake, to carry the guilt and the memory. The woman had tried to signal her. Had she been trying to save herself or Storm? It was the kind of question that would haunt her nights.

But she was tough. She'd survive those nights. All the things she'd lived through had made her exactly what she was and had led her right to this point. Yes, the woman was innocent, and killing her was wrong. But she had not killed her. The guilt was Howard's. Her kills were clean. They were in the service of justice and of the innocent.

Storm sighed deeply. "Okay, Howard, you have a good point, and yes, I guess I do owe you one. But we'll do it my way. I'll select the target. Got it?"

"Not too old or ugly," he said, sounding like someone at a drive-through placing a special order. Hold the pickle, no onions.

"No, of course not," she promised. "I'll set it up. But this is the last time, you remember that. After this one the justice killings stop. You hear me?"

"Loud and clear," said Howard. "Over and out."

CHAPTER ELEVEN

TUESDAY, according to studies, is the most productive day of the work week. That was probably why, on that Tuesday, Storm found herself staring at three files arranged across her desk.

Each of the files represented a woman in her caseload. They all shared similarities. All three were reasonably attractive, as Howard had requested. Each had been suspected, but never convicted, of child abuse or neglect. Odds were they would continue being abusers, destroying innocent lives and never fully paying for it. They'd all been arrested on drug charges, done some jail time, and been freed to make their children's lives a living hell again.

Studying the files, Storm realized that choosing one of these women as a target was different than her other choices. For one thing, she knew them. She had met with each of them at least twice, and though that was not the basis for a warm and fuzzy relationship, it did make them seem more real and therefore harder to pronounce sentence on—and turn over to Howard.

On the other hand, since whichever one she picked would already know her, there was no need to take all the convoluted steps to guarantee the target would later recognize her as an officer of the court. Something Storm felt added a certain legitimacy to carrying out the sentence they deserved.

Furthermore, in the beginning, she'd been absolutely sure she was doing the right thing. The evidence of what those people had done to their kids was in their files, complete with police reports and graphic photographs.

This time, she wasn't as sure. She had to be honest and admit that this one was less about justice and more about appeasing Howard.

This would be the last one, she promised once again—just four. There had been four rules, and there would be four killings. The symmetry seemed like a good sign. After this, she would be free of Howard and of finding and killing targets. In fact, if what Tom said was true—that she'd be able to quit her job—she would soon be free of probation and parole entirely. No more dealing with offenders. No more glimpses of children with haunted eyes and scarred bodies.

She fantasized about what she'd do after she quit the

department. Stay at home with the kids? It sounded good for the short term. There were some projects she'd been putting off. But after that, maybe part-time somewhere? She could take a class. She'd thought about an art class, maybe watercolor?

There was a watercolor in the cafeteria of the Washington County Public Service Building across the street from the courthouse where she worked. She walked over there a couple times a week to buy coffee from Cappuccino Corner, the coffee shop just inside the main doors. She preferred their blend to the ubiquitous Starbucks on the corner. After getting her coffee, she'd wander down the hallway to the lightly used cafeteria to admire a row of paintings someone had donated for display there.

The first time she'd seen them was during a retirement party held in the cafeteria. Their realism stood in contrast to the other donated art around the county building, mostly modern pieces that looked like a child's temper tantrum in bas-relief.

Her favorite watercolor was a snow scene. It showed the distant roofline of a barn, the tops of fir trees, and in the foreground, a snowy hill with a few stalks of yellow hay poking through the snow. The smoky-gray clouds and sense of stillness was calming. She would have loved to have been able to paint like that.

Sensing a presence, Storm looked up from her desk to see Carrie, the young receptionist, standing in the doorway. She was a freckle-faced natural redhead, who kept her hair braided, rolled, and pinned like Heidi from the old Swiss story. She tended to wear baggy sweaters and pants that were too short. Poor Carrie was also obviously and embarrassingly in love with Big Ed, who was, as far as Storm knew, very happily married.

"Hi, Storm. Norma's out sick, so I'm delivering the mail," she explained, stepping into the room and laying a handful of large inner-office envelopes and a single standard white envelope on her desk.

"You could have just put it in my mail slot," Storm noted, feeling slightly annoyed but not sure why.

"Oh, but I wouldn't get to say hi, and besides, I'm bored. Not much to do today. Always slows down around the holidays, doesn't it?"

"Yeah, I guess. Well, thanks," Storm said, and turned toward her computer, trying to appear busy. Carrie looked like she wanted to talk, but Storm wasn't in the mood, and reluctantly, Carrie seemed to realize that and left her office.

For a moment, a very short moment, Storm had been thinking about such pleasant things. Carrie had pulled her out of her daydream and into the nightmare of her life. She had to join Howard for one more high-risk justice killing. No, call it what it is: another killing. How could it be justice when she wasn't even sure about her choice?

The woman she'd finally selected, Angela Ruiz, did have the Department of Human Services Child Welfare Division involved in her life. From what Storm could tell, DHS had been called in more than once to determine if Angela's kids were safe.

Once, a year earlier, all four of her kids had been removed, but only for a couple of weeks. She'd kicked out the guy who had given her oldest daughter a black eye, and that was proof enough for DHS to believe she'd made her kid's welfare a priority. Storm wasn't so sure.

She'd only met with Angela twice, but the woman hadn't made the best impression. She was tiny and a little overweight. Despite that, she wore blouses so low-cut, they showed the string of lace-edged hearts tattooed across her breasts and jeans so tight they pushed a roll of fat over her belt. Her shoes had four-inch heels, and she smelled like she bathed in gallons of perfume.

She also looked hard, and her attitude was just on the edge of hostile. Her dark eyes, rimmed in charcoal-black liner, never seemed to make contact. Most of the time she just stared at her long, perfectly manicured nails and answered, 'uh-huh' or 'nu-huh' to every question Storm asked. Sometimes she'd flick her ironed, Cher-length hair back over her shoulder and make brief eye contact, but there was no real exchange.

The problem was, Storm didn't want to select someone one the basis of an active but personal dislike. She continued to struggle with the knowledge that her selections, up to now, had been made carefully, based on plenty of information and a sense of outrage sometimes shared by her coworkers. This one . . . was this one even justice?

Sighing, Storm picked up the file. She'd made the selection. Angela Ruiz was young and attractive. The women in the other two folders were older, one in her late fifties, the younger one with a face ravaged by years of using meth.

All three had histories that made them potential targets, but only Angela fit Howard's criteria. Is this what It had come to? Storm tried not to think about it as she took the file to the copy room and scanned the page with the information they would need to find Ms. Ruiz.

Once they found her, Howard would incapacitate her, Storm would tie her up and help get her to the kill room. After that, all she wanted was for it to be over, and fast.

She guessed, however, that it wouldn't go that smoothly. Storm suspected that Howard would drag it out, use every moment of the 'special' time he'd demanded. She knew the most horrific thing wasn't whether she'd help Howard rape and kill Ms. Angela Ruiz. She knew she would. The only real decision was whether she'd force herself to watch.

For the first two killings, she'd made herself stay and be a silent observer, flaying her conscience and refusing to hide from the result of her choices.

This time it felt different, and it was. The victim was less chosen by her own actions and fate and more by Howard. But perhaps that was only a justification, a way to give herself an out so she didn't need to participate, even as a witness, in what was sure to be a brutal and violent death.

At least it would be the last time. Storm dreaded what he would say when she made that clear. Luckily, she'd been trained in dealing with conflict, knew how to stand firm. He would, inevitably, have to deal with it. Still, it wouldn't be pleasant.

Storm felt restless. She got up and grabbed her coat. She wanted to move. The walls felt like they were closing in. She decided to walk across the street and get some good coffee. The stuff they made in the break room smelled like burnt tar and gave her heartburn.

There were usually two or three pleasant young women working at Cappuccino Corner, but that day the owner, Dan, was at the front counter. She always liked seeing Dan. He started running the café about the same time she'd started at the county, so in a way, he was one of her oldest work friends.

He was tall, not hard to look at, but most importantly he was invariably friendly and had an inner calm that seemed hard to ruffle.

"How's your day going?" he asked, "And what's your poison?"

"Fine," she answered. "Sugar-free vanilla latte. Extra foam, please."

"You got it, sister." He flashed a wide smile as he reached for the coffee measure.

"How's your day?" Storm asked.

"Beautiful, just beautiful." His smile seemed completely sincere.

Storm marveled, not for the first time, at how Dan managed to keep so steady. Even when he was upset about something, he didn't show it, except perhaps for a slight crinkling around his eyes.

"How do you always manage to seem so darn happy, Dan?" she asked.

She expected an evasive answer, but he seemed to consider it carefully and said, "I guess it's because I'm a born-again Christian. I know, I know. I'm not preaching here. But you asked the question and that's the answer. I wasn't always this easygoing, so I guess there's something to that saying, give it up to God. I mean, when you give up all the stuff you're carrying around, the anger and the negative stuff, well, it makes every day a pretty nice one. That'll be three ten, by the way, unless you want something else?"

"No, that's all. Thanks." Storm said and handed over her preloaded coffee card.

Coffee in hand, she wandered into the cafeteria. 'Cafeteria' was something of a misnomer, because although the room was full of tables and chairs, there was no food service. She wanted to look at the watercolors. Unfortunately, her timing was bad, and the room was unusually crowded with people nuking their lunches in the two available microwaves or sitting at long tables, eating bag lunches or reading.

She headed back to work, pushing through the two sets of double doors and into the chill November wind.

God. Religion. Those were topics she didn't want to think about. How would God look at her justice killings? What religion would accept them as necessary?

In a way, it was funny. Religion had always seemed to her to be nothing more than just another set of rules, judgments, and punishments. Of course, wasn't that what she had been doing? She had judged the people who had broken the rules of a decent society, hurting the very people they should have been kindest to, and she had punished them.

She looked at her targets the way some people looked at cop killers. If a person could kill a man sworn to protect him, well, that person would stop at nothing and was a danger to everyone.

The ones she had gone after weren't that different.

They had hurt the innocent, the children in their trust, and if they could do that, what weren't they capable of?

Someone had to protect children from such monsters. Someone had to eliminate the threat to innocence these monsters posed. To hell with people and religion and their judgment of her.

God, though, was a different story. Was there a creator who saw all and judged all? Would he, she, or it, really judge her actions or her intentions? Was there even such an entity?

She didn't know. All she really knew was that she was freezing. Dashing across the street, jaywalking like every cop, lawyer, or judge returning from getting coffee, she hurried back to her building.

After a quick ride up the elevator, she checked in on the board. She hung her coat on a hook and was back at her desk, wide awake and ready to do some work.

First things first: she picked up the envelope on the top of the stack of mail Carrie had placed on her desk earlier. The white envelope was marked, *State of Oregon, Department of Corrections.*

She picked up her silver letter opener, ripped the envelope open along the top crease, and pulled out a single sheet of white paper.

Storm unfolded it and read it, then read it again, her face slowly paling until it was nearly the color of the paper. Chewing her lower lip, she placed the document on her desk. She slid her hand across it, smoothing out the folds, and read it again:

This is to inform you of the release of Joseph Don Dean.

Storm carefully folded the letter along its fold original

lines.

This is to inform you . . . may pose a risk . . . parole board . . . has served . . . Joseph Don Dean . . .

The words pounded through her head like a roll of thunder. She could not stop them. Coffee forgotten, she stood up, grabbed her coat, and slipped it on.

"I'm not feeling well. I have to go home," she told Carrie at the front desk.

"Oh no. Are you okay to drive? Do you need anything?"

"I'm fine. Cramps," Storm whispered. In her normal voice, she said, "Actually, could you call Big Ed and let him know I had to leave early? You don't have to say why. He won't care."

"Of course," Carrie said, her face lighting up with the prospect of calling him. "I hope you feel better soon. You look terrible."

Storm gave her a wan smile. "I'll be fine. Probably in tomorrow. Goodnight."

"Night."

Sitting in her car, Storm felt like the whole world could see the expression on her face, read the fear, and wonder at it.

She knew she was being crazy, paranoid, but she couldn't help it. The parole board had released him. The stupid, idiotic, evil parole board had released Joseph Don Dean.

Her father.

CHAPTER

TWELVE

JOE DEAN, ex-military, booted out after fourteen years and one too many fights. That all around good guy—most of the time.

That guy, who came home on his first leave and looked up one of his high school sweethearts, not the girl he planned to settle down with, but the neo-hippy chick with the good weed.

After busting ass for six weeks, the weed went a long way, made it easy to ignore a torn condom. That led to a quick wedding and, soon after, a baby girl.

By the time she was thirteen, that baby girl knew she was smart and thought she had the world figured out. Sure,

Dad's drinking was a problem, but it was episodic. You kept your head down, stayed quiet and out of the way, and you would get past it. Find yourself on the other side.

It was like a summer lightning storm. The rumble of thunder a long way off, you knew it was just a warning. Then the lightning came, a crackle of sound, a harsh snap, like the crack of a belt across bare skin.

Seeing a bottle of Johnny Walker Red Label Scotch at home, that was thunder, but Joe Dean noticing you—that was lightning.

So many of the kids at school played the my-old-man's-a-bad-ass game. She'd sit out at recess, her hand cupped around the stub of a cigarette, counting on the chill wind and the laziness of teachers to keep her from being caught smoking, and listen to them.

"Man, you know what he did Friday? He told me I've got a ten-o'clock curfew on the weekend."

"On the weekend? No shit!" some admirer would say.

"Yeah, well . . . mine took away my car keys and said I don't get them back until I get my grades up."

"No wheels? Dude."

"Yeah, well, mine . . ."

And so the game would continue while Joe Dean's daughter sat, tired and cold, squinting into the smoke. Unbidden, her thoughts would slip backward to the previous night, lying in bed and listening to the sound of slaps and her mother's voice pleading quietly, the sound bleeding into the night.

There was no conflict, no confusion, no choice to be made. There should have been. A war should have raged between fear and anger. Between hiding under the covers or going to the kitchen for the turkey knife.

Shame shivered through her body at the memory of that night and others before it because there had been no inner conflict, only cowardice. The memory of that sat like an icy fist in her stomach, sending waves of cold through every vein and artery. Lying there, her blankets pulled up around her, head buried under her pillows, she had shivered as if she were buried in snow.

When the noise stopped and the heavy silence of the early hours settled over the Dean household, only then did the coward slide free of the icy sheets and reach cautiously into a drawer for a flashlight.

Holding the flashlight under the pillow so that no one could hear the snap, she turned it on, lifted it clear, and set it, oh so carefully, on her nightstand. The light reflecting from the chalk-white ceiling was feeble but enough.

Opening her Star Wars lunch pail of treasures, she took out the single-sided razor blade she'd stolen from the garage. She hadn't taken a new one, afraid he'd notice. She pulled one from the trash and disinfected it with rubbing alcohol. It was shiny, clean, and sharp.

Cutters cut their arms. She'd seen them at school. They looked like they'd been playing some sort of game, a boring, unidirectional tic-tac-toe. She was much more creative. Besides, she couldn't risk getting caught. Her cuts had to look like accidents.

Pinching the razor between her thumb and the first two fingers of her right hand, she sliced across the back of her left hand, scoring a diagonal line from the base of her pinkie to her wrist. Blood beaded along the cut.

She cut twice more, shorter but deeper slices, placing

the cuts one on either side of the first. She held her arm up and watched the blood gather and slowly slip down her arm. It was warm against her frozen skin.

Then the cuts began to hurt—sharp, biting pain that made her smile.

Roses. Thorns. It was easy to explain the scratches when her mother saw them. Because she had the world figured out, a lot of things were easy.

This storm would pass.

On the Friday, she spent the night at Annie's. Her dad liked Annie. Sometimes, when the thunder rumbled, she would signal her by toggling the back porch light switch up and down several times.

If Annie saw the signal, she would go over and be polite, sweet, and very attentive, causing a slow rise in the barometric pressure and a delay in the appearance of the lightning.

That day, Annie didn't have time to go in. She'd walked around the block with her friend but then hurried on to meet another schoolmate to get some notes for a class she'd missed. So when Storm got home, late the next morning, she was alone.

"Where's your buddy?" her father asked as soon as she closed the living-room door.

He was sitting in his chair, oriented to face the fireplace and television. On the cigarette-scarred end table next to him sat half a bottle of Bacardi 151, an ashtray with two smoldering cigarettes, his Zippo lighter, and a plate with a sandwich that looked untouched.

His hand was wrapped around a tumbler of amber liquid and he sat erect, legs crossed, corduroy slipper dangling from his foot.

Joe Dean's daughter recognized his body language. Her father was drunk—beyond drunk. He was in that quiet place, somewhere between tempest and passing out. Being wise, she knew all she had to do was be calm, be still, and let the eye of the storm pass.

"So what you and that girl do, you spend the night with? You lesbians? You like to play with each other?"

The accusation was so unexpected, so inappropriate and tasteless that it was like a fresh wound, something so raw, she had no time to develop a defensive scar around it.

Shocked into forgetting prudence and even fear, she raised her chin in defiance, stared into his dark eyes and spat out the words. "Fuck you. Fuck you, you fucking bastard." With tears blurring her vision, she moved to run past him, to seek the cave of her bedroom and the sharp, shiny relief of the razor.

But he was fast, surprisingly fast for a drunk. He caught her blouse in his fist and yanked her back against him, into the chair and onto his lap. The same lap where she'd snuggled to read stories, to have a band aid placed on a scratched elbow, to fall asleep when a summer barbecue lasted too long.

He wrapped one arm around her narrow waist; his watch dug sharply into her ribs, and she couldn't catch her breath. His breath, hot and rank with rum and tobacco, was in her ear. "What did you say to me?" he demanded, his voice gravel, all fury and hurt.

Her arms flailed and she kicked her feet. The heel of one of her shoes came into contact with his shin. He grunted and wrapped his other arm around her, squeezing harder. She coughed, fought for air but couldn't get enough. A wave of dizziness swept over her. She stopped struggling as a gray blur began to move in from the periphery of her vision.

"That's right," her father growled. "That's how you behave. You do what you're told. I say jump, you ask how high. I feed you. I buy your clothes. I work my ass off for you. I own you. I own this. Not some fucking lesbo."

As he spoke, he moved one of his hands to her chest, found her breast and enclosed it, his fingers pressing into the flesh. "This is mine," he said. He squeezed so hard, she couldn't help the moan of pain that escaped her. "I want to touch it, I touch it. Me, not your lesbo bitch friend."

Releasing his hold around her waist, he slid his other hand up to grab and torture her other breast. "This one too," he snarled.

She whimpered as fresh pain shot through her body, but she was too terrified to move. A lifetime of obeying the monster in the lightning was not easily abandoned, even when everything screamed for her to fight, to break free.

But she was a coward, so she slumped against him, every nerve and muscle tense, her body poised for flight but caged in fear.

He continued to knead and squeeze her breasts but not as painfully. When she didn't move, he loosened his grasp even more. Instead of hurting and punishing her, his touch grew tender. He cupped her small breasts gently, ran his thumbs across her nipples.

The pain she could survive. This, she could not.

Twisting, she sank her teeth into his arm, and ground in, her jaw clenching. She felt her lower teeth slide across bone. He grabbed her shoulders, pushed her away and tore loose. She attacked mindlessly, her teeth snapping, looking for a fresh hold. She was facing him now. Her hands, curled into small hard fists, struck at his face, his shoulders, anywhere she could reach.

He grabbed a handful of her hair and jammed her face against his chest. He held her close, making her fists ineffectual.

The cold splash of liquid against her back was a shock. The strong smell of alcohol told her what it was.

Reaching awkwardly, he fumbled for the lighter, grabbed it from the table, flipped the top, spun the wheel with his thumb.

Her shirt went up fast with a whooshing noise. It startled him, and he pushed her away. As he explained later, "I was surprised. I mean, it happened so fast. I was drunk, but it was crazy. She was mad, mouthing off, told her old man to get fucked. Hell, I'm not even sure I was the one with the lighter."

Mrs. Dean walked through the door a few minutes later, took in the sight, and dropped the two bags of groceries she was carrying.

"I put her out," her husband boasted, his shirt covered in blood stains and soot. He was sitting on the scorched carpet clutching the blanket he'd used to smother the flames. His daughter was on the other side of the room, where she'd rolled trying to escape the pain and him—Joe Dean—her loving father.

CHAPTER
THIRTEEN

THANKSGIVING was the one holiday Storm felt she had nailed down. The turkey was in the oven, baking. No fancy brine, no deep-frying, just an old-fashioned turkey, its skin bathed in butter and rubbed with a mix of spices.

The table looked like something out of a magazine, with white tableware, red goblets, a centerpiece the kids had helped her make out of evergreens and red candles. Every place at the table held a setting, ten in all. Six guests were expected, none of them family.

The Mackenzie tradition had always been Thanksgiving with friends, Christmas with Tom's family in Boise, Idaho. For the first time, Storm actually looked forward to getting out of town and driving to Boise. Every time the phone rang or there was a knock on the door, she was sure it was her father. The one she'd told Tom was dead. The one she'd said was a policeman, out of some weird belief it would make her own fascination with criminal justice seem more natural.

She had certainly never divulged that her father was in prison doing ten to twenty for aggravated vehicular assault.

The doorbell rang, announcing the arrival of their first guest. Storm swept the door open to find Nicky, a vision in pink mohair, black ski pants and white, furry, knee-high boots, standing beside her plus-one. "This is Jackson," she said, gesturing to an incredibly handsome African-American man in an expensive tailored suit and a gorgeous fur-lined leather jacket.

"Jackson Wallace," the man introduced himself.

"Come in. Come in. It's freezing out there," said Storm. "Tom's tending bar and dying to actually mix a drink, so if you give me your coats, I'll put them in the guest room and you can go straight back. You know where the kitchen is, Nicky."

"Yes, but I'm pretty sure Jackson can find it all by his little self. He's a man and does not need directions. Right, baby?"

"That's correct, honey." He shrugged out of his jacket and handed it to Storm with a smile. Storm smiled back and rolled her eyes. She felt an immediate sense of kinship.

Jackson moved down the hall to the kitchen while Nicky followed Storm to the guest room, where she tossed the coats onto the bed and turned to her friend. "Oh my gosh, you never told me he was. . ."

"Tall?" Nicky asked impishly.

"I was going to say gorgeous and follow up with freaking rich."

"I know, right? He's something and a half."

"And this is the guy you break up with every five minutes?"

"He has baggage!"

"Who doesn't? What kind of baggage?"

"You heard his name, Wallace."

"So?"

Nicky waited a few seconds, but when Storm didn't immediately get it, she said, "What if I told you Jackson Wallace is an attorney?"

"I'd say he has a good name for an attorney. It's the same as Shirley Wallace."

"His mother!" Nicky exclaimed. Like the most famous lawyer in Portland, and guess who the other Wallace in Wallace and Wallace is?"

"Holy cow!"

"Tell me about it."

Only Storm wasn't thinking about the prestigious law firm, she was thinking about how close she'd come to trying to involve Nicky in the justice killings. "I need a drink," said Storm.

"Me too," said Nicky.

By six, everyone had arrived. The guests consisted of Nicky and Jackson; Tom's partner, Rylan, and his boyfriend, Evan; and their closest neighbors, an elderly couple, Alex and Grace Goodenoff, both retired professors. With all the company, Tom and Storm and the two kids, the house was full of voices.

Storm felt as if she were moving through a lucid dream. Like a Stephen King scene where the loving family gathers around the warm kitchen, unaware the howl outside is more than just the wind.

More than once, her nerveless fingers dropped things: a knife, two forks, the cutting board, even a precious red goblet with gold etching that shattered into a hundred pieces when it hit the kitchen's ceramic-tile floor.

"Hey, we're just your friends. You don't have to be that nervous. We're not judging you," said Nicky, after the goblet fell.

"Actually, we're always judging," corrected Grace as she swept the tiny shards into a dust pan. "Yes, judging, testing, looking for patterns."

"Don't listen to her," said her husband standing at the bar between the dining room and kitchen, with a cup of eggnog in one hand. "She's always overanalyzing things. Clinical psychologist," he explained, nodding to Jackson and Nicky, with whom he'd been chatting a moment earlier.

"Oh, like he's much better. Don't ask him anything about interfaces. Please, I beg of you."

The Goodenoffs looked like a sweet, elderly couple who had slowly, over the course of decade, morphed into each other's doppelganger. They were both, stout, plump, tweedy, and kept their hair cut short and styled in a way that might, generously, be called windblown.

Storm saw them most often out in their garden, pulling weeds or planting flowers or rows of vegetables while holding lively conversations with each other. Their large corner lot held an astonishing amount of plants and not one blade of grass. At other times, she'd see them wandering alone, muttering to themselves.

At first she'd thought they were eccentric or even slightly demented. That was before she'd had a conversation with them.

Storm felt the need to explain. "Grace was a professor of psychology at Portland State University. She's kind of famous for her studies on women in leadership."

"Because she overanalyzed that too," joked her husband. "Bored them into giving her that award so she'd go away."

"Boring, huh?" she asked, glaring at him and shaking the cane she'd started carrying since a fall two weeks previously. "Just don't ask him about structural equation models or meta-analytic methods," she warned.

"Grace, that's not going to be a problem, I assure you. Not one person here has a clue about what you just said. Was that French?" Tom had come into the conversation. His tone and sober expression made them all laugh. The silliness was contagious. The kids got excited and started running around the room, scampering under the dining-room table and hiding under the folds of the tablecloth.

When they'd recovered and Storm had made sure the last of the glass was picked up, Grace continued. "Your friend was right. You really don't have to be nervous. We judge that dinner was wonderful, you made too much pie, and the coffee smells like heaven. Decaf, right?"

Storm nodded.

"Well then, judged and given the gold star. Hand me a cup, my dear."

Ever since receiving the letter announcing her father's

release from prison, Storm felt as if she were moving in and out of the world—connected to it one moment, detached the next. When she was disconnected, sound was muffled, light was dim, and all she knew was a quiet, focused waiting. In the other, there was too much noise, light, and motion, but still she tried to absorb the evening, the laughter and chatter and the good-natured jokes.

What an odd couple Jackson and Nicky made, she pondered, in one of those moments. He was so tall and dark, with big, white, feral teeth while Nicky, with her short pink hair and mohair sweater, was like a fluffy bunny sitting too close to a predator, oblivious to the danger.

Yet Storm also saw how Jackson looked at Nicky, and she wondered if the dangerous one might be the bunny in this case.

The kids were having a blast. Uncle Rylan had bought them early Christmas presents. They were inappropriately expensive electronic games that he seemed to enjoy playing as much as they did. He spent a lot of time on the living-room floor, teaching them this or that move, while his handsome, Nordic-looking friend with the chiseled cheekbones sat at the table, drinking wine at a steady rate, pointedly checking and rechecking the expensive watch he wore and sighing.

Since Storm hadn't liked him from the moment he'd given her home an unpleasant lookover and squeezed her hand while avoiding all eye contact, ignoring his discomfort did not detract from the evening's pleasure.

Jackson was eventually co-opted by Alex and Grace, who soon learned he did estate law and planning. They wanted to know everything he could tell them about reverse mortgages and how they could finance a move to a warmer, drier climate. Thrilled with what he told them, they left early with plenty of smiles and leftovers.

After dinner, Joel fell asleep on the couch, and Tom carried him to bed. When he returned, Storm dimmed the living-room lights and turned up the gas fire. Everyone sat around the living room in companionable silence, full and content. A Christmas song began playing on the radio, and Nicky sang along with it softly. After a moment, Jackson chimed in. Soon everyone was singing Jingle Bells, followed by Auld Lang Syne.

As she sang, Lindsay crawled into her mom's lap and shut her eyes. Storm stroked her hair and let the warmth of the room and of friends and family sink into her bones. Outside, the wind howled, the victim she and Howard had targeted was eating her last Thanksgiving feast, and her father walked free like an ancient curse.

This night was not a cure for the cancer eating through her life. It was just a mixture of vitamins, fortifications against what was coming.

For the moment, it had to be enough.

CHAPTER FOURTEEN

"WHAT DO YOU WANT?" Storm asked as soon as Howard was close enough to hear her. He wore jeans, a burgundy rain jacket, and a brown cap. He looked like someone on a lunch break, out for a stroll.

She'd agreed to meet him at the Jackson Bottom Wetlands Preserve, a 635-acre wildlife preserve located within the city limits of Hillsboro, a quick, ten-minute drive from work.

"Take the far right trail and walk until you get to the third picnic table," he'd instructed.

She hadn't realized how far from the parking lot the third table was. She also hadn't expected the park to be so empty of people or so dark. The trail took her into the deep shadows of the ash and fir trees along a creek the mottled color of burnt steel. The sky was low, clouds seeming to touch the horizon in every direction.

She hadn't wanted to go, but he had insisted, and she definitely didn't want him to go to the office. There was no reason for him to make such frequent appointments. Someone might have noticed. How would she have explained?

No, the wetland was a good idea, private enough to talk, yet public enough to make her feel safe. Or so she thought.

"What do I want?" Howard said, repeating her question. "That's not a very friendly hello."

"Sorry. Hello. What do you want?"

Howard's smile melted. "You know what I want," he said. He stepped around her and climbed onto the table, sitting with his feet on the bench, hunched forward, his forearms resting on his legs.

"A new target?" Storm asked

"A new target," he agreed.

"You know how the last one went. How close we got to real trouble. They may not still be actively pursuing Helena Smith's disappearance, but they're suspicious. We shouldn't do anything for a while. Maybe a long while," she said, broaching the topic she'd been avoiding and nervously waiting for his reaction.

He didn't seem to react at all, just chewed on one of his ragged fingernails, tore a bit away, and spit on the ground. Finally, he sat up.

"One more," he said. "One more and then we take a break. Maybe three, four months."

"Why one more? Why not no more and we take the break now?"

"A couple reasons," he said, holding up two fingers. "No, I take it back, three reasons. One, you broke in on me with the woman I picked up in Portland and you blew my fun with her."

"But you—"

"Hush, it's my turn." He didn't raise his voice, but his tone silenced Storm, nonetheless. "Two, you broke the rules, way more rules, with that last one. I helped you. Saved your ass, in fact, and had zero fun there. Three, you've been thinking you're the queen around here for long enough. When we're in your office, I may have to eat shit and do what you say, but out here, out here we're partners. Partners help each other out. Partners have each other's backs. I had yours. Now it's time for you to step up."

"One more, then we stop."

Howard looked up; his eyes met Storm's. "One more and we take a break."

"A long break."

"A break. Jesus, woman, what do you need to hear?"

"Four months, at least."

"Fine. Four months."

"Okay. I have someone picked out."

A smile broke across Howard's face. A twinkle lit up his eyes. "Now you're talking."

"Her name is Angela Ruiz," Storm explained and told Howard all she knew. She took the address she'd tucked into her purse and handed it to him. "You can follow her, figure out the best way to get to her."

"So we're going after this one because she's what . . . a

serial dater?" Howard scoffed.

"She's a mom who keeps dating gang bangers and putting her kids in danger. We know of at least one incident where one of those boyfriends beat up her oldest daughter. Why did he hit her? Maybe she was fighting him off? Who knows what Mom's letting those boyfriends get away with."

"You got a sick fucking mind, lady."

"Yeah, well try working in P and P awhile."

"No thanks," Howard joked. "I'd never want to deal with a bunch of freaking criminals."

"Funny, Howard. Real funny." Storm reached into her purse and pulled out a phone. "This is what the cop shows call a burner," she explained. "It's a phone that comes preloaded with minutes. No contract. You want to call me, use it. My number's programmed.

"Classy." He took the phone and slid it into the back pocket of his jeans.

"Okay, so we're agreed. After this one we take a break."

Howard didn't answer right away, and when he did, it was not to say what Storm expected.

"Who is it that you hate so much you gotta keep killing them?" he asked.

"What?"

"You know what I mean. You say you want a break and I know you believe that, but I also know you won't be able to wait too long. Who is it you see hanging from the ceiling? Who am I whipping? Who do we incinerate?"

Storm took an unconscious step back. "I don't know what you're talking about."

"You do," he argued. "I saw it in your eyes just now. You were seeing someone, a face. You know exactly who it is. You just won't share it with me."

"I have to go." Storm, rubbed her hands together, as if to warm them. Glancing at the sky, she said, "It looks like it's going to start raining any minute."

Howard stood up on the bench and then leapt to the ground. "Want me to walk you to your car?" he asked, dropping the subject. "It's getting pretty dark. I don't want you to be afraid."

"No thanks. I'll be fine." Storm didn't dare say out loud that the only thing in the park she was afraid of was him.

CHAPTER

FIFTEEN

AS SOON AS SHE shut the door to her car, the sky opened up, and rain fell in torrents. Storm hit the auto lock on her doors, started the car, and sped away.

Howard was . . . perceptive. Yes, that's what he was. She figured, as a sociopath, it had probably been smart for him to study people. Under the mask of an average, not-too-smart guy just trying to get along was a different Howard, a Howard who was keenly intelligent, perceptive, and extremely dangerous.

His disguise was so clever and perfect, she was sure he'd get away—had gotten away—with many horrible things in his life. She thought there was probably only one thing that could reveal what he was—his addiction. He had a real need to hurt the people they took. True, they were abusers and deserved to be punished. They needed to learn empathy through the same suffering their victims had endured. To Storm, this was a balancing of accounts.

The extremes to which Howard took things, however—there was no balance there. Yes, he was addicted to torture and pain as surely as so many of her clients were addicted to drugs. It was just another way to chase a high.

Howard pretended that what he'd been denied was sex with his last two killings. Storm was pretty sure it was his need to hurt that was actually driving him. Or maybe some sick twist of his mind had braided the two into one. He probably couldn't have enjoyed sex without inflicting pain and not the kind of pain a normal sexual masochist would have been willing to endure.

Normal masochist—had that thought just gone through her mind unquestioned? She was absolutely losing it.

Thank heavens for Tom's gift. The day after Thanksgiving, he had presented her with a Christmas card showing a snow-covered tree in the woods. In it were reservations and lift tickets. His parents had decided to take a Christmas cruise, so they weren't going to Idaho, after all. Tom had made reservations for the family at Timberline Lodge at Government Camp near Mount Hood.

"How in the world did you get reservations on such short notice?" Storm had asked.

"Your husband is a very important man," he'd replied. Breaking under her doubtful stare, he admitted, "The folks told me months ago, around the time they booked their cruise. I swore them to secrecy and booked the trip on the off chance we might be able to afford it by then."

"And we can?" she asked.

"We can."

Storm was tired. Tired to the bone and she hadn't realized it until just that moment. The idea of escaping from her everyday life exhilarated her. Though she didn't ski (it was Tom's thing), she would be happy to take the kids sledding, or snow tubing, or maybe they'd just hang around the pool.

There were plenty of things to do, and she imagined at that time of year, the lodge would be beautiful.

In fact, the lodge met all her expectations. Arriving after a short but exhausting drive over snow-packed roads, the family was relieved to park the car and drag their luggage to the check-in counter.

The lodge was decorated for the holidays. A giant Christmas tree stood in the lobby, dressed in shining ornaments and strands of twinkling white lights. Red velvet bows were tied along the timbered bannisters and railings that circled the huge room and to the handles of baskets of freshly cut pine boughs and giant pinecones. A fire of leaping orange and red flames crackled in the huge fireplace. The air was filled with the slightly smoky scent of burning logs and cinnamon.

The children were asleep in the queen-sized bed they were sharing. They were exhausted from their first day in a strange place and didn't put up much of an argument, especially after their warm baths. Storm tucked the blanket around them, making sure their hands were underneath.

Joel always had such icy hands.

She closed the door to the bedroom and moved into the adjoining suite. Tom sat at the desk, a newspaper spread across it, but he wasn't reading. It was too dark. She stood behind him, her hands resting on his shoulders as she looked out the window.

In the cone of light from a street lamp, she could see fat flakes of snow slowly drifting to the ground. In the distance, Mount Hood was a dim blue shadow against a darker-blue background. Tom reached up and took her wrists, pulling her gently forward until her cheek was against his. She tilted her head and kissed his neck.

"Nice out there," she murmured. "Going night skiing?"

"Too late," he said. "Ends at nine and it's what, eleven or so?"

"Pretty late," she agreed. "Kids are out."

"Long day for them."

She nodded, raised her eyes to look out at the fresh snow, so unsoiled, and so perfect.

"Yeah. This was a good idea, bringing us he . . . he . . ." Her last word broke into a sob and tears slipped unexpectedly from her eyes.

Tom, reacting to her weeping, let her go and turned in his chair. "Babe, what is it?" When she didn't immediately answer, he stood up and put his arms around her. "Stormy, tell me what's wrong?"

"Oh, God," she moaned. "What isn't?"

Concern growing, Tom led Storm to the far end of the room, where a selection of overstuffed furniture was oriented to face a carved oak mantle that held a gas fire. He led her to the couch and helped her sit down. The flames in the fireplace burned low, a blue flicker that made their faces seem pale and convoluted.

"You look cold," he said as he covered her legs with a blanket he took from one of the two armchairs. Storm knuckled away her tears, staring down at the black bears woven into the blanket. Tom picked up a remote from the coffee table, and suddenly, the dim fire grew up, casting a welcome golden glow.

He sat beside her and put his arm around her shoulders. "Now tell me," he said, "tell me why you're crying."

"I . . . I don't . . ." Suddenly the lie she'd been about to tell felt like acid on her tongue. She couldn't do it any more, couldn't keep the truth hidden from Tom. He didn't deserve lies.

Fresh tears cascaded down her face. This time, she didn't try to hide them.

"Stormy. Honey, what is it?"

"Not St . . . Stormy. Not m . . . my name," she sobbed. She pulled away, just a little bit, just enough so she could breathe. She couldn't look at him. She looked into the flame as she told him the truth for the first time.

"My name isn't Storm. Or at least it wasn't always. I was born Willow, Willow Tina Dean. Tina for my dad's mom, Willow because my mom just liked that name.

"When I was little and I'd had a bad day, my mom would tell me everything would be fine. She said willows were tough, that they would always bend in a storm. Only, see . . ." she said, turning to look at Tom to make sure he understood, "I didn't want to bend. I didn't want to be the stupid bendy willow. I wanted to be the storm."

Her voice grew stronger though not louder as Storm found the courage to continue.

"So you changed your name?"

"Yes, when I was eighteen, but there's more."

Tom nodded. He waited quietly.

"When I was thirteen, my dad . . . my dad set me on fire."

"What? What do you mean, set you on fire? Your scars?"

"Yes, of course my scars," she said bitterly. He was drunk and I made him mad. But of course he was always mad when he drank," she said, half to herself.

"But you told me there was a car accident."

"I lied. There was no car accident. No perfect parents who died trying to save me."

"So, your parents . . .?"

Storm wiped her palms across her damp face. "My father has been in prison for the last twenty years. After the accident, once I was released from the hospital, I was taken to my Great-aunt June, my mom's aunt, and my only living relative. Child welfare was investigating what happened, you see."

"So they put your father in prison for hurting you."

"No. Of course not," Storm exclaimed. "That's not how it works. In our family you didn't share family business with anyone—ever. No, I told everyone it was an accident. I was fooling around with Dad's liquor supply, somehow splashed it around, and set fire to my shirt. Dumb kid stuff. You know?"

Tom shook his head. She knew he was having a hard time processing all the information she was giving him. He was such a good father. The very idea of a father doing that to his child must have been almost impossible for him to imagine.

"I was still at Aunt June's when my mom disappeared. My guess is they had a fight about what he'd done. She'd come home from shopping right after it happened, so she knew the truth. I think he killed her."

"That's horrible."

Storm nodded. "It was awful, but they couldn't prove anything, and eventually the child welfare people came and took me home." She didn't share that for that short period of time she didn't mind the scars. They made her ugly, untouchable. She didn't think her father would try to touch her again.

Storm looked away from Tom, back into the flames. She closed her eyes, watched the after-image sizzle and fade behind her eyelids. "He's out," she said. "They just let him out."

"He killed your mother and they let him out?" Tom asked, eyes wide with shock, firelight sparkling in them.

"He was never convicted for killing my mother," she explained. "Accused yes, but they couldn't hold him. They let him out of jail and he kept on drinking. He was—he is—what they call a binge drinker, and until he was good and ready to stop, he'd keep drinking. So, even though he'd set his kid on fire and put her in the hospital, even though he'd killed his wife and somehow disposed of her body, well, that was not enough reason to stop.

"He stayed drunk until he fell asleep at the wheel. His car jumped a curb, and he hit a woman out walking her dog. She didn't die, but she was hurt really bad. I imagine that didn't stop him either. I know you can get booze in prison. I wonder if he was always first in line?"

Tom took Storm's hand. She curled her fingers tightly around his.

"They charged him with aggravated vehicular assault, and he was supposed to do ten to twenty. He was not a model prisoner. He kept getting in fights, hurting people. He did the full twenty. I have a friend who works in the prison system. We went to college together. I asked her to flag his record, so if he ever got released I'd be notified. I just found out."

"I don't know what to say."

"It's all been a lie, Tom. Everything I told you about my family, my childhood. I'm a liar. I come from a white-trash, dysfunctional family, and I won't blame you if you want to leave me."

"Oh Stormy, why in the hell would I ever want to leave you?"

Storm turned away from the fire once more, her eyes locked on his, trying to find the truth within them. "Do you mean it?"

"Am I thrilled you kept this from me? Of course not. Do I understand why you did? I think so, sort of. You've always tried so hard to make the best possible home for me and the kids. You've always tried harder than anyone I know. I thought that came from losing your parents so young. Maybe you didn't have time to hear them say how much they loved you, how proud they were. I was so wrong. You weren't trying to make them proud, you were trying to be nothing like them."

"Oh yes, you do understand," Storm said. Excitement

brought a sparkle to her eyes, a wash of pink to her pale-as-snow cheeks. "I never wanted you to know how terrible my parents were. How awful my dad could be or how much my mother lived in denial, pretending it would all get better. I never wanted our kids to know a moment of a life like that."

"My poor baby," said Tom as he pulled her gently against him.

"What will we do?" Storm whispered, exposing her greatest fear. "What will we do if he comes to the house?"

"Why would he do that?"

"To see me. To see his grandchildren."

"I will make him go away. And if I can't, one of your cop friends will. Remember, Storm, the work you do, the people you know. Hell, half your friends are police officers, judges, lawyers. All you need to do is make a call, let some of them know what's going on."

"I guess you're right."

"Hell yes, I'm right. Damn, Stormy, no wonder you've been acting so weird lately."

"Have I?"

"It's like you weren't even there half the time. I was starting to think that . . . well, that you'd found someone else."

"Someone else?"

Tom smiled. "Don't look at me as if I've grown another head. You're a very beautiful woman, and I've always been worried that eventually you'd figure that out. You are way out of my league. Plus, you do go out late at night a lot and without any good reason. I mean, who has a Tupperware party until midnight?"

"Tupperware usually morphs into drinks with that crowd. You know that. But you're right. I do sometimes have to go out to walk or run. It helps me think. Lets me work things out."

"Because you think you have to work them out all alone. You don't, Stormy. You have me."

"I'm so glad. I was feeling sort of, I guess, disconnected," Storm said. "In the same house but miles away."

"Well, you're right here, right now, and so am I." Tom leaned forward and kissed her softly. "You taste salty," he joked. "Very tasty." He kissed her again.

Almost dizzy from the emotional ups and downs of the last ten minutes, Storm let herself fall into the kisses, let a surge of desire wrap around her, filling her with something that was much more welcome than fear—lust.

Storm slid her hand tentatively down his stomach, waiting to see if he pushed it away. He did not, and she fumbled awkwardly with his belt buckle. He reached down to help her, and she knew it would be all right.

The buckle made a clanking sound and Tom stilled it. They sat breathlessly until they were certain the sound had not roused the kids.

"Close the blinds and turn off the fire," said Storm. Tom scrambled out of his jeans and ignored her. He hooked his fingers inside her jeans and panties and stripped them off. "Not this time," he said. "No more secrets."

Storm had no fight left. She fell back on the couch, reached for Tom as he climbed between her legs, and slid inside her. It was not so bad, making love in the light. Within a few moments she was able to forget her scars and join him, move with him. She didn't think an orgasm was likely; she was too attuned to catching the sound of her children if they stirred in the other room. Still, she enjoyed the bliss of knowing Tom still loved and wanted her.

It was only when Tom stopped, pulled out, and rose to his knees that she began to feel the old fears rise up. "Show me you trust me," he said.

The fire's warm, golden light was like a searchlight tracking across her skin. With her eyes closed so she couldn't see Tom watching her, Storm turned awkwardly onto her stomach.

She was grateful she still wore her long-sleeved shirt that covered most of her scars.

As if he'd read her mind, Tom grabbed the edge of the shirt, slowly pushed it up above her shoulder blades, and unhooked her bra.

Tom took his shirt off and slipped onto the couch beside her. He put his arm around her and pulled her against him. Her scarred back was against his chest.

She could feel his skin against hers, something she had always avoided. He held her, not speaking, not moving.

Her heart beat began to slow. She relaxed against him. Only then did Tom kiss the edge of her shoulder, the back of her neck, the slope of her shoulder. Her anxiety rose again, but only for a short time. Slowly, carefully, he coaxed her onto her stomach and began to make love to her again. It felt good, so very good and perfect and right.

Afterward, they spooned again. Storm drifted, all tension gone. All she knew was the warmth of the fire, its golden light flickering across her skin. She felt the weight of Tom's leg thrown across hers and the softness of his breath against her neck.

She would have fallen into a deep sleep, but Tom nudged her. "The kids."

Groaning, they struggled into their clothes. Tom lay down, his back to the couch. Storm was nestled between his warm stomach and the fire. She had not been so relaxed and content in months.

As she drifted off to sleep, she realized she'd crossed a threshold with Tom. In some hard-to-describe way, she was no longer on a pedestal—a fragile and precious thing—and that felt a bit like a loss. She was not the clean and pretty princess she'd been an hour ago.

On the other hand, she now seemed—in some fundamental way she also couldn't fully explain—a bit messy, far from perfect, but somehow more real.

Yawning, she tried to further analyze the events of the last hour, but sleep took her before she could frame another coherent thought.

CHAPTER

SIXTEEN

HOWARD CALLED on a Saturday in early January. His timing was perfect because it was one of those rare times when she was home alone. Tom had taken the kids to Out of This World Pizza and Play to give her a break and some quiet time to work on their taxes.

Closing her eyes, she pressed the throwaway cell phone to her ear and listened to his plans. The excitement in his voice was contagious.

"She lives with her sister and her sister's husband. Plus, I think either a boyfriend or just some random guy that's renting a room or something. There's, I don't know, maybe six, seven kids in and out. Not sure who belongs to who. They might mostly be the neighbors, but I think at least five live in the house."

"So the house . . ."

"Yeah, the house is out. Way too many people. But, that's not going to get in the way. There's a better place. It's busier, but it will work for us. Your friend's a drinker. Did you know that? Oh, of course you knew," he said, correcting himself. "She's a real fish, that one. Goes to the same bar just about every Friday and Saturday night. A place called The Cooler. You know it?"

"Not really. I've driven past it twice a day for several years on my way to work and back. I'm not big on hanging around in bars. You'll have to tell me why you think it's such a good place to grab her. It seems to me like there would be too many people around."

"That's true," he agreed. "What with TV Highway being right there, you've got lots of traffic going by, as well as people pulling into the lot. But look, if you were on probation and your PO showed up in the parking lot of the bar you were heading out of, what would you do?

Storm shrugged. "Head back in?"

"Or pull your shit together, act sober as a judge, and say hello."

"Maybe."

"No maybe. I got it all worked out. I'll pull through one of the parking spaces so I'm nose out and able to take off quick. You park closer to the door. We'll both watch, and we'll be on our phones so you'll be able to tell me when you see her. When you do, you'll get out, call her over, and start chatting.

"Once you get her attention, you work her back to the

side of your car or, I don't know, whatever car is handy. Tell her you're there to check out one of your clients, not her, and you don't want him to spot you. Ask her to step out of view of the bar. See how easy this is?" Howard enthused.

"Soon as you get her out of view of anyone coming out of the bar, I'll step up, give her a little tap on the head. When she drops, you'll help me get her to her feet. After that, she's just our drunk friend we're helping out. We'll walk her to my car and put her in the back seat. No trunk this time. Too many witnesses. Brilliant, right?"

Storm thought about it. There were plenty of ways in which Howard's plan could have gone wrong. Primarily, she was afraid of being seen and recognized. Most of the clients she worked with had problems with alcohol, and The Cooler was just the kind of place that would appeal to them. Still, it wasn't a bad plan. Once it was over, she'd be done with the justice killings and, except for one more small task, done with Howard.

Nodding, she said, "I don't know about brilliant, but yes, I think it might work."

"Damned right it'll work. We'll do it Friday night," he said, as happy as a boy learning snow was falling and school was cancelled.

Annoyed by his enthusiasm for another kill, she asked, "And if she isn't there Friday night, or if she is there but she's not alone?"

"If she isn't alone, we wait and try another time—but she'll be there. That I can almost guarantee. I don't think she misses too many Friday nights. I suppose if you want to be sure, you could ask her to come see you Friday. That way she'd be plenty pissed and have a good reason to tie one on."

"No thanks," Storm told him. "I want as much distance as I can between us. I'm not crazy about being this connected as it is."

"But you still agree with me that it looks odd that you're the only person on your team who doesn't have a missing client?"

"Oh yes, I agree. If they ever notice there are missing clients. So far, it's just the last one that's seemed suspicious to them. We need to keep it that way."

"We'll keep it that way by following your rules," he said, sarcasm heavy in his voice. The fact that this was his way of reminding her she'd broken most of them was not lost on her.

"That's the only reason you talked me into doing this," she said. "I screwed up, and this is my way of making it up to you."

Which, Storm knew, was a lie or, at best, a half truth. Storm did think Howard was right about how funny it would look if the only missing people were from her teammates' caseloads. She also felt she owed him for helping her with the last kill. But there was more to it than that.

Joe Dean was out there somewhere, a threat to her family, to her peace of mind, and to the life she'd created. Thinking about the possibility made her stomach twist, her hands clench into icy fists and her heart pound as if she'd just done five miles at a dead run.

She had shared her fear with Tom, her concern that Joe could have shown up at their home and introduced himself to their children as their grandfather. Tom seemed to think she had a magic list of friends who would stand guard at her door and provide security for her children. He thought being a probation officer gave her special protection.

The truth was that in her work world she was exposed to the worst in people. She knew exactly what the species was capable of, and she never felt safe or protected. There were monsters out there, and one had to be hyper vigilant and ready to defend their family. She also knew that the best defense was a good offense; Howard was that offense.

She was going to ask Howard to kill her father.

The idea of that—of having her father killed—filled her with warmth and a sense of well being. For the first time in days, she felt she could breathe.

CHAPTER SEVENTEEN

STORM HAD PARKED in The Cooler parking lot at 10 p.m., expecting a long wait. The place was bright as daylight. There was light from the cars, from the front doors, and, like a row of minor suns, from the two rows of spotlights highlighting the billboard that straddled the lot.

She had pulled in alongside one of the thick concrete legs holding up the billboard. The nose of her car was facing the front door, and a shadow cast by the post helped disguise her presence to anyone going in or coming out of the bar.

Howard had shared that Angela Ruiz liked to close the place down or at least, come awfully close to it. She rarely left before the early hours.

The lot was not as full as it had been earlier. She'd driven by several times. Her nerves dictated she check out the area as thoroughly as possible. She had even gone on Google Maps and looked at pictures taken of the building and surrounding area from both the sky and the ground.

It was just as Howard had described it. The place where he planned to park would allow him fast access to TV Highway—not highway in the strict sense of the word but a four-lane main through street, where the top speed was 45. They would definitely not be breaking any speed limits.

Storm was to park close enough to see the front door but not too close. They had agreed they should arrive early before it got too busy, but since pulling in over an hour before, only three cars had joined the five already there. Customer parking was the striped asphalt at the front. Staff parked along the side of the building among the weeds and gravel. Four cars and an RV with a flat tire sat there, half hidden in the shadows.

Only two people were in sight, lounging under the roof of the open-air smoking area to the right of the door. They didn't seem to know each other and stood apart, not speaking and smoking their cigarettes as if there were a contest to see who finished first.

She didn't recognize either of them, though with the flickering light and changing shadows, she wasn't certain. One of her fears was running into a client. The Cooler had a bad reputation and was just the kind of place to attract many of her addiction-challenged clients.

Her phone chirped and startled her. She picked it up

from the passenger seat where she'd placed it.

"You didn't see me," he said.

"I haven't seen your car," she agreed. "Where is it?"

"You see the gray pickup that just pulled in?"

"Yes."

"That's my car for the evening. Borrowed it for the occasion. Don't worry," he said, forestalling her complaints, "No one will miss it for days, and by then I'll have returned it. Just thought it made more sense than driving my car in case someone caught my plates."

"That's probably a good idea," she agreed.

"You look nice," Howard told her. "Checked you out when I drove by."

Unconsciously, Storm twisted a long strand of dark hair between her fingers. She had tried to look like someone who might hang out there, someone waiting for a date. She'd left her hair down and lined her eyes with dark pencil.

She had also traded her usual ubiquitous garb of designer workout clothes, known locally as 'The Beaverton Mom' look, for faded jeans and a stretched-out gray knit sweater with a hood, worn over a black tank. Only her Nikes seemed familiar and comfortable. She had considered wearing platform heels but had worn the sneakers, in case she had to run.

"Haven't seen her yet, have you?" Howard asked.

"No, haven't seen her. There have been a few people, and a couple guys who were outside smoking just went in, but I haven't seen anyone else.

Sitting in the parking lot, talking to Howard in low tones, made Storm feel very much as if she were taking part in a secret tryst with a lover.

"Her car's here," said Howard. "Black Range Rover about three cars from you toward the bar. See it?"

Storm nodded. Realizing he couldn't see her, she said, "See it. I'll call you if I spot her." She hung up, tossed the phone on the passenger seat, and sat back.

Near the end of the first hour, Storm grew increasingly worried that someone would be curious about why she was just sitting in her car. Her invented excuse—that she was waiting to meet someone—wouldn't wear well if she sat there much longer. No one was worth this sort of wait.

In the middle of the second hour, Storm started yawning. She hadn't been getting much sleep, and the rhythmic sound of the cars passing on TV was becoming a lullaby.

Three hours went by, and traffic into the parking lot picked up with each of them. On one occasion, she caught the profile of a man who reminded her of her father. She caught her breath until the man turned, and she realized he didn't really resemble him. She shook it off. Paranoia was not going to help her get through this.

After a while, the adrenaline rush from thinking she'd seen her father faded. She was tired, and the car seat was warm from her body. The heat seemed to wrap around her back and shoulders like a hug. She sank back into it and let her eyes close. Her thoughts drifted lazily and illogically. There were yellow squares under her lids, the after-image of the lights in the parking lot. She studied the shapes, saw a dresser, the moon, a capital A. Now she was lying in an open field, a warm wind blowing across her face. A wide wheel rolled across the hills, heading leisurely toward her.

She welcomed the weight of the thing as it pressed her into the ground, rolling slowly over her feet, up her legs, over her torso. The ground was warm, welcoming. She was asleep.

Storm woke up with a jerk. What the hell was she thinking, drifting off like that? This wasn't some dark movie theatre. Tom wasn't there to nudge her awake. This was a woman's life, or rather . . . death. It was an occasion that deserved more attention and surely more respect than curling up for a nap.

Adrenaline-charged and guilt-driven, Storm fumbled across the passenger seat to search for her phone and checked the time. How was she going to explain this night excursion to Tom? 'I couldn't sleep and decided to go for a drive and I had a flat' didn't seem like the kind of excuse that would cut it with him anymore.

The door of the bar swung open several times, spilling light and noise into the parking lot. Each time a group or individual emerged, she became more and more nervous. But none of them was their target.

Barely able to sit still, frustration an ever-tightening knot in her stomach, she was about to call Howard and suggest they try again another night.

That was when the door opened. She heard loud high-pitched voices and spotted Angela Ruiz and five or six women staggering from the bar into the parking lot. They were laughing, bumping hips, having a great time.

Storm watched as the entire group of women climbed into Angela's car. They didn't pull away immediately, but Storm knew that, for all intents and purposes, Angela Ruiz had made her getaway.

CHAPTER

EIGHTEEN

FOR THEIR SECOND attempt, Howard stole a dark-gray van. "White would have looked sort of suspicious, you know. The killers in books always drive those white panel vans," he explained.

Not in a mood for levity, Storm had clenched her teeth and managed a painful smile. She couldn't think of anything to say. At least this time she realized there was no need to arrive so early. The Cooler wasn't that popular a night spot. Parking was not going to be an issue.

She'd also made up a better excuse for Tom. One of the admin staff was retiring after thirty years, and as was customary, several of her coworkers were joining her for drinks at a local watering hole. Such events could go on pretty late. She ran home before going out, ostensibly to change clothes.

"Don't wait up for me," she told him. "So glad I don't have work tomorrow. Why don't you think about something fun for us to do?"

"Will do," Tom agreed. "Promise you'll call if you need a ride."

"I will. But don't worry. You know the plan—drink early, drink much, spend the rest of the night sobering up."

"Totally sober, or you call," he said.

She rolled her eyes. "Yes, dear." Feeling like a kid sneaking out, a mixture of excitement and guilt rolling through her stomach in a not completely unpleasant way, Storm escaped.

Despite the lights around The Cooler, it was definitely nighttime. The shadows were deep and black. There was also a stillness and chill to the air and on the street, an air of Friday-night impatience.

Storm rolled her shoulders, pressed her head into the headrest of her car seat, and sighed with impatience. If it didn't work, she would have to tell Howard it was over. They'd have to find someone else to take. There had been three women under consideration. She'd obviously made a bad choice.

As she was considering whether to phone Howard and suggest they call it a night, the door to The Cooler opened, and Angela Ruiz stepped out. Alone. She wore a tight black leather skirt, a white tank top that blazed under the lights, and platform heels Storm thought looked like horses hooves. Storm wondered if the woman was too drunk to notice how inappropriate her clothes were for the frigid night.

Storm fumbled for her phone and dropped it twice before grasping it with both hands and hitting the call button. Howard answered before she heard it ring.

"She's here and she's by herself. I'm going now." She hung up without waiting for a response, opened the door, and stepped out. Her legs felt heavy, half asleep. She'd been sitting for too long.

As she walked toward Angela Ruiz, Storm tried to keep the pace of someone going somewhere, but not in a huge hurry to arrive. Realizing her hands were shaking and damp, as if she were about to deliver a speech to a large audience, Storm took time for a couple deep, calming breaths.

Easy, this is just your client, she reminded herself. Becoming annoyed with herself, her tone changed, and she admonished herself. *Stop being such a baby*.

Stepping around the trailer hitch on the back of a dusty pickup, she spotted Angela lighting up a cigarette, inhaling deeply, and then dropping what must have been a lighter into her purse. As she looked up, Storm said, "Angela? Ms. Ruiz."

The woman's head snapped up, and eyes black as a moonless night sky stared into hers. Recognition dawned, and the tension faded to be replaced by a frown.

"Hey, Ms. McKenzie. How's it goin'?"

"Fine. Just great. How have you been?"

"Good. Real good."

"Look," said Storm, moving into the next part of Howard's plan. "Could we maybe talk . . . I mean, could you come with me, just over here?"

"What? Why?" the woman asked, her natural instinct for self-preservation kicking in.

"I need a favor. You think you can help me?" Storm asked.

Storm watched the woman mull it over; it took less than two seconds. Who wouldn't want their PO to owe them a favor?

"What do you need?"

"Right now I need to get away from the door. Someone might come out and see me."

Accepting that, and after casting a quick glance over her shoulder toward the door, Angela followed Storm. A van with darkly smoked windows was parked near the bar and would have made a good shield, but Storm decided that an SUV and the old pickup would work just as well. She backed between the vehicles' shadows, and Angela continued to follow her. Storm wondered where Howard was. The same street noise that masked her approach also covered his.

They had moved into the shadows between the cars. From which direction would Howard come? Should she try to maneuver Angela Ruiz so she had her back to where Howard's stolen van was parked? Would he work around the car or maybe just walk past as if he were simply heading toward the bar?

"What is it? What you want from me?" Angela Ruiz asked.

"I'm here to check on a client," Storm explained, just as she'd rehearsed. "I'm trying to determine whether he's breaking his court order and is still drinking. If he is, I need to warn his wife. He's a very violent drunk, and he almost killed her last time."

"She ought to leave him."

"She did. But that doesn't stop him from trying to find her," Storm improvised.

At that moment, three things happened. The door to the van with the smoked windows opened and a heavyset. African-American woman climbed out and started running toward them. Howard moved past Storm, startling her with his sudden appearance, and lunged for Angela, who screamed.

Uncertain how to react, Storm froze. Howard bumped into her with his hip, slamming her so hard she spun a quarter turn and would have fallen except she managed to catch the edge of the pickup's bed.

From the corner of her eye, Storm caught the motion of what looked like a kid's baseball bat being swung down at Angela Ruiz's head. The woman moved like a cat, despite the high heels. The bat bounced off her shoulder, and she gave a shriek of pain.

Turning away from the car, Storm saw Howard catch Angela's wrist. She was still screaming, cursing in Spanish and trying to break away.

Wanting to help, Storm shoved Angela toward Howard. He brought the bat down again, and this time it slammed down on Storm's forearm. The impact made her arm go numb. It fell to her side as if it had become disconnected, but then the connection was restored and pain, sharp and sudden, told her she was hurt. Instinctively, she backed away, but found herself unexpectedly blocked by a trio of women with flailing fists.

Trying to protect her arm, Storm kept her back to them. She was trapped on two sides by an SUV and a pickup. Howard had his arm around Angela's throat and was dragging her away. Behind her, women slapped, clawed, and punched in an effort to get past her and reach their friend.

Storm was pushed against the SUV, and pain shot up her arm and into her shoulder. A sharp-toed boot or shoe cracked into her shin, and she tried to push her way free. She was suffocating under the press of bodies. Incongruously, she was surrounded by the scent of flowers: jasmine, rose, lilac, and a trace of vanilla.

Someone grabbed her hair. A fist was driven into her stomach. As Storm doubled over, the person whose hand gripped her hair had no trouble dragging her the rest of the way to the ground.

"What the hell is going on out here?" a rough voice called. He repeated the question in Spanish. "¿Que diablo esta pasando?"

Her hair was released, but someone stepped on her hand, driving the thin point of a stiletto into her palm. She jerked her hand back, tearing her knuckles on the asphalt. The woman who'd stepped on her teetered and fell, driving a knee into Storm's stomach.

She rolled away and heard the woman hiss, "Ala gran puta" as she climbed awkwardly to her feet.

Afraid the woman would try to stomp her again, Storm tried to squirm under the pickup. Everything was chaos, but in slow motion and high definition. In the shadows, under the truck, she could make out rusty metal parts and smelled dust and oil.

Her shoulders were under the van, and she tried to slide sideways to get the rest of her under cover. A large hand grasped her ankle and dragged her unceremoniously into the unforgiving light of the largest flashlight she'd ever seen.

"¿Senora, que diablos esta pasando?" asked a male voice. She stared at the large bald man uncomprehendingly and shook her head. "On your feet," he said in perfect English. "Get up."

Tentatively, grasping her elbow with her good hand and keeping her bad arm tight against her side, Storm managed to sit. "I think my arm is broken. Can you help me?"

"Si," the man said, reaching down for her. She took his hand and pulled her to her feet. With each movement her left arm, from elbow to wrist, burned and throbbed.

As she hobbled from between the cars, she saw the women who had attacked her. Another man, who was shorter but with broader shoulders, stood in front of them slapping a flashlight into his palm over and over.

"You gotta go after Angie!" one of the women yelled.

"He's getting away, you idiot!" shouted another.

"Who is getting away?" the tall man asked. This set off another flurry of shouting, and it took some time before the men realized someone had been kidnapped from the parking lot and called the police.

Everyone seemed to calm down once they realized the police were on the way. The men, who said they worked security for the bar, stood between Storm and the women, who seemed convinced she had something to do with their friend's abduction.

Storm looked at the women, who stood beside one pillar of the billboard and stared back with jutted chins and an attitude that promised a fight.

Two could have been sisters, except that one was black and one white. They were short, heavyset, and wore nearly identical jeans with short, black, leather jackets and boots.

The black woman held a water bottle in her fist like a weapon. The white one juggled two purses. In front of the two stood a diminutive, curvy, Hispanic woman, her dark hair streaked with blond highlights. She held a broken shoe in one hand and cursed nonstop. From the small amount of Spanish Storm knew, she gathered that the woman was more angry about the broken heel of her shoe.

Dressed more for a dinner party at some upscale Portland restaurant in an obviously expensive, knee-length, green dress, off-white pumps, and a black fur shrug, she seemed out of place at The Cooler. She fiddled nervously with her necklace, the light glinting off the stones. Then she lifted her shoe and shook it in Storm's direction. "Ija de puta me quebraste el tacon." The combination of elegance and street language was disconcerting.

"Where is our friend?" demanded the woman with the purses as soon as Storm stepped out of the shadows and into the light. One of the men asked her to settle down.

Several other people were now milling around, spilling out of the bar, all asking what had happened and adding to the general craziness.

"You hear me?" the woman asked, ignoring the bouncer, her voice becoming a screeching wail that rose above the crowd's chatter.

"What are you talking about?" Storm shouted back, still holding her bad arm tightly and wondering if she'd be able to drive and escape from this disaster.

"We saw you and that guy jump our friend. We saw you helping him kidnap her. Where you take her? She don't have much money, so you didn't take her for that. What are you, some kind of perverts or something?"

"I don't know what you're talking about," Storm repeated. "I was talking to my client, Angela. All of a sudden we got jumped by some man. Next thing I know I'm on the ground and you and your friends are kicking me. I think my arm's broken. That man hit me."

"What do you mean, your client?" asked the attractive Hispanic woman, who obviously spoke English just fine and had picked up on the word. "How do you know Angie?"

"You mean Angela Ruiz? I'm her probation officer," Storm said. The simple truth felt scary, like a secret had been ripped open, a hidden fear exposed.

"But we saw you and that man attack Angie," protested the black woman, shaking her bottle of water toward the parking lot.

"We called the cops. They'll get it figured out," said one of the bouncers.

Storm could hear a siren and saw red lights flashing from the windows of the businesses across the street. An ambulance was approaching from the direction of Beaverton, the nearest town to the east. It pulled into the parking lot, and mercifully, the sound was shut off. The flashing red lights continued, however. They pulsed in time with her heartbeat and the throbbing pain in her forearm.

The paramedics made her sit in the back of the ambulance while they took a quick look at her injuries. They put a brace on her arm and were helping her put it into a sling to further immobilize it when a Washington County Sheriff's patrol car pulled in, red and blue lights rotating.

Two officers approached, one stopping to see who'd been injured, the other moving past to speak to the other women. The bouncers had continued to encourage them to stay where they were. All three spoke at once, frantically explaining that their friend had been taken, dragged from the parking lot to a dark van, black or blue, that was driven away with her inside.

Storm heard the officer get on his radio and report.

"Excuse me. Could you tell me what happened here tonight?"

Storm dragged her attention back to the officer standing in front of her.

He was about six feet tall, fairly slender, with wide shoulders, buzz-cut hair, hard eyes, and tight lips. Despite his appearance of youth, Storm thought he was probably older, had been around longer, and had seen and heard more than she suspected. She would have to be careful.

Trying for the right level of cool professionalism, Storm listened to the policeman's question while in the back of her mind a voice, her own, was screaming, *Where is Howard? Did he get clean away? Has he had time to get to Evergreen?*

"I'm a probation officer," she told him. "My identification is in my purse in my car. I think someone was kidnapped from the parking lot. I got in the middle of it and got hurt. I can explain later. You need to go and do whatever you can to find the woman who was taken."

It was hard to urge someone to chase Howard when it was the last thing she wanted. All she could do was trust that Howard had had enough time and that no one would track him to Traynor Chemical.

"We've asked for other officers to be dispatched. Let's concentrate on what happened to you," said the officer, not so easily brushed off. "Can you describe it?"

"I guess." Storm took a deep breath. She realized she was trembling but decided it was an appropriate response and would not have seemed odd. "I was driving by and saw someone who looked like a client, a multiple DUI. He shouldn't have been near a bar. I thought if I drove up, let him see me, that maybe it would be enough to sort of, I don't know, scare him straight, I guess. Dumb idea."

"So, you pulled into the parking lot."

"Yes, like I said, I thought he was one of my clients. He'd been doing really great in recovery, and I didn't want to see him blow it.

"I didn't get there in time. He had already gone inside. I was about to drive off, but I remembered he was a smoker. I figured if I sat around a little while, he'd be bound to come out for a cigarette and if he did, I'd do my little drive-by, maybe have a few words with him, staying in my car, of course. At minimum I'd have a good reason to get a UA next time and see just how far off the rails he'd slipped."

"Can you get your identification please?"

"She can't use that arm," supplied one of the two male paramedics. They were both young, blond, and unbelievably gentle. "We're about to transport to Tuality

ER for treatment."

"If you could get my purse out of my car?" Storm said, "I'd be happy to show it to you."

"In a moment," he answered. "So now you're sitting and waiting for your client. So how come you got out of the car? You just said you planned to stay inside your car in order to stay safe, right?" asked the annoyingly perceptive policeman. So far, any camaraderie Storm had hoped might exist between fellow officers of the court was entirely absent. The officer's face was as lacking in emotion as an experienced poker player's.

Storm shook her head. "No reason. He wasn't coming out. Thought I'd get out and stretch. Sitting in a cubby all day, the first thing you want to do is not sit. Wasn't really thinking about it. Got out to stretch, was going to get back in and head home when I saw Ms. Ruiz."

"Another client."

"Yes. Most of my clients have drug or alcohol problems, so finding them at a bar isn't much of a surprise. Still, no one likes running into their clients. It's embarrassing knowing that much about a person. Just because someone is on probation—well, they did something wrong, sure, but public humiliation isn't part of the sentence. Everyone deserves their privacy. When Ms. Ruiz spotted me, I just wanted to say hi, sort of reassure her I wasn't checking up on her."

"How did she react?"

"Fine. In fact we were just sort of chatting. You know, the usual stuff. How was your week? How are the kids? She said she was doing great, that her kids were doing well. Next thing I know, there's a man swinging a bat at Ms. Ruiz.

I grabbed her and sort of pushed her out of the way. It hit me instead. I tried to grab Ms. Ruiz and back away, but these women—"

Storm raised her injured left arm to gesture toward the women and winced at the shooting pain in her elbow. "Those women are friends of my client and I think they believe I was involved. That I was with the man who attacked us."

"And you were not?"

"Of course not."

"Can you describe this man?"

Storm paused as if she were thinking. "Not really. It was dark between the cars. I don't know. Let me think about it."

Realizing there was no harm in giving a general description of Howard, who looked like about half the men she'd ever met, Storm went on to give a very general description of his height, weight, hair color, and what she could remember of his clothing. She was sure the women would be asked the same question, and if her answers weren't similar, it would have looked odd. Maybe not too odd, though, considering they had already reported the van as black or blue when she knew it was dark gray. Crime witnesses had notoriously bad memories of events.

Looking pointedly at his watch, the paramedic said, "We should transport now."

"No, you don't have to do that," said Storm. "I'm sure I can drive myself to the ER or an urgent care myself." She stood up, and suddenly, all the blinking lights and shadows began to spin in a very unpleasant way. As she started to slide toward the ground, the police officer caught her and helped her sit back down.

"Or maybe you should do that," Storm said, realizing she had little choice.

In order to be transported, Storm had to suffer the further humiliation of lying down on a stretcher and being strapped in. At least they promised not to run the siren or lights.

Lying there, amid the beeps of the machinery and the unmelodious harshness of voices over the radio, Storm wondered what story she would have to invent to keep Tom happy. She had to stick closely to the story she'd told the police. Tom thought she was out celebrating a coworker's retirement, but she was supposed to be at McMenamins Grand Lodge in Forest Grove, several miles west. She couldn't even say she'd stopped on her way home because she'd have had to pass home to get to The Cooler.

As she shifted to a different position, a jolt of pain shot up her arm. The palm of her 'good' hand ached where she'd been stepped on, and her knuckles stung. She had a headache, and the base of her skull ached. She wanted to cry or scream. It had not been her best night.

CHAPTER NINETEEN

THE EMERGENCY CENTER waiting room was painted in decorator colors: sage green, slate blue, and cinnamon. Mahogany-veneered tables and comfortably thick padding on the chairs added to the sense of style. After three hours of waiting to be seen, Storm was wishing they'd passed on the designer fees and hired more medical staff.

She had called home and gotten no answer. Not a big surprise given the hour. She left a message saying where she was, that she'd be home soon, and not to worry. It was what she'd have done if she really had been attacked in a parking lot.

Finally, she was called from the front waiting room to

the back waiting room, where she got to rest on a gurney with a ridiculously thin mattress while she spent her time trying to figure out what all the strange machinery was for. She didn't try too hard, since she really didn't want to know.

Lying there gave her too much time to think and feel. The planning, the boredom, the dread, and the guilt had all taken their toll. The pain, the odd and ugly feeling that her body had been assaulted, broken, she held all of it, buried it inside. She couldn't risk losing control, so she couldn't share her feelings with anyone. The sense of loneliness that engulfed her was like being caught in an undertow in a black churning ocean. It threatened to take her down, so far down she might have gotten lost.

Even before the fire, she had learned how to remove her emotions, compress them, and send them deep into an empty darkness at the bottom of her soul. From there she could stare out, a wretched feeling beast, and be safe, protected by the very same sense of detachment. After the fire, she had become an expert at disconnecting from emotions.

Trusting Tom had allowed her to inch out, bit by bit, a thin-skinned creature afraid to venture too far from its shell.

Working with Howard to avenge and protect had allowed her not to creep from the dark but to explode from it, crashing forth in a blaze of anger, not afraid, not tentative, but fully alive and filled with righteousness.

She had no faith, but she wondered if that feeling of passion was similar to the religious fervor she had read about in the histories of zealots and martyrs. Certainly she had no trouble finding the guilty and making them pay for their sins.

When she thought she might have been one tick of the clock from losing her mind, a nurse arrived to take her to x-ray. From there, things moved more quickly.

After a series of x-rays, she was taken to a third room, where her arm was set in a cast. Before it was fully firm, the curtain was swept aside, and a nurse came in. Tom was right behind her.

"Your husband was worried about you," the petite, red-headed nurse told her. "I told him you'd been very brave."

"You make me think you're about to give me a sticker or a lollipop."

"Do you want a sticker?" the woman asked.

Storm shook her head. "No, just joking."

"Okay. Someone will be back soon to sign you out."

Storm nodded, a little taken aback. The woman had no sense of humor.

Tom had taken a seat on a rolling stool beside the bed, and now he reached up and took her right hand. His hand was cold. She smiled at him. "Don't look like that. It's just a broken bone, not a death sentence."

"Stormy, what happened? Your call didn't make much sense. A fight in a bar? What the hell?"

"Is that what I said? Well, no, there was no fight. We left McMenamins early, but a couple of the girls wanted to stop at this place called The Cooler, just to check it out, and I let them talk me into going along."

"What were they thinking? That place has a pretty bad reputation."

"Does it? They said it was a good place to go dancing. I didn't get a chance to find out either way. I saw one of my clients in the parking lot, stopped to talk to her, and all of a sudden this man came out of nowhere, hit me with a baseball bat or something, and grabbed her. It was horrible."

Tom stood and wrapped Storm gently in his arms, careful of her injured arm and bandaged hand. "You must have been scared out of your mind. Where was your gun?"

"My gun?" asked Storm. She never carried her gun. It was an odd question.

"Yes. I noticed just this morning it wasn't in the lock box. I was getting my hard hat off the shelf and moved the lock box. It felt empty.

"Oh." For a moment she felt as if he was setting her up, trying to catch her in a lie. She was so careful with all the little lies, all the half-truths she told him. It was terrifying to think he wasn't oblivious to her deceit.

"It's locked in the trunk of the car. I was planning to go to the range last week, but I forgot."

"You hate going to the range. Tell me the truth."

Shaken from the night's activities, her injuries throbbing, wondering if Howard had gotten away free or if he'd been caught and the police were coming for her, left Storm unable to respond. She couldn't even come up with a reasonable story. The truth that she'd started keeping her gun in the car since the night she'd crept into Helena Smith's house and found herself outmatched, well, that was a truth she'd keep to herself.

"It's your father, isn't it?" Tom asked, letting her go and sitting down on the edge of the gurney. "You've been so tense since you found out. I knew something was wrong, but until you told me about him being released . . . how did I not see how hard this has been on you? I hate how scared you must be. So scared that you feel like you have to carry a gun with you. God, Stormy, can you ever forgive me?"

Dumbfounded, Storm could only stare open-mouthed at Tom as he continued.

"I should have seen how upset you were about your father. I should have offered to help you find the bastard, hired a private investigator or something. Instead I left you to deal with it on your own, like I always do. Stormy do the taxes. Stormy pay the bills, plan the menus, cook the dinners, buy the presents, keep up the housework. Why you put up with me I will never know."

Stormy reached out with her bandaged hand and gave Tom an awkward pat on the head. "You're an idiot, Tom McKenzie", she said, a sense of lightness filling her, or maybe it was just the pain pills kicking in. "Now go find someone and get me the hell out of here."

CHAPTER TWENTY

MARTIN LUTHER KING, Jr. Day was a county holiday. A day set aside for observance and community service. Storm was meeting with Howard. It seemed fitting, since she believed the result of their association had been, in a way, a service to the community.

After all, they had put an end to four child abusers, offering at least a little hope that the children who had been in the care of those monsters had a better shot at lives free of threats, fear, and pain. Storm had no regrets, but she was ready to end her double life.

They met at the picnic table at Jackson Bottom Wetlands. Storm grimaced at the aptness of the name. All around her, the ground was soaked, puddles forming even on the higher ground above the marshes. The marsh itself looked like a lake, with trees growing from the water. The creek that ran alongside the trail, usually at a leisurely pace, was now swollen with rain, and it rushed past, churning up a dirty white froth and making a low-pitched roar.

Pulling the cord that tightened her raincoat's hood, she watched Howard trot up from one of the many trails in the park. Just as he reached her, the clouds opened up and a bar of sunlight broke through, dazzling reflections bouncing off the mirror-like face of each puddle and drop of water it touched.

"You made it," Howard said.

Shielding her eyes, Storm said, "Of course. I need to hear how it went with Ms. Ruiz."

"Fine. Just fine. Down to the last detail. Just the way you outlined. Is that a cast?"

The elastic at the end of the sleeve of Storm's coat was stretched wide to accommodate the cast, which covered her arm from just below her elbow to the base of her thumb and fingers.

"Yep. Want to guess how I got it?"

"I thought maybe I hit you. Things were happening so fast. Did I actually—"

"Yes, you actually. You broke my arm."

"Holy crap. I never meant for you to get hurt out there. Damn."

"It's okay. Should be out of the cast in four or five weeks. Not the end of the world."

"Still. Must have hurt like hell."

Storm shrugged. "Tell me more about Ruiz. I didn't get to see much of what happened."

"Sure. He looked at her, his eyes narrowed against the sun. All around them, from every surface, a wispy mist began to rise. Water dripped with no discernible rhythm from the nearby trees.

"I missed her with the bat," he said. "She was fast. Knew how to duck. Finally, I just grabbed her, got a lock around her neck, and dragged her to the van. She kicked the hell out of my shins on the way, so I punched her out and tossed her into the car. Her friends saw everything and would have been right on me except they had to get past you first. I saw you get knocked down, or you fell down, but anyway, it slowed them up enough so I could get the hell out of there.

"She started coming around when we reached Evergreen. I didn't hit her again. It was easier to let her walk than to carry her. She tried to run, but I got her into the building okay. Once I got her to the room, I tied her up like usual, but it didn't work for me. You can't have sex with a corpse, and every time I grabbed her ankles and pulled her legs up she started to choke, you know, huh?"

Storm swallowed hard, trying not to imagine the scene in all its graphic detail. "Just tell me you got rid of her body and cleaned up."

"I'm getting to that. Anyway, I took the noose off her neck and hung her up by her wrists. That worked fine, except she kept fainting. Man, I thought she was tough, but hell, by the time I cut her down, she was so out of it. All I had to do was drop her in the cart. So, yeah, I got rid of her body and all her stuff. I dumped the van and everything went like clockwork."

"She was still alive? You burned her alive?" Storm asked, her eyes staring with a disquieting intensity, her voice nearly a whisper.

Howard leaned forward to hear. "Burned her? Oh, hell no. I snapped her pretty neck first. You taught me that. Don't want anyone coming to outside the room, moving around, making a mess, huh? Why you gotta worry so much?"

Storm shook her head, unable to speak. Clouds crossed the sun, and a shadow took away the painful glare. Storm dropped the hand that had been shielding her eyes to her hip. "You know what they do to people who kill people? How can you ask why I'm worried?" She drew her lips back scornfully and shook her head at the ignorance of his question.

"I just meant, why don't you trust me? You'd think by now I'd have earned some trust. I helped you with that woman you tried to take out by yourself. I come up with a good plan to get that Angela woman. What's it gonna take?"

"The question isn't whether I trust you," said Storm. "It's just how far can I trust you. We had an agreement about who we would target, but you broke that agreement. You killed that woman, the one you picked up in Portland, the one that hadn't done a damn thing to get herself killed. Maybe that did a little something to my trust in you."

"Okay, I guess I can see that," said Howard, uncharacteristically agreeable.

"Can you. Well, good." Deciding it was time, Storm said, "It won't come as a complete surprise when I tell you we're done. I've decided it's time to stop the justice killings."

"You always say that."

"What?"

"You do. You say that after every one. We aren't going to do another. We've been lucky so far. We shouldn't push our luck."

Storm, hearing her words echoed back to her, was dismayed. It was true. She had said those things, just as Howard repeated them, each and every time.

"But this time I mean it," Storm argued, sounding peevish and unsure even to herself. "We really have been lucky. And this last one . . . it felt wrong. I don't know for sure this woman was an abuser. She put her kids in danger, yeah. But she didn't hurt them herself. At least, not that I could see. Maybe it was even a one-time thing, a complete accident."

"Sure, I can see that," agreed Howard. "I wondered about it myself. So you feel bad now, but what about the next time you hear about some kid getting locked in a closet or some meth freak leaving his kid on a furnace to slow roast and walking away free and clear, huh? You think you'll be able to walk away? You never have before."

Storm hugged her bad arm to her side protectively. It still ached, and sometimes a sharp twinge of pain traveled from forearm to shoulder, reminding her that the injury was recent and far from healed.

"You look . . . you get this look sometimes," said Howard. He stepped forward and raised his hand toward her face. She flinched and he said, "Shhh, it's okay." He took a strand of hair that had come free and slid his fingers down its length.

She stepped back. "Don't."

"Don't what? Don't be nice? Don't tell you the truth?"

"Don't touch me. I don't like it."

"Are you sure about that? I remember that kiss. I think about it every night. I thought about it when I was banging that little Mexican chica."

"Were you thinking about it when you stuffed her in the oxidizer and hit the button?"

"Nope. I was thinking about her at that particular moment." Howard smiled, and Storm's stomach twisted and sank. She had felt like this once before, on a roller coaster. Just as the ride reached the crest of an impossibly high climb, it paused, and she knew it was about to fall backward and down, a long way down.

Her stomach made the fall first, and she realized then, and she still knew that the anticipation, the moment before the fall, was the worst moment of all.

Now she was there again, stalled at the very top, ready to fall into the abyss, except this time Storm knew the abyss was inside and she could fall forever.

She didn't want Howard. She wanted Tom. He was her knight in shining armor. If she could have transported herself back to their room on the mountain to the night she'd told him about her father she would have. That night she'd steeled herself, expected shock and anger, but had received sympathy and acceptance instead. That was what had kept her going ever since.

When she let him, Tom was the strong presence beside her that made it easy to face the night, to sink into bed and fall away, give up control, and float into a welcoming darkness. He was the warm body who held her when the nightmares came and shook her from that slumber.

For a short time, she'd been disconnected from him. She had been hollow. All the little moments of happiness that made life more than just something to tolerate held no worth. They were simple things, like the smell of fresh ground coffee, the feel of sun on her face after a long week of overcast days, the taste of Tom's dessert invention: waffles dotted with syrup and covered in whipped cream. Even Waffle Whips were tasteless when she felt detached from Tom.

Then they made love, and somehow, as she went through the motions, through the act of joining bodies, she rejoined him. "Where have you been?" he'd asked.

"Far away," she admitted. "But I'm here now."

"I'm glad," he said. "I missed you." He whispered all those little endearments that were links in a metaphorical chain that held them together and separate from the rest of the world.

She couldn't risk losing that connection to Tom again. Her fear of drifting into the darkness and not returning was as real as other people's fears of closed places, or spiders, or death.

It was true she'd felt a moment of—something—when she kissed Howard. There was the sick thrill of danger, a compulsion to step off the cliff and see how far she could fall. The cost of learning could have been pretty high: Howard and the justice killings or Tom and her children. There was really no choice to be made.

"You know what I like about you?" Howard asked.

Storm shook her head, not caring in the least, but

curious where this was going.

"Well, there are lots of things I like. I like that you're tall and that you have long dark hair that you hardly ever let down because you've got that stern librarian thing going on. But I can see by the look you're giving me that you don't want to hear about that kind of like." Howard gave her a crooked smile.

Storm crossed her arms and waited.

"Mostly, I like you because you like to pretend you have it all under control, but the truth is you're rarely sure of yourself. You're not like those people who think they got it all figured out. Come on, you know the kind I mean, huh?"

Storm nodded.

"Once they get to that idea, that they know it all, that's when they get stuck. They're done, as far as I'm concerned. They can live a hundred more years, but they're basically just a lump of dried-up clay, hardening a little more every year but not really changing.

"People like you, though, you're never sure you're right. You're always looking for the path, the one way, but you never find it. You'll change your pattern and shift this way and that, and by the time you get old, well, you won't be anything like who you are now."

"And that's a good thing?" Storm asked.

"That's hella good," Howard agreed. That's where all the creative stuff comes from. The outside-the-box stuff. Nothing about you is set in stone."

Now it was Storm's turn to give a twisted grin. "Is that a line that works on a lot of women?"

"Don't be a bitch," Howard warned, his voice suddenly going low and the same hard look back in his eyes. "I'm trying to give you a compliment. You suck at taking them, obviously, so I'll just say this. I'm not ready to quit yet. I'll let you know when I am. In the meanwhile, you get back to your office and you find us another waste of air."

"I told you. I don't want to do this anymore."

"I know what you said, but you aren't the boss. I'm not saying I want to do this forever, either. I'm not a fucking serial killer, huh? What I do want is some respect from you. I've held up my end, hell, more than my end of our bargain. I'm not going to let you lay down the law about when we stop."

"So what are you saying? You want one more killing to show that I'm not in charge? One more death will make you feel like a man?"

"I'm saying," said Howard, enunciating each word in a forceful tone she'd never heard before, "that I will be the one who says when we stop. Until I say so, you will keep finding targets, and I will keep pulling the trigger. That might mean one more—that might mean ten more."

"And if I don't want to go along with this?"

"I will be very, very upset with you."

They stood there while the warmth of the sun sent mist curling around them, face to face, like two friends out for a stroll in the park, who had met each other by chance and stopped to chat. Only someone very observant would have noticed the crossed arms, stares that lasted too long, flared nostrils, and fighting stance each had adopted.

Storm knew one way to end the hostilities was to distract him. She dropped her arms to her sides.

"Fine, okay, maybe you're right. Maybe we aren't done yet."

"That was a fast turnaround," said Howard, his disbelief apparent.

"I need a favor."

"I see," said Howard, waiting.

"I just found out my father got out of prison."

"So?"

"So, I want you to kill him," she said without preamble.

"What?" asked Howard, taken aback. "Why?"

"Because I want him to be dead," she answered simply.

"He's that bad."

"That bad."

Storm shivered. Howard took off his coat and, standing in front of her, slipped it around her shoulders. His hands stayed pressed against her back, and he moved forward until she was held firmly against him. She didn't try to break away.

As much as she wanted Tom, there was something she needed from Howard. It would be stupid to antagonize him. Besides, his coat was warm. It smelled good, like dial soap and citrus aftershave. Not sure why, she suddenly began to cry, deep sobs that left her shaking. She pressed herself against Howard. He held her, made soothing noises, and let her cry.

"You don't have to be afraid anymore," he told her after a while. "Howard will kill all the monsters for you."

"Will you?" she asked, her lower lip trembling like a child's.

Softly, he leaned in, kissed the corner of her mouth and whispered in her ear. "I will," he promised.

CHAPTER

TWENTY-ONE

THE STREET WAS WET, but it had stopped raining. It was cold, misty, and miserable. A distant glow was either the rising sun or the lights of Portland.

Running had been a challenge that morning. Getting out of bed had been almost painful. The cast on her wrist, which she'd had to put up with for over a month, made Storm feel like screaming. She had no desire to face the cold gray streets.

Ever since the night at the bar, when she helped Howard take Angela Ruiz, her mind had been playing tricks on her. She was seeing her father everywhere.

It had happened for the first time that night, in the

parking lot of The Cooler. She'd seen a man in profile who looked like her father, but when he got out of his car, she realized he wasn't. A week later, she thought she'd caught a glimpse of him near the back of a grocery store. She'd called up her courage and pushed her cart in that direction, but when she got there, she was alone. Now, nearly every day she saw a face in a crowd, a blur reflected in a window, and she was scared.

The fear, she knew, was unreasonable. She was no scrawny thirteen-year-old. She was a grown woman and no victim. In fact, part of her strength came from her very conscious choice to never be a victim again.

Her father was nothing more than a stranger, who happened to live in the same town. It was a big town; they didn't have to bump into each other. So why did they? Or was it all just her imagination? Maybe the problem was that she wanted it to be true. If her father was stalking her, didn't that mean she had every reason to use the handgun she'd begun to carry? Maybe Tom hadn't been completely wrong about that.

Storm was an officer of the court, and even though Washington County didn't want their probation officers to be armed, she'd gone through the same training required for police officers and had even put in extra time on the firing range because she hated it and was therefore bad at it. It was a weakness, but she eventually overcame it. Now she knew how to handle a weapon, how to load and sight and pull the trigger. Part of her wanted to put that knowledge to good use.

The other part of her—the rational, logical, mom part, who would have a difficult time explaining why she had killed her children's grandfather—made her realize her wish would not be granted. She couldn't kill her own father.

Luckily, she had Howard. Or did she? Howard had been quiet all week. No phone calls. No dropping into the office unexpectedly. This time, it didn't seem like a peaceful break. This time, it felt like abandonment.

She realized her moods were a little bit erratic, jumping from anger at Howard for not calling, to fear that he'd found and confronted her father, who was now lying dead in some dark alley. Then she would decide she was being melodramatic and far too inventive.

The best course would be to forget her father, forget Howard and the justice killings, and make the best life for her and her family as possible.

After all, she had a duty to make sure her kids were not messed up the way she was. Her father? Fuck him. He wasn't going to ruin her life. He'd done enough of that.

When she got home from her run, she was surprised to see activity in the kitchen. Why was everyone up so early? A stab of anxiety lanced through her, and she ran up the back porch steps and burst into the kitchen.

"Happy Valentine's Day, Mommy," sang out her family.

The scent of chocolate and freshly brewed coffee filled the air. Tom turned from the stove and set a plate at her place at the kitchen bar. Joel sat, swinging his legs while Lindsey put forks out.

"We made Valentine pantakes," shouted Joel.

"Pancakes," corrected Storm automatically. "Wow, do they ever look good."

"They're hearts," Lindsey told her proudly, "and they

got chocolate chips. Come on, Mommy, eat."

"I'm eating. I'm eating," Storm reassured her daughter. "Wow, this is really something." She looked at Tom and sent him a grateful smile. "I totally forgot about Valentine's Day."

The meal was fun. Tom had made pancakes in the shape of hearts, dotted with chocolate chips. He served them with a drizzle of maple syrup and a ghastly amount of whipped cream.

"Well?" he asked, after she'd taken a bite. "Do you like them?"

"Do you, Mommy? Do you?" asked the kids.

Storm set down her fork, chewed extravagantly, swallowed audibly, looked at her waiting family, and said the magic words. "They're even better than Waffle Whips."

The kitchen erupted into a total uproar. It didn't last long, as the kids, who'd apparently nearly starved to death in the twenty minutes they'd had to wait for their mother's return, fell quiet as they gorged on pancakes.

As she sipped her coffee, Storm picked the chocolate chips out of her pancakes. They were too sweet for morning. She wished someone with a camera could capture this scene. It belonged in a frame on her desk. 'The Perfect Family at Breakfast' would have been the title. Maybe she would paint it from memory someday. Thinking about this imaginary painting, she studied her family with a critical eye.

Tom wore his worn red-and-black checked robe over white flannel pajamas decorated with bright-red chili peppers—a birthday gift from his daughter. He'd been losing hair, and though it bothered him, Storm wished it would hurry up and all fall out. He would be a handsome bald man, and eventually he'd realize that.

Joel looked as if he'd gone to bed with his hair still damp from his shower. One side was plastered to the side of his head. The other stood up in random spikes. She wanted to get a spritz bottle and a comb but stilled the impulse.

Lindsey cut the edges off her pancakes with her fork. She hated edges and not just the ones on bread, like most kids.

Sometimes, Storm saw herself reflected in her daughter's quirks. Pointedly, she picked up her fork, sliced off an edge, and ate it.

"Oh, I almost forgot. A package came for you yesterday," said Tom. "Alex brought it over. Grace told him it showed up by mistake. Oh, and he said to tell you they're sorry they forgot to bring our casserole dish back. The one from Thanksgiving."

"They're so sweet," said Storm. "If I need the thing I'll go next door and get it. I wonder what's in the package. I don't remember ordering anything."

"I figured maybe a Valentine's gift from a secret admirer? Or maybe a gift for a really thoughtful husband?"

Storm shook her head. "No to both, I'm afraid. Where is it?"

"Hold on, I'll get it. It's sort of heavy."

Storm acknowledged Lindsey's questioning look with a shrug. "I don't know what it is. You think your dad might be pulling a trick."

"I don't know. He didn't say he was," said Lindsey, impressively serious. Storm wondered if she was pretending not to know. "You're going to be a good poker player someday," said Stormy.

"I already am," bragged Lindsey. "I beat Dad and Rylan at five card draw."

"Me too," said Joel. "I played five card drawed."

"Draw," corrected Storm and Lindsey at the same time. They exchanged amused looks.

"That must have been fun," Storm said to her youngest.

"Here you go," said Tom, setting a brown cardboard box large enough to hold a German shepherd puppy on the bar top. Storm looked at it suspiciously, but it didn't move or make any noise, so she figured she was safe. Tom had been hinting at wanting to get a dog for the kids. A puppy they could grow up with.

There was a mailing label, but the name on the return address wasn't familiar, and the address itself had been torn off by something by the looks of it, probably something with metal teeth.

"Want me to open it for you?" Tom asked Storm.

"Please," she said, moving her plate aside and standing so she could see inside once he had.

He took a knife from the magnetic holder on the side of the fridge and sliced through the tape. Then he stepped back to let her open it.

The scent of lilacs should have been enough of a clue to whom had sent the box. However, it wasn't until she slid aside the felt wrapping and revealed the jewelry box at the top of the file folders that she knew.

Aunt June was her mother's aunt and the woman who had raised her after the accident. This had been her jewelry box. There could have been only one reason it had been sent to her.

The realization that her aunt must have died struck Storm with the force of a sucker punch. She didn't have time to hide her reaction, which was fierce and overwhelming.

"Nooo," she said, the word stretched out, then dwindled to a whisper, a moan of surging pain. Eyes shut, an agony of regret filled her as the memories came flooding in.

"Get off my porch, Don." That was her aunt, old but unbent, standing on her front porch, a rifle resting in the crook of one scrawny arm. "My niece was an ass for marrying you, and I'm an ass for letting you live. Get yourself gone."

Aunt June, or properly, Great-aunt June, standing between Storm and her father, was one of Storm's best memories. She'd been the only person who had ever tried to protect her from her father, though certainly not the only one to guess that Storm and her mother were being abused.

Another memory came to the fore. Aunt June scolding. "Of course you'll go back to school. You didn't burn off your frontal lobe, did you? Get your clothes on and get on that bus."

Later, when the letter came, "The court says you belong with your dad. They think it's good to keep family together. If you told them the truth about that day . . ."

But Storm had pressed her lips together tightly and shook her head. She would not talk about it, not to her aunt and certainly not to strangers.

Storm remembered how she brushed her aunt's hair. The long chestnut strands mixed with threads of silvery gray were beautiful. Storm liked taking out the big rollers, brushing out the loose curls that flowed to the middle of her aunt's back.

"Old women don't have to cut their hair short so they look like boys. Whoever had that idea was a woman who didn't like competition!"

Her aunt had all sorts of ideas and little sayings like that, things that had stayed with Storm and which she continued to practice.

"You don't earn happiness, you choose it. Cook corn six minutes on a full boil, no more, no less. When you put your spare tire on, tighten the bolts in a star pattern, first with your fingers, then a wrench. It's as easy to fall in love with a rich man as it is a poor one. If a horse throws you, buy a nicer horse."

Storm's elbows were propped on the table, her face buried in her hands. Tom was rubbing her back. The kids were fussing, concern and fear in their voices. The plaintive sounds finally broke through her grief.

"I'm sorry," she told them. "Mommy got some bad news, but it's going to be okay." She hugged them, gave them love pats, let them crawl into her lap for reassurance. She even managed to dry her tears on the paper towel Tom got her, drank a glass of water, and even tried to smile.

A little while later, while Tom drove the kids to school, she took a shower, washed her tear-streaked face, dressed, and called in sick. Not a complete lie since the emotional storm had left her with a headache and an upset stomach. She'd cried more in the past month than she had her entire life. She didn't like it.

Three ibuprofen seemed like a good idea. She drank another glass of water, feeling dehydrated as if the tears had drained all the moisture from her.

Finally, she opened the cardboard box and removed the jewelry box. It was covered in gold leaf, the inside lined with rich purple cloth. It held a strand of matched pearls, a diamond and ruby ring that had been her aunt's prized possession, and a palm full of brooches and other costume jewelry.

Attached to the box in a see-through plastic holder was an envelope with her name typed across it. It was a letter from the nursing home director—or at least signed by her.

'I am sorry to inform you . . .' it began. It said that her great-aunt had passed away, leaving instructions that the box be delivered to her. The letter assured Storm that they were happy to carry out her aunt's wishes and that they were sorry for her loss.

Storm sat at the edge of her bed, rocking, clutching the letter in one hand, the jewelry box on her lap. It was such a pretty thing: old-fashioned, a little worn, a little fragile. A lot like her aunt.

Regret was a worm that chewed through her heart, leaving holes, hollow tunnels. After agreeing to marry Tom, she had turned her back on her Aunt June. Not a gradual process of one birthday forgotten, one Christmas card not mailed.

No, Storm had wanted a complete break from her past and from everyone who had ever known her as Willow. She had fulfilled that wish, and now she regretted it with every painful breath. Dear Aunt June. She had thrown her out, the baby with the bathwater, the good with the bad. Willow may have been a coward, but she, Storm, was an idiot.

Eventually, Tom returned home.

"Do you want to tell me what other secrets you've been keeping?" he asked, as he stepped into the bedroom and found her sitting on their bed.

She cradled the jewelry box on her lap.

"My great-aunt died."

"You told me you had no relatives. I assume from your reaction to this news that not only do you have a relative but that you were close." Tom's words were clipped, his annoyance palpable.

Storm nodded, unsure of her feelings. Guilt was one of them: anger, sorrow, regret, mourning, nostalgia. She could list them. She just couldn't sort them out. For instance, should she have told Tom she was sorry for holding back a few things when she told him about her father? Or should she stand up, walk calmly into the kitchen, get the gun out of her purse and make the need for explanations go away? One well placed bullet in the center of his forehead should do it.

She looked up at him, said nothing, and knew that her eyes reflected her dark, unnatural thoughts.

"Do—do you need anything?" he asked.

"Water?" She took the empty glass from the bedside table and held it out to him.

"You got it, honey," he said. "We'll get through this."

Storm smiled, or rather she forced the corners of her mouth up.

CHAPTER TWENTY-TWO

"MAN, I NEED A VACATION," said Nicky, standing in the door to Storm's office.

"Oh please. You just got back from one. What you want is an early retirement. Like thirty years early."

"You said it, sister."

"I have to admit I can't believe our Christmas getaway was just two months ago. It feels like it's been years since I've had any fun."

"I didn't want to say anything, but you have seemed sort of down lately. Anything you want to share?"

"No, not really. Nothing is going on. Tom and the kids are good. I think it's just the nonstop freaking rain, the gray. I get so sick of it. Why the hell do we live here?"

"The rain", said Nicky, laughing. "Anyway, the green stuff that comes after the rain and those flowers—you know—that stuff."

"Yeah, well, flowers don't stop suicide. We have one of the highest rates in the country."

"Oh boy, you really are a laugh riot today."

"Sorry. Maybe I just need more coffee."

"Yep, because as we know, caffeine solves all." Nicky's watch beeped, and she looked down at it as if it were sending a message she could read. "Shoot, got court. See you for lunch later this week?"

"Of course. Send me an email, days you're free."

"Will do. Have a better day, sweetie." Fluffing the short spikes of her wild pink hair, Nicky turned dramatically and literally skipped down the hall.

Storm smiled at Nicky's silliness. Making friends had always been hard for her. Her father's army career had kept the family moving so frequently that she'd never had a chance to learn how to maintain a long-term friendship. After the accident, she'd felt even less inclined to let someone get close.

Nicky, though, was special. She was Storm's opposite in so many ways and not just in the superficial and obvious ones. Tall or short, brunette or blond, slender or curvy, didn't really matter. The important differences could be found in their personalities. Where Nicky was filled with optimism and positive energy, Storm was cynical and downright somber. Where Nicky was carefree and fun-loving, Storm was controlling and tedious.

Being around Nicky forced Storm in a new direction.

She always felt more balanced after spending time with her friend. She wondered if maybe she was like a house plant on a windowsill that had to be turned now and then. Nicky kept her from leaning too far in one direction.

Smiling at her fanciful metaphor, Storm dug in her purse for her coffee card, and then, hesitating, placed it on her desk. She'd go in a moment, but before she forgot . . .

Storm clicked a few keys on her keyboard and opened the law enforcement database. She had found her father was on post-prison supervision and had been living in a halfway house but had moved out. He was supposed to have reported change in residence but not enough time had gone by for anyone to be worried. Well, aside from Storm. She was worried.

Her usual methods of discovering someone's whereabouts had failed. Not that much of a surprise. After all, it wasn't as if he had been part of society for a few years. He had no credit cards, probably not even a library card. He'd joined no online organizations, neither for his old squad or his high school. She'd discovered no paper trail at all—at least, not yet. Storm hoped for a parking ticket, half expecting a DUI. With his lifelong quest for the next buzz, eventually he'd screw up and she'd learn where he was.

She ran his name, but again had no luck. Coffee sounded better and better.

Standing in line at the coffee shop, Storm fidgeted. There were five people ahead of her. She hated lines.

"White chocolate mocha, please."

That voice. It was familiar. Storm peered around the shoulder of the man in front of her just as the woman who'd placed the order turned to walk to the counter where the barista would place her drink when it was ready. Their eyes met and they both froze.

Storm decided to do nothing. Forget the woman was even there. She sidestepped back to where she'd been in line, her view the back of a suit jacket. The woman had obviously made a different choice.

"Psst." It was more hiss than word.

Storm saw that the woman was now standing nearby, boldly staring at her. "Did you say something?" Storm asked.

"You were at The Cooler that night," the woman said. Storm had immediately recognized the diminutive Hispanic woman with her dark skin and blond-streaked hair.

"You work here?" Storm asked, surprised.

"Upstairs," the woman replied curtly, giving nothing more.

"Small world," said Storm. "Have you heard anything about your friend?"

The woman's eyes narrowed, and she looked Storm up and down as if she might find an answer of some sort if she just stared hard enough.

"Nothing," she finally spat out. "It's been a month and the police haven't said anything. They talk to you?"

"Yes. They followed up with me because I work in P and P, and they wanted to be sure I wasn't the one he was after. He broke my arm after all." Storm held up her left arm. Her sleeve was rolled back to mid forearm to accommodate the thickness of the cast, now decorated with faded magic marker drawings of flowers and a smiling sun.

"Hmm," said the woman, whom Storm remembered was called Celine, "I think you have fast answers to every question. Maybe too fast."

"Yeah, well, I think you and your friends weren't much help that night. You got in the way. You assaulted me. You're lucky I don't sue you."

Storm took a shallow breath and kept her eyes locked on the woman's. She was nervous and still felt a little guilty about how she'd selected Angela Ruiz, this woman's friend. But acting too nice wouldn't have helped anything—it would have only allowed her guilt to show through.

"White mocha," rang out the voice of the barista.

The woman looked Storm up and down once more, and tossing her head, moved off to get her drink.

Two customers later, Storm placed her order. Still rattled but determined not to show it, she moved up to the counter and asked for a wet cappuccino and a bran muffin, though she no longer wanted either.

Back in her office, Storm worked steadily through the pile of files on her desk. The coffee she'd bought grew cold, the muffin stale. She wanted to shut off her mind, throw herself into work and nothing else.

That woman, suspicious and far too close by, added another level of misery to an already rotten day.

She should have known it would be an awful day. She'd had the dream again last night—the good dream, or the bad dream, depending on how she looked at it.

The dream always began the same way, and the images seemed so real, she was sure it was based on an actual memory.

She was very young, no older than Lindsey, maybe even as young as Joel. It was a quiet day. A dreadful emptiness filled the house, and she wondered if it would be like that forever.

There was a reason it was so bleak. Her father had left again. Just like that. There one day, tossing her onto his shoulder and carrying her around like the queen of the world. The next day, gone, leaving an empty space where sound echoed but had no real voice.

In the dream, she found his room, the one with the big bed, so very tall, but she managed to climb onto it anyway. She pulled back the blankets and found his pillow, buried her face in the mingled scents of Old Spice, hair oil, and rum. The tears had come. Slow, warm tears that made her feel a little better. Eventually, she fell asleep, the pillow hugged tightly against her chest, not happy but content, at least.

She woke from the dream each time with the same longing ache for a father who didn't exist, except as a child's flawed memory, and a blinding anger at her loss.

That morning was no different. The pang of nostalgia, the child she had been, was still present, still able to remember and hurt. This bothered the grown-up that was Storm.

She didn't love that child. She wanted to spit on her, slap her, force her to act. She wanted to save her. Too many of her memories held that child cowering in a corner, hiding under a bed, sneaking around the edges of a life of fear. There was no pride there, no fighting spirit. That child made Storm sick to the core of her being.

CHAPTER TWENTY-THREE

IN THE MONTHS since landing the county project, Tom had fallen into the habit of taking Storm to lunch on Mondays. It was the day he usually met with the county's project manager to discuss progress on the new building. Storm always looked forward to those lunches. Since the kids had come along, they rarely had alone time.

On a blustery day in early April, she and Tom ate lunch at Baker's Burgers, a local family-owned restaurant that made burgers like the ones they remembered from childhood.

"We'll have to bring the kids here," Tom said. "I don't think they've ever had an old-fashioned burger or a cup of fries." He held up the cup, fries spilling from the edges. "What do you think is the idea behind this?"

"That's funny. I asked the counter girl that same question. She said it's so you can put them in the cup holder in your car."

"That's brilliant!" Tom enthused, his architect's mind thrilled by the functionality of the idea.

Storm smiled at his enthusiasm. How nice to be able to spend a relaxed moment free of the need to analyze every nuance. There were no lies to tell to cover late returns or unexpected absences. Since her last meeting with Howard, when she'd cried like a baby for no reason at all, he'd left her completely alone.

Because Howard had been compliant with all his court-ordered sanctions, and since his fines and fees were being paid on time, she had no reason to call him in. She was starting to think he had given up pressuring her into resuming their partnership.

She'd even begun to give up on her fear of running into her father. He was an old man—well, at fifty-three, an older man. Twenty years in prison was a long time. Odds were good that he wouldn't want any trouble and she was simply being paranoid. There had been no letters or phone calls in all the time her father had been in prison. Aunt June had forbidden it and Storm hadn't minded.

"I'm sorry, I was daydreaming," said Storm, when she realized Tom had asked her something. "What did you say?"

"I was asking if you read the paper this morning."

"No. Why?"

"I was looking at one while I was waiting for you

earlier. I read about this grandmother they think drowned her grandkid and buried her in the back lot. They found the body yesterday. Wondered if you'd heard about it."

"I did actually. Didn't the grandmother call the police to report her granddaughter was missing? Are they saying she did it?"

"Seems like. Though everything is worded so carefully. Wouldn't want to come right out and say it, I guess. Not without plenty of evidence. I just wondered if your office will be involved."

"Doubt it. We don't handle the people going into jail. We just handle the ones coming out."

"I knew that. I guess I was curious if you had insider information. How could a grandmother kill anyone, much less their own grandkid? Sort of blows your mind."

"Sort of makes me sick to think of it." Storm looked at the half-eaten burger sitting on the tray. The yellow paper wrapped around it was stained with grease. She pushed it and the nearly full cup of fries away and took a long sip of her iced tea.

"Let's talk about something more cheerful," suggested Tom. "What are you planning for Easter? Should we take the kids to the Alpenrose Dairy's egg hunt this year or to the zoo, like last year?"

"I don't know. I guess we can try the dairy."

"You don't sound very enthused," said Tom.

"Well, you know I've never like the whole egg-hunt thing. I hate the competitiveness. Some kids get lots of eggs, some get a few, and some get pushed around. Do you really think that sounds like fun?"

"We'll keep an eye on them, Stormy. I don't remember

being traumatized by hunting for Easter eggs, and I had lots of competition. We always held ours at the church."

"I'll think about it."

The throwaway cell phone in Storm's purse rang at 4:45. Howard's voice: "Did you hear about the woman who killed her grandkid? She's just been released. We can't let this stand."

Storm sat quietly, the phone gripped in her hand. "Yes," she finally said, "We can."

She switched off the phone.

The phone in Storm's house rang at 6:30 p.m., but when Tom answered it, the caller hung up. It rang again at 7:15 with the same result. At 8:00, when it rang the third time, Storm was ready and snatched the cordless from its cradle.

"This is Storm," she said, a warning in the tone of her voice. There was a click in her ear as someone hung up. In the next five hours the phone rang five times, and each time it was answered, the caller hung up. The last call came at 12:45 p.m.

Tom pressed *69 after the third call, and a number had appeared, but neither of them recognized it. When Tom dialed it, there was nothing but an impersonal recorded voice suggesting he leave a message for the phone's owner.

Storm was not fooled. She had purchased a throwaway phone for Howard. There was nothing to keep him from buying another.

After the sixth call, Tom tried to call the number back to leave a scorching message, but Storm stopped him. She didn't want Howard angry at Tom.

In the morning, they were bleary-eyed from sleeping

too little and too lightly. They had turned the phone off after the 12:45 p.m. call, but they needn't have bothered. According to its memory, there had been no further calls. It was as if the caller knew he couldn't bother them anymore.

Storm got the kids ready and told Tom to sleep in. She dropped them off on her way to work. She was eager to get to her office, a private place where she would be free to call Howard.

Unfortunately, as soon as she reached her office, the phone rang. It was Carrie.

"You've got a client waiting."

"Already?" Storm was certain it was Howard waiting to apologize or threaten.

"Yep. Sorry. His name is . . . let's see . . . Eldon Shatterly."

"Oh." Storm was both disappointed and relieved. She took a quick glance at her appointment book. Eldon did have an appointment, though not for another half hour. "He's early, but I guess I'll go ahead and see him. I'll be out in a minute."

"Okay."

Eldon Shatterly: the client who'd been in the wrong place at the wrong time. He must have been getting eager. There was only a week left until the end of his probation period. She'd asked him along for an exit interview. They'd go over everything just to make sure he'd pass through the system with the least amount of friction.

"I'm glad to see you doing so well," said Storm, once they'd finished going over the necessary forms. "Your new job sounds great, and didn't you tell me last time you were here that you turned in a financial-aid application for college?"

"Yes, I did. I got accepted to a couple schools, and now I'm just trying to figure out which one is giving me the best deal. It feels like a whole new start."

His smile and enthusiasm were infectious. Storm found herself smiling back. She'd tell Tom about this later. He hated the people she had to interact with and worried about her all the time. Eldon was the kind of person he'd want to hear about, someone who had earned a second chance. Furthermore, despite having more reason than most to hate the system, he'd done all that the court asked of him and hadn't projected his sense of injustice or anger back on her.

After escorting him down the hall and back to the reception area, with the usual admonishment to stay out of trouble, Storm returned to her office.

Storm's coworkers were busy and noisy, so to escape them, she closed her office door, sat down in her ergonomic chair, and stared blindly into the middle distance. She wondered what, if anything, she could do to earn a reset of her life. Maybe she'd already made a start. She listened to Tom's story about the abusive grandmother, and though it made her angry and upset, she hadn't felt the need for further research or to take action.

Let someone else deal with the evil people in the world, she decided. She was tired and wanted nothing more than to raise her children, be a good companion to Tom, and do her job. This horrible path she'd strayed onto, the anger that drove her there, were both things that should stay in the past, like everyone's mistakes.

Thinking about the past few months, there was a part

of her that couldn't really believe what she'd done. It was as if there were two Storms or, maybe, one Storm and one Willow.

The strange thought caught her imagination. Storm and Willow, but which was the killer? Willow, of course. The one who'd been burned, spent all that time in the hospital, dealt with the surgery that followed. Willow was a little girl having a temper tantrum and demanding revenge or justice.

Storm was just a mom who wanted a quiet life and good times with her family, a person who stood aside fearfully and watched from some dark corner of Willow's mind. Storm would never have done what Willow had. She'd never have taken part in any kind of killing, and she'd never have become involved with Howard.

Blinking, Storm rolled her shoulders, sat up straighter, and looked nervously around her empty office. These were the kind of thoughts crazy people had, and she wasn't crazy. She didn't have a split personality or hear voices. She was just a person who had seen too much crap and decided to do something about it. Well, to be honest, to get Howard to do something about it.

Yeah, that was the truth. If she hadn't talked to Howard, found that first number, agreed to go with him to serve as lookout the first time, none of the killings would have happened. People had those kinds of thoughts, but they didn't act on them. She would never have acted on them if it weren't for Howard.

Howard. He was the key to all of this. A truly damaged person if ever there was one. She thought of him with his nasty whip, spittle flying from his mouth as he reared back and then swept forward, blood and screams at the end of each horrid stroke. This was the man who had her phone number and was calling her home. The place that sheltered everyone she cared about.

She thought of his smirk, his smug expression, and suddenly she could see him as clearly as if he stood in front of her. She thought of the unwelcome touches of his hands and lips. A sense of disgust bordering on hatred filled her. God, what had she allowed herself to get into? How dare he call her home? Shaking, she swept her right hand across her desk. Eldon's file flew across the room and smacked into the wall and to the floor.

Storm wanted to hit something else, break something or someone. He'd reached right into her house—the son of a bitch.

Taking the special cell phone from her pocket, she punched his number with her forefinger. She heard one ring, and the call went directly into voice mail. Taking a deep shuddering breath, she said, in the calmest voice she could muster, "Don't call my house again. Don't call me again. After I hang up, I am going to throw this phone away. I'm also transferring your case to a coworker. He will contact you soon. We are done. We are finished. If you call me or try to contact me in any way . . . well, trust me, you will not enjoy the outcome."

Feeling proud she'd kept her temper and said what she had to say, Storm set the phone down. Her hands shook, but she knew she had done the right thing—finally.

Tuesday. Wednesday. Thursday. Each day that went by without a reply from Howard added another layer of anxiety.

Howard was not a person who avoided conflict. He dealt with conflict directly, immediately. She knew so little about him, but she knew that. This march of days with no response was so unlike him, or so she believed.

Now that she thought about it, she realized how little she knew about Howard. A few pages in a case file told her next to nothing. No matter how well one knew people they were often enigmas. Hitler was a vegetarian who liked to paint. The worst sex offender she'd ever met had baby-blue eyes, chubby cheeks, and a job that kept him in sports cars and Rolex watches. People were annoyingly unpredictable and complicated.

At least she had followed through on one of her promises. She'd taken the SIM card from her cell and thrown it and the phone away. What she hadn't followed through on was asking a coworker to take Howard on as a client. It seemed like a good idea, and she might still have done it, but the truth was she and Howard were bound by their partnership in a way that was inescapable. Damn it, she wished he'd call.

She regretted tossing the cell phone. Maybe he was reluctant to call her at work. The last time he called her there, she'd jumped all over him. She had not handled him very well.

The more she thought about it, things like his demand to let him be the one to decide when they stopped, made a certain kind of sense. He was expressing how he disliked being made to feel like an underling, and she couldn't blame him for that. Maybe if they talked it out and she explained calmly, without being bossy, her reasons for them taking a break. Or, what if she gave him some incentive to do what she asked? She could pass him through probation without a hitch. If he got the job in Seattle or one like it up there, maybe she could help him with some money for a first and last on an apartment or something.

That was the thing to do: treat him like a friend, not like a minion. Convinced she was on the right track, Storm decided if she hadn't heard from him by Friday afternoon, she would drive to Traynor Chemical and have a talk with him.

With that resolved, Storm opened the door to her office and got on with her workday.

* * *

The table was set, and dinner was being placed on it when Storm walked in. "What's all this?" she asked.

"We're celebrating spring," explained Tom. "You will note that the forsythia are in bloom."

Storm saw a jelly jar had been placed at the center of the table. It held half a dozen thin branches. They were almost bare except for rows of tightly closed leaf buds and several bright-yellow flowers.

"The goofy things. They're blooming early."

"Aren't they pretty, Mom?" asked Lindsey, who stood next to Storm's chair. "We picked them for you."

"I helped. I helped," insisted Joel.

"I said we," Lindsey said, exasperation clear in her voice.

"She did," agreed Storm, pulling her daughter close and hugging her. "That was very nice of you to remember that your brother helped."

"Who's ready to eat?" asked Tom. "We've got some

nice broccoli casserole here, followed by eggplant soup, and dessert will be a yummy Brussels sprout pie." He smiled as he recited the list of foods the kids disliked.

"Eww, that's gross," said Lindsey.

"Pie, pie, pie," sang Joel happily.

Storm shook her head at all of them and felt her spirits lift. It was so nice to be home.

"How was your day?" she asked Tom, after everyone had taken their seats and were working their way through macaroni and cheese casserole.

"Good. Helped Rylan on his project, and he's coming out tomorrow to work on mine. We've decided he'll take lead on the bank in Tigard and I'll be lead on the county project. Should keep us from bumping heads too much."

"Sounds smart."

"We like to think so. I was also a good husband and got the back forty mowed and the flower beds raked out pretty well. Not exactly all the spring cleanup, but a good start."

"Sounds like a productive day."

"Yeah, my back says it was productive."

"Don't forget to say about Mommy's friend," said Joel.

"Mommy's friend?" Storm asked.

"Oh yeah, totally forgot. A friend of yours came by and dropped off the seeds for the kids."

"The what?" Storm asked.

"The seeds. He said you ordered them a while ago from one of his kids, one of those fundraiser things parents get suckered into. Anyway, he said to tell you thanks. His son didn't win, but he had a good time learning how to harass people into buying stuff they didn't want. Nice guy."

"Yeah." Storm made her voice calm, but a dreadful

coiling was going on somewhere deep inside. "What did he look like, this nice guy?"

"I don't know. Just a guy. Pretty average. Medium build. Brown hair. Sorry, I can't remember his name or if he even gave me a name. Why? Don't you remember who you bought the seeds from?"

"What are you talking about?" Storm insisted, pushing hard past Tom's puzzled look, searching for an answer she didn't want to hear. "What did this nice guy give you for our kids?"

"I told you. Seeds," Tom said. "Packets of seeds for the garden. Simple things that anyone could grow—zucchini and corn and some flowers. The kids were excited about planting them. That's why I thought I'd get started on the yard work. What's wrong?"

"We have to leave," Storm said, her voice still calm but her eyes, wide with terror and locked on his, transmitted her fear more clearly than any words. "I need you to help me pack a few things for us and the kids. We have to get out of here."

CHAPTER
TWENTY-FOUR

"DO YOU HAVE ANY IDEA who the man was?" The investigator's piercing blue eyes studied her. A notebook lay open on the table before him, waiting to capture everything she said.

"No. No idea," Storm said. She hadn't wanted to call the police, but Tom insisted. Now, Tom was in their room with the kids, and she was in the hotel's empty breakfast room, being interviewed by an investigator from the detective division of the sheriff's office.

The detective looked so calm in his dark-gray suit and blue tie, so confident and relaxed. Seated across from him, she rested her forearms against the cool granite surface but could not help tugging at the ragged cuffs of her sleeves as she tried to express the reason for her fears.

"I have no idea. All I know is that I didn't order any seeds. I probably wouldn't have thought much about it, but lately I've had this creepy feeling. It's as if someone's watching me. You know how you get that feeling sometimes and you turn and there's someone looking at you?"

The detective nodded.

"Well, when I turn around to see who it is, no one is there. It's odd, but I don't think I'm imagining it. Now this. I know I didn't buy any seeds, and I'm starting to think one of my clients is harassing me."

To Storm, this embellishment seemed worse than simply lying about knowing who the mysterious man might have been. Of course it was Howard, and of course she had to get the kids and Tom out of the house. She even had to follow through and call the police, just as she would have if an angry client had figured out where she lived and shown up there. But did she have to send the police down a blind alley and waste their time?

The answer was yes, if she valued her freedom. Of course, she could just opt to tell the truth. She could simply say that Howard Kline was the visitor. That he'd been angry when she put an end to their killing spree. Somehow she didn't think that would get her much help. No, this one she'd have to handle all alone.

"I probably sound crazy to you," Storm said with a wry grin. "Going off about someone following me. Pretty dumb, huh?"

He shook his head. "No ma'am. I teach defense classes,

and we always tell our students if they feel funny or uneasy, or if they get that hair-standing-up-on-your-neck feeling, they should trust their instincts."

"My instincts are on high alert," said Storm. Some of the people I work with . . . well, you know."

"Yes ma'am, I sure do."

They spoke for a short time longer. He jotted down a few notes but inevitably said what she'd expected. "If you don't know which of your offenders came to your house, if that's who it was, there isn't much we can do. We'll send more cars to drive by your house, but you might want to consider installing a security system."

"Thank you. We'll think about that," she said. "I need to get back to my family now. They stood up, and she was happy to see him leave.

"So they aren't going to do anything?" Tom asked a few minutes later. Storm heard disbelief in his voice. "Aren't you, I don't know, like, one of them? Don't they get all protective of their own?"

"Oh honey. I'm not one of them. I'm just a probation officer. There isn't much love lost."

"They could at least think about the kids," he whispered furiously.

She saw him glance at the kids lying on their stomachs on one of the two queen beds watching television and scribbling in coloring books with crayons.

Storm thought the kids were treating the whole thing as a special getaway. They begged for trips to the snack machine or the ice machine, and they loved the strange room with the sink in the same room as the beds and the teeny bars of soap.

She was not enjoying it, not one bit, and she was sure the kids wouldn't for much longer. The novelty would soon wear off, and they'd become restless and cranky. Also, she'd caught an expression of fear on Lindsey's face when they'd first climbed into the van. They had tried to shield the kids from the truth of why they were spending the night in a hotel, but Lindsey might have understood more than she and Tom realized.

Her suspicion, that Lindsey was playing the happy older sister as a way of keeping her little brother from sensing her fear, seemed very grown up. Storm bitterly regretted the necessity.

"I think it's our job to think of the kids," she said to Tom. "That's why I wanted them out of the house."

"How dangerous do you think this guy is?" he asked.

"I'm not sure. I don't know which guy this guy is. I make people mad a lot, and this week was no different. I think I may have some ideas, though, and I'm going to make some calls in the morning." She hated lying to Tom, but what was one more after the hundreds she'd already told him?

"Maybe we should do what they said and get a security system installed."

"Can we afford it?"

"I have no idea what one costs, but we can afford it if we have to. Damn it, Storm, I wish you'd give up that stinking job."

"I know."

After a few moments of silence, in which the kids continued scratching away at their coloring and the television provided a mundane backdrop, Storm placed her hand on Tom's.

He sighed, looked up, and gave her a small smile. "I guess we'll get that security system. I'll also invest in a baseball bat, a nice Louisville Slugger. Unless you'd like to loan me your gun, that is."

"A bat it is," she said, curling her fingers around Tom's. She could see it, Howard sneaking into the house, Tom striking out with the bat, one single, lethal blow.

She shook off the fantasy. Tom was gentle, like a sleepy-eyed basset hound. Howard was a fight-trained pit bull, savage and untrustworthy. Tom would never have been prepared to defend himself against Howard. He'd never have expected the level of viciousness and lack of conscience that Howard brought.

No, the only way to make sure this ended was to end it herself. She would have to make Howard go away. The good news was that she was more than angry enough to make him go away forever.

"Tom. I know it's late, but I have to run to work and print up some information for the police. They'll want to contact some of my clients in the morning, and I need to make it as easy as possible. Will you stay here and make sure the kids—?"

"They'll be safe," he told her. "You go do what you need to do."

"I won't be long," she promised.

CHAPTER
TWENTY-FIVE

IT HAD JUST turned 11:00 p.m. when Storm drove into the parking lot of Traynor Chemical, the time they felt it was safe, when the building would be free of employees. Her timing was perfect. The lot was empty except for Howard's car.

She parked badly askew, took up two spaces, climbed from the car, and slammed the door. Each step she took toward the building seemed to drive her anger harder and deeper into her body. It rose from the base of her spine to her brain, hammering through each vertebra, thrumming through each cluster of nerves as she fought to walk slowly, to keep her cool.

After she unlocked the door, she pushed it open with her left hand. Her right was in the pocket of her coat, wrapped around the butt of her Glock 22.

She went straight to the shower room. The space was empty. She retraced her steps and turned down the main hallway. She'd walk the halls until she found him.

She found a door marked OFFICE, and opened it. The space was dark, but a motion sensor detected her presence, and a row of fluorescents flickered on. They highlighted walls the color of hay, decorated with framed photos of colorful electronic circuitry. To the left, were two chairs with a small table between them. On it was a fan of magazines. To the right was a wooden door marked STAFF ONLY. Directly in front was a tall reception desk with two workstations.

She entered the office, walked around the workstation and opened the staff only door. She found herself looking down another hallway, this one with a row of doors on the left. The prospect of checking each room was frustrating. She was reaching for the first door when one near the end of the hall opened, and Howard stepped out. He paused when he saw her. Then, smiling, he strode toward her. He seemed eager to reach her, happy to see her.

"Stay right there, you son of a bitch." Storm pulled the gun from her coat and held it at the ready. She aimed at the center of his body. Her plan was to shoot him center mass three times and put a final bullet in his head just for the reassurance.

"What the fuck!" Howard raged, still moving toward her.

Storm slid her finger into the trigger guard. Howard

flung his hands up and stopped in his tracks.

The others they had killed had earned their deaths. She had told them so. Each time she'd given them the reason. Howard deserved as much.

"Howard Kline, you went to my home. You talked to my husband, to . . . to my children. This is not forgivable."

"No, Storm, no. You got it wrong."

"You went to my house, didn't you?"

"Yes, I did, but not to hurt anyone. I did it to protect them."

Storm said nothing. The ugly black thing that burned inside snarled from its home in the dark well of her soul and was not easily contained.

"It was your father, Storm. I followed your father there, to your house. I didn't even know it was your house until I saw your husband come out for the mail. I recognized him right away. I've seen you two together, having lunch plenty of times. Put the gun away, and I'll tell you all about it."

"Why didn't you tell me about it before?" Storm asked, her arms beginning to tremble from holding the gun straight and steady on her target.

"I tried, but you didn't answer the cell phone and you've got me all paranoid about calling you at work. I was going to come to the office and see you Monday. Come on, Storm, I didn't even know where you lived. Honest. Don't shoot me until I tell you what your dad was up to. You need to know."

Storm lowered the gun, the muzzle pointed at the floor halfway between them. "Talk."

"I found your dad. He was staying at a halfway house

off Baseline."

Storm nodded. So far, he was telling the truth.

"I have a friend in recovery staying at a house near there, almost next door actually. I talked to him, and he took me over and introduced me to some of the guys who lived with your dad. Hell, it doesn't take but a half rack of beer to get all the information you need from an alcoholic. You know that, huh?"

"Did you talk to him? To my father?"

"No, he wasn't there. Found out he had a girlfriend and was staying at her place. I went there, parked down the street, watched him for a few days. Sort of the same way we stake out our targets, you know?"

"I know." Storm continued to hold the gun at the ready, though she was beginning to believe she might have been mistaken about Howard's motives.

"So, one day he leaves and I follow him. He drives toward Hillsboro and into a neighborhood. I see him pull up and park, so I figure I'd better do the same. But there's no more free street parking, so I pull into someone's driveway.

"After a while, I realize he's not getting out of the car. Then it hit me. Shit, he was watching a house, just like I'd been watching his. Got me curious, so I stuck around. Finally, I saw your husband come out and get the mail. I knew him right off. I've seen you and your man around Hillsboro often enough. You go to lunch with him at that Thai place on Main."

Storm let the gun fall to her side, her finger resting alongside the trigger guard. Her hands were shaking even more; the adrenaline that had coursed through her system was fading, leaving her feeling weak. Her limbs felt heavy, filled with sand. "What . . . what did he do? What did my father do?"

"Nothing. He just sat there. But then this car pulls in next to me. Scared the hell out of me. Guy comes over to the car, asks me what I'm doing there. I tell him I'm lost, come up with some address off the top of my head. I don't think he bought it. Anyway I got out of there, drove around a little while. When I came back, your dad's car was gone. I took the spot where he'd been and watched your house awhile. It was quiet. Didn't see anyone. I got nervous. What if your father did something? I decided that I should see and that I'd need something better than the being-lost story."

"And the best you could come up with was seeds?"

"Why not? Some guy at the halfway house was selling seeds for his sister's kid. I bought some because I wanted those guys to like me and tell me what they knew. They were sitting there in the car, and well, that's where the idea came from. I went in and told your husband I was delivering the seeds you bought for your kids. Got to see your kids, by the way. Great-looking kids, huh?"

"Yeah, they're great kids all right. That's why I don't want you anywhere near them." The handgun's muzzle moved as if under its own volition, rising slightly.

"Hey, come on now. I told you, I was just trying to make sure they were all right. I don't know what the hell the deal is between you and your dad, but if he's badass enough to bother you, well, he bothers me too. Besides, what if your family was dead in that house? You think I want you to find something like that? I know you don't believe it, but I do think we are more than just partners. I like to think we're also friends."

Storm put the gun in her pocket.

"I'm not so sure we're friends," she said. "But we are partners. I just wish you hadn't made all those phone calls. Those calls felt very threatening, Howard. They pissed me off."

"What calls?" asked Howard, his forehead wrinkling as his brows drew together.

"That day you called about the grandmother who killed her grandkid. I said no and you got mad and called me all night, hour on the hour."

"Bullshit. That never happened. Sure, I was ticked and I did call and tell you that, but I'm not in high school. I don't phone-prank people. I waited a few days until I cooled off and called. Only I didn't get through. I just got this canned voice telling me the subscriber is out of the service area. It's been like that ever since, which is why I couldn't reach you to tell you about your dad."

"If it wasn't you, who was it?"

"How should I know?" Howard asked, his attitude much less deferential now that the gun was out of sight. "My guess? Your father did it. Maybe he just wanted to hear your voice, huh? He's your dad after all. Been away for twenty years. Maybe he wants to hear his kid, see her, maybe see his grandkids."

"That," said Storm forcefully, "is not going to happen."

"I gathered that," Howard said. He looked up and gave her a smile full of warmth and understanding. The kind of smile only someone close to you can give.

Storm sighed. She had been forced to reassess her

feelings about Howard yet again. "Thanks for looking out for my family. I know you understand why I was so angry. What we do together, the justice killings . . . that's not the sort of thing sane people do. It makes it hard to believe you're not crazy or that you won't do crazy things."

"Same goes for you," said Howard.

"Yes, it does," she agreed. "Plus, there's that other thing."

"What other thing?" asked Howard.

"You know, the way you're always hitting on me. I'm married and I'm not interested, but you're a dangerous man. How do I tell you I'm not interested? How can I be honest without being afraid?"

"Damn, Storm. I never meant to make you feel like that," Howard said, closing the distance between them. He stopped within arm's reach. "Don't you get it? We're partners, huh? We got this stuff to do and we get it done. You see me for who I am and you don't turn away. That makes you special to me. I know I wanted more, but when you made it clear that no was no . . . well, hell, Storm, I thought you understood I was backing off."

"I'm sorry, Howard. I should have trusted you more."

"No need to be sorry. I wasn't listening to you. Telling you about that crazy killer grandma right after you told me we had to lay low. That wasn't right."

"It really wasn't," Storm agreed. "But I could have handled it better myself." Storm smiled. It was a genuine smile that reached her eyes. She had just realized her kids were safe. Her father was not going to harm them. If she was lucky, he'd never even get a chance to speak to them.

Howard was not the problem; he was the solution

she'd been looking for.

"What now?" he asked.

"Now we both get what we want. If you can find my father once, you can find him again."

"I can," Howard promised.

CHAPTER
TWENTY-SIX

"HOW MUCH TROUBLE am I in?" Storm asked Big Ed, who had managed to lower his oversized frame into one of her visitor chairs.

"No one's in trouble," he assured her. "Look, we all make mistakes now and then. You forgot about buying the dumb seeds. You don't remember who you got them from, but at least you do know the guy was legit. That's got to make you feel good. There's no longer a threat."

"It does. But it also makes me feel like a total ass. I called the police. I called you. I dragged my family to a hotel."

"If you're waiting for me to say you did the wrong

thing, you'll be waiting a very long time," said Big Ed. "If you're afraid for your family or your own safety, you take steps, you take action. That's what you did, Storm. Now, stop making me repeat myself, or it will start to seem like you're fishing for a compliment." Ed shot her a big smile and Storm felt better. Then he made her feel worse.

"What I'm more concerned about is what you told the police about feeling as if you're being followed. What is the basis for that? Do you have anything you can share with me?"

Storm crossed her ankles, crossed her arms, and leaned forward, staring down at her desk. What should she have said? The truth? That she'd felt as if she were being stalked from the moment she'd learned her father was out of prison? She wasn't about to tell him that. She'd rather let him and everyone believe one of her clients was the stalker or even that she was being paranoid.

She put her palms flat on the surface of her desk. She could smell Big Ed's cologne. It was nice, but a bit overpowering in the confines of the small room.

"I've been thinking about quitting," she said softly, looking up and meeting his eyes. "My husband hates that I work with offenders, and I think this whole thing shows I'm sort of freaked out."

Big Ed seemed to consider this and said, "Storm, you had your arm broken recently. You haven't been out of a cast for very long. A dustup like that—the memory must still be pretty fresh."

"No. This was going on before that. It didn't help, of course. But I don't think getting hurt that night and working here are related. That was just me being in the wrong place at the wrong time."

"I see. Have you considered taking some time off? Maybe you're just tired and need a break. We could arrange a leave of absence."

"Maybe," Storm agreed. "I'll have to think about it some more. Talk to Tom."

"Of course."

Carrie popped her head inside. "Big Ed, there's a call for you. It came into the main line."

"Can't you just send it to my voice mail?" Ed asked, noticeably annoyed.

Blushing, Carrie said, "It's someone from the FBI.

Big Ed rolled his eyes. "They're people. Carrie, just people." But he got up and ducked through the doorway anyway. "I'll talk to you more about this later. Okay, Storm?"

"Sure. That would be great."

* * *

The Mackenzie family swung through the drive-through pizza on the way home from the hotel, picking up a pepperoni for the kids and a vegetarian for the adults.

"Pizza. Come on, you guys. No pizza dance?" Storm watched Tom try to get the kids to cheer up. It was painfully obvious he was failing.

"Pizza sounds good," said Lindsey, "but I'm not very hungry."

Even Joel was quiet, and apparently engrossed in opening and closing the lid on the backseat cupholders. Snap. Click. Snap. Click.

When they got home, they ate, and Storm was glad when it was over and the kids moved into the TV room to play on their game system.

Storm hated to park kids in front of electronic babysitters, but there were times she needed it, and this was one of them.

"I'm so sorry about putting you through that," Storm told Tom as soon as they were able to speak alone.

"I'm just happy we're back home," said Tom.

"Kid's aren't so happy. They were having fun, and I went and ruined it by remembering I did buy those seeds. God, I feel like such an idiot."

"Well, if you're an idiot, I'm right there with you. I should have tried to keep you calm, given you time to think. We both know you haven't been yourself lately. This thing with your dad and then your aunt. It's been rough. I'm so used to you being logical, reasonable. I should have been there for you. I should have been the voice of reason and logic for once."

Storm nodded, but she was wondering how reasonable and logical Tom would have been if he knew what she knew, that her father not only had their address, but had been watching their house.

No doubt, Tom would have wanted to lie in wait and have some words with the old man. He'd probably have told tell him he wasn't welcome, would never be allowed to speak to his grandchildren, and would have to leave or have the cops called on him.

Tom's belief in the efficacy of the system and in a world where good conquered evil was both sweet and almost fatally stupid.

He reached across the table and took her hand. "It's going to get better, I promise."

"The only way it will get better is if I take up Big Ed's offer of some extra time off and you take me on another much longer trip to the mountains,"

"Liked getting away from here that much, did you? Can't just stay home and rest for a few days?"

"Boy, you just don't get it. This house is another job to me. I can't relax here. There's always something that needs to be done, fixed, cleaned, something."

"You're right," said Tom, unexpectedly. "And since we can't afford to jet you off to some foreign destination with fantastic room service, we're going to have to prove you wrong. We're going to have to prove you can be a lazy, slovenly, vacationing mess at home."

"It will never happen," scoffed Storm.

"Ah, but it will. Saturday, you'll get up, but you'll stay in your pajamas all day. No cooking. You'll be waited on by your willing staff. No cleaning. We'll take care of that too."

"I'm starting to like this idea," said Storm, meaning it. Absently, she reached for the box she'd received from her aunt's nursing home. It was too heavy to slide toward her with one hand, so she got up and grasped it with both, dragging it across the table. She opened the top and reached inside, remembering it was half filled with what appeared to be folders containing documents. Though once important, they were probably no longer of interest to anyone.

Storm took out the top folder. "Looks like car stuff. What do you think?" she asked Tom, sliding the folder across the table to him.

"Yep. She must have been one of those people who keep every receipt for everything she bought or had done for her car's maintenance."

"I don't think she even drove the last five or six years. Funny, the things people hang on to," said Storm.

The next file held copies of tax returns dating back twenty years. The one beneath that was a thin photo album, but rather than the expected photographs, it was filled with cards, old ticket stubs, and the faded remains of a few dried, pressed flowers.

A puff of dusty musty scent filled the air, and Storm sneezed. She closed the box and pushed it away. "I think there might be a better day for me to deal with this stuff. Let's go hang out with the kids and pretend yesterday never happened."

"You mean forget that you totally lost your mind and made us go into hiding? No way."

"Oh boy," said Storm, "Something tells me you're going to be using this one a long time."

"A long, long time," agreed Tom. "But for the moment, if I'm nice, can we have popcorn?"

Storm stood up and slapped the top of the box of folders. "I'll make a deal. You put this box away in the bedroom closet and I'll pop your corn."

"You always do," said Tom, waggling his eyebrows suggestively.

Storm dug the air popper out of a bottom cabinet while Tom carried the box into the bedroom. She measured out the kernels, let them slide into the machine, and enjoyed the sound they made as they fell into place.

There was a muffled crash and Tom's voice. "Damn—I mean—darn it," he said, catching himself.

A moment later, he entered the kitchen. "Drop

something?" Storm asked, keeping one eye on the popper while reaching for a bowl to slip beneath it as the first kernel popped.

"Let me do that," said Tom. "Here. He handed her a white envelope and took the bowl from her hands. "The bottom of the box fell out, and this was in it."

"I think whoever packed it flipped the contents over. I'm pretty sure this letter was meant to be on the top. At least, it's addressed to you."

Storm took the white business-sized envelope with her name scrawled across it in her aunt's shaky handwriting.

What had she written? She could only imagine the anger and the pain it contains. "Do you mind?" she said to Tom, looking toward the now frantically popping corn.

"No, you go," he said.

Storm, her mouth twisting, nodded. Stiffly, she walked to the bedroom, shut the door, and fell across the bed.

Taking a deep breath, she steeled herself, ripped open the small end of the envelope, and fished out three lined pages covered in her aunt's familiar handwriting.

Dear Storm,

I know this is going to come as a shock to you, and you've already had more than your share of those. I feel like your life has also been filled with partings. Losing your mother, not being able to continue your relationship with me—and your father, well, that was a parting as well.

I'm sorry for any role I had in making your life hard. It is sometimes difficult to know what is right and what is wrong, where to place your loyalties and your trust.

Your mother was not just my niece, she was also my

friend. I have remained loyal to her and kept promises I made to her for a very long time, but I cannot go to my grave knowing you might never know the truth.

I had hoped some day you would come back into my life. When that day came, I planned to tell you everything, but the years have slipped by, and I understand your need to distance yourself from a past you have not been able to forgive or forget.

I do not ask or expect your forgiveness but hope you don't hate me even more when I finally unburden myself of this terrible secret.

I know that you believe that your father killed your mother in a drunken rage while you were in the hospital. That is not true.

Your mother was unable to cope with what your father did to you. She went to see you in the hospital. They were keeping you unconscious, and when she saw the burns, she simply couldn't deal with it. I'm still not sure how aware she was. Was it some sort of disassociation, her mind shutting off the memory of who she was? Or did she just run away? The truth may be somewhere in between. I don't know, and I guess I don't want to know.

After your mother disappeared, she ended up in a series of homeless shelters. At the time, I wasn't aware of that. I too thought she had been killed and her body hidden.

It was only later, after she and I reconnected, that we were able to reconstruct where she'd been during some of those lost years. She had made calendar entries. We found some notes in a diary and a few other things.

The first I knew that she was alive was three years after she'd disappeared, when one of the shelters contacted me.

They'd found my number in her things and took a chance and called. She was very sick, and they sent her to a hospital. The hospital said that it was lung cancer and that she had very little time. I was in shock, of course. I couldn't believe she was alive. It was a miracle. But she was dying. It was horrible.

I decided not to tell you. You were doing well in school. You seemed to be putting things behind you. Your father had been sent to prison for driving drunk and hitting that poor girl. Telling you that your mother had run away seemed too cruel. Asking you to watch her die was unthinkable.

I told you I was going away to help a sick friend for a couple weeks, remember? I didn't completely lie. When I got to the hospital, I found out they'd made a mistake. Your mother didn't have cancer, she had pneumonia.

She was still very sick, but with a warm place to stay and decent meals she eventually regained her health and slowly regained her memory. However, even with her memory back, she knew she was in no shape to be your mother. She'd been using drugs and wasn't sure if she could stop. She felt you'd already had to deal with one addicted parent and didn't deserve another.

I want you to know that she did straighten herself out, though it took another year before she managed to stop for the last time. By then, you were in your final year of high school.

Your mother and I kept in touch. I sent her pictures of you, lists of your accomplishments. She never stopped caring. I hope I haven't implied that she did.

We kept meaning to tell you, but one year went by and then another, and well, after a while, you met your husband

and you seemed happy. You didn't need me and I was sad, but also happy for you.

So now, here I am. Cancer finally got one of us, but it wasn't your mom. What a funny universe we live in, full of irony and bad jokes.

She doesn't know I'm sending you this letter. I didn't know what to tell her. I didn't want to make her run away again. She's been hiding a long time.

She lives in Crescent City, California, where she runs a lodge-style bed and breakfast out in the redwoods. It belonged to an old man she took care of, and when he passed on, he left it to her.
It's called Flat Lake Lodge. You won't have any trouble finding it if you look. I really hope you do.

Take care of yourself. I have always loved you like my own. I hope there are still some shreds of love for me in your heart after you read this.

Love always,
* Aunt June*

Storm waited for some sort of emotion: shock, anger, pain, hurt—something. She was numb.

When Tom entered the room to tell her the popcorn was ready, he found her tying the laces of her running shoes. She'd already changed into shorts and a T-shirt.

Handing him the letter, she said, "I have to go for a run."

She ran and ran and ran.

CHAPTER TWENTY-SEVEN

NICKY SAT BACK against her seat. Sunlight glinted from her sunglasses, and Storm wished she'd take them off. She wanted to be able to read her emotions.

It was unusually warm for the season, and the sun was a bright white presence. They'd decided to sit outside. The place they chose for a quick coffee break—a cozy wine bar and restaurant with the curious name Primrose and Tumbleweeds—provided wrought-iron chairs and tables under their wide green awning.

"You have got to be kidding me?" Nicky said, and she did remove her sunglasses, sweeping them aside and staring at Storm with wide unblinking eyes. "This is so . . .

well, so much to take in. I mean, I kind of figured your parents were dead. You never talk about them. I had no idea your dad was in prison or your mom a suspected homicide victim. That's terrible."

Storm didn't know how to respond, but the concern in her friend's eyes told her she'd been right to trust her with her well-guarded childhood secret. "I know you think trying to find her when she hasn't done a thing to contact me is crazy. Tom thinks I'm setting myself up to be hurt, and he's upset that I'm going without him. He doesn't understand why I can't wait until he's able to go, but he's tied up with his job, and I don't want to wait. Finding out my mom's alive changes so much—it changes everything."

Nicky shook her head, jeweled beads sparkling from thin braided sections of her spiked pink hair. "You have to go. Of course you do. Maybe I should go with you."

"You just told me you are out of vacation time, remember?"

"Oh yeah, that. I've got to hurry up and get married to my rich man so I can quit this stinking nine to five."

"You'll go insane."

"I know. That's why I've talked to Dorothy about doing a job share. She's big as a house, and I know once the kid's here, she'd like to work half-time."

"You mean it?"

"Yep."

"Oh, that's great news. I was already starting to think about missing you, missing this."

"You won't get a chance to miss me. Sounds like I made a good choice in deciding to stay. I mean, I'm getting married and settling down, ho hum, but your life is turning into a great big soap opera."

"Is this a good thing?" Storm asked, with a wry smile.

"Good? I don't know. Entertaining? Oh yeah. So when are you leaving?"

"Tomorrow morning. I'll have to tie up some things at the office. Get someone to cover for me. I'm out of vacation time too, so I'm requesting a week of unpaid."

"HR isn't going to like that."

"HR can bite me," said Storm, crossing her arms defiantly and almost knocking over her coffee. She grabbed it just in time.

"Hey, you can't steal my expressions," said Nicky.

Storm just smiled. "Bite me."

Nicky laughed. "Okay, maybe you can." Her watch beeped. "Damn it. I guess we'd better get back." She drained the last of her coffee and tossed the cup into a nearby can. "Two points," she said. "I'm glad you suggested this restaurant. The coffee's better here."

"It sure is." The image of the suspicious woman she'd first met in the parking lot of The Cooler, and later in line at her former favorite coffee place, filled Storm's thoughts. It replaced some of her good mood and darkened the day. She didn't tell Nicky it was the dread of another encounter with the woman and not the difference in coffee that had affected her choice of coffee options. Some of Storm's secrets connected too closely to other secrets that could never be told.

Storm returned to work believing the rest of the day would drag by. That knowing she was driving to California and wanted to get home and pack would make each minute crawl. Luckily, there was enough to do to distract her and the day sped by faster than expected. It was 4:30 before she knew it, and she had only one thing left to do.

It had become Storm's habit to run her father's name through the law enforcement database at the end of the day. She was certain he'd turn up eventually.

Of course, now there were other things to worry about. Her mother was alive. She could barely hold onto the thought. When she did, it brought such a surge of emotion, such light and happiness, that it threatened to spill into tears.

Such unrestrained joy was alien to Storm's nature. It left her shaken and nervous, and yet . . .there it was: that glint of light. It was as if a door had been opened in a dark room allowing a thin sliver of light to stream in. Storm could only stand a glimpse of such a vision. The thought of throwing the door open wide made her mouth go dry.

Storm clicked her way into the system and typed in her father's name. While she waited, she slid open the bottom drawer of her desk, took out her purse, and set it on her desk. There was a small beep. Looking up she saw that an icon was blinking on her screen. She opened it.

She read every word. It came down to one thing. Joseph Donald Dean had been taken into custody in Brookings, Oregon, and cited for driving while suspended. He had been held for about twelve hours, probably to give him time to sober up was Storm's guess, and was released at 11:00 a.m. the following day.

"Got you," she said, her response to the information like that of a hunter hearing a well-placed trap spring shut. Then she caught the date. She read it again and again. March 15th, the day Howard said he'd followed her father to her home. The day he'd gone inside and spoken to her husband, met her children.

An icy chill ran down Storm's back, a visceral response to learning that the monster under the bed, the face in the dark window, the footsteps following you across a parking lot late at night, were real.

Fear filled her, sank its claws into her chest, and closed her throat. But this wasn't fear for herself. The monster was not after her. It was after her family.

As she sat staring blindly at her computer screen, the sense of panic that filled her began to transform. Her anger was growing, pushing away the fear, the sense of helplessness. She was no child cowering in a corner. She was a grown woman, strong enough to seek justice, to make others pay, to take lives.

Righteousness rang through her. Rage grew and served as an accelerant burning away the last vestiges of fear and leaving nothing but the coiled black hatred that she kept buried deep inside. It was a dark, ugly, and evil thing that only rose to the surface occasionally, to laugh in glee behind clasped hands and downcast eyes as the whip tore flesh, or a scream was muffled by a length of duct tape, or she pressed the button on the oxidizer.

Storm checked her purse. The gun was there, tucked inside its holster. She removed the slender belt around her slacks, threaded it through the holster and put it back on. The gun now rested at the small of her back, a bit to the left so that she could draw it easily with her right hand.

Digging into her purse again, she pulled out one of the two throwaway phones she'd purchased during her lunch break. She'd planned to give one to Howard, a sign of trust and appreciation.

"How did it all get so fucked up?" she asked the empty room.

There would be no trip to find her mother. She had cancelled her request for unpaid leave. She had also called Howard, and he'd agreed to meet her at the Jackson Bottom Wetlands Preserve after she got off work the next day.

There were more people at the park than the previous time. As she waited, one large group was leaving and walked by on their way to the parking lot and, she guessed, the bus that was waiting there.

Several of them had binoculars for spotting birds and other animals. Storm was certain they'd had good sightings. While waiting for Howard at the picnic table, she saw a red-tailed hawk soaring above, a family of ducks in the creek, dipping their beaks into the water as they slowly paddled by, and the usual robins and starlings flitting through the trees.

The park seemed like the very nexus of life, with its numerous animals and plants. There were so many varieties of trees, shrubs, and grasses, so many shades of green, that it made her eyes ache. What a strange place to choose for a killing ground.

A runner pounded by, his face red, sweat dampening the neck of his white shirt. A group of elementary school kids went by with a harried-looking woman. Then a family of three, with a mom and dad who held hands while a red-haired boy ran from flower to pinecone to rock wall touching them all with equal delight. It was as if he were discovering the world for the first time, thought Storm, and maybe he was.

The next person she saw was Howard. He walked briskly down the path, his shoes throwing up puffs of tan dust with each step. He smiled when he saw her, his head back, his expression without guile.

If there hadn't been so many people around, Storm might have taken the gun out and shot him right then and there. Only her impulse wasn't to aim center mass as she'd been trained, but to aim right at his smiling face.

"Hey, got here as fast as I could," said Howard, taking a quick look at his watch. Sorry you had to wait."

Without preamble, Storm said in a soft, conversational tone of voice, "You lied to me. You didn't follow my father to my house. My father wasn't even in town that day. You went to my house to mess with my family. To what? Prove that you could? Maybe to threaten me later?"

Howard's smile vanished, his stride faltered as her words, so at odds with her tone, got through to him. Storm continued to lean against the end of the picnic table, her hands resting on the table's surface, close to her gun that was hidden under her windbreaker.

He took a few more steps, stopping in front of her. "You figured it out, huh?" he said. "Didn't expect that."

"I bet. So what was it? What did you have in mind going there?"

"Nothing bad," Howard said, his shoulders dropping, hanging his head in a submissive posture she didn't believe. "Just curious. Wanted to see how my partner lived."

"Wanted to find some bargaining chips is more like it," said Storm, surprising herself by her poise. A couple on bikes pedaled past. The woman studiously ignored them.

The man raised a hand and gave them a friendly smile and wave. Storm waited until they had gone by. "Well, it turns out I've got some bargaining chips of my own," she said.

"What do you mean?

"Remember the four rules, Howard? No body, no weapons, no trophies, no connections. Remember that?"

"Sure, and between us we broke most of them, didn't we?"

He seemed to be trying to establish some sort of camaraderie, but Storm was having none of it.

"The one I want you to concentrate on is the no-trophies part. You see, I've been collecting trophies right along, right from the first. I've got a nice little collection. Gloves from the Malino killing. Remember how he bit you and you got your blood on the gloves? His blood and your blood all there, all together on the gloves that I've kept in a nice, tidy, plastic sandwich bag.

"Of course, there was also poor Mr. Everett. That whip you invented and built for him was pretty horrific. Even the twine you wove it from was rough, prickly. I bet it tore a few epithelial cells off your hands when you worked with it. Your blood, his blood, a few inches cut off, wound up in a freezer bag and tucked away somewhere nice and safe.

"I didn't get to keep a trophy from dear Helena Smith, but that's all right. Remember that woman you brought in from the street? You're so predictable. How hard was it for me to find a used condom in the cart? DNA is pretty easy to extract from semen, or so I've heard. I wrote the rules for a reason you know. Trophies are very, very bad things."

Howard's face revealed a range of emotion as she spoke, going from anger to surprise, to something like fear.

Maybe, thought Storm, he isn't such a sociopath after all. Of course, last she'd heard, there really weren't any sociopaths, just people with severe personality disorders. One had to laugh at how the mental health profession loved to name things and rename them.

Howard finally seemed to settle on one response—threats. "If you turn me in, I'll drag you down with me. I know too much. Things I couldn't know if you hadn't been involved.

Storm laughed. "You think I care? You really think I won't go to prison to protect my family?"

Howard stared hard into Storm's eyes. She stared back, unflinching and still and strangely calm.

Finally, he nodded. "Okay, you win. What do I have to do to get those trophies back, huh?"

"Oh, you don't get them back, not ever. Those are my insurance. We all need insurance. As long as you stay out of my life and far, far away from my family, those items will stay well hidden. Someday they might even find their way to you, when you're old and gray and harmless. For now you'll just have to trust me."

"Trust you," scoffed Howard. "You're a murdering bitch. How am I supposed to trust you?"

"Not my problem," said Storm.

A young couple, seeing them and sensing that all was not well took a shortcut through the brush to avoid passing near them on the trail. Storm barely noticed. Her focus was locked on Howard.

"I guess I got nothing to say," said Howard. "I think you're wrong. I never wanted anything but for us to keep doing what we started. We were doing something good, something big."

"I know," said Storm, softening for a moment. "But it has to end, Howard. It's not for us to make those decisions. Life is hard, it's unfair, and no matter what we do, there's always going to be someone else who gets away with it. We can't change that."

"You used to think we could,"

"I know, but putting my family in jeopardy or risking them hating me if they ever found out, it's just not worth it."

"That's your final word? We're through."

"Final word," said Storm.

Howard nodded, put his hands up, and rubbed at his neck. Storm almost reached for the gun but realized he was only stretching. He rolled his shoulders as if trying to shrug off tension and dropped his arms to his sides. "I guess there's nothing more to say." He shrugged again, shoved his hands into the pockets of his dark gray hoodie, and without another word, turned and walked away.

Storm stood away from the table and realized her arms were shaking. She watched Howard until he disappeared behind the trees. The confrontation had gone so much better than she expected. Still, it had left her wrung out, completely exhausted, and emotionally drained. She wanted to go home, crawl into bed, and sleep for three days.

CHAPTER
TWENTY-EIGHT

ON HER SATURDAY morning run, with the air just cool enough to be pleasant and a cloudless sky promising an afternoon of grilling on the back deck, Storm felt content. Peace. That was the new theme of Storm's life. Or so she'd decided.

It would only be another two weeks before Tom would be free to go with her to find her long-lost mother. She had hated postponing, but given her recent poor decisions, maybe he was right. Maybe waiting until he could go with her was a good idea. She wasn't sure what the reconciliation would be like, but she hoped it would give her some sort of closure.

Once in a while, she caught her mind wandering down some fantastic daydream, where she and her mother saw each other and then, as if in some weepy, made-for-television movie, ran to each other with hugs and tears.

When those thoughts filled her mind, she immediately shut them down, chided herself for her ridiculously high expectations, and reminded herself of the pain she was setting herself up for.

When Tom asked for her thoughts about seeing her mother again, she told him she was very excited about the idea and wondered if this was how adopted children must have felt on finding their biological parents.

What she had not shared with him was the unfamiliar sense of glee which she could not seem to talk herself out of. It was frightening to fly so high, especially when she knew—not suspected or was afraid of—but knew, with every cell in her body, that the experience was going to toss her to the ground so hard, she might never get up again.

As for her past with Howard and the justice killings, she was doing all she could to get beyond it and to look at that period of time as a strange aberration. All she had to do was make sure she wasn't drawn back into someone's story, some sad victim who made her so angry and vengeful that she'd . . .

But no, she wasn't going to think about it. She had resolved to stop reading the paper and stay away from the local news. Stories she heard at work she would pretend were fiction or, at the very least, sad things she could do nothing about.

It was time to become a normal person and a good

wife, mother, and friend. There was a list of things waiting for her to do. One of the things on the list was to shop for a few new blouses. She'd worn the cuffs on most of hers to a frazzle. Stress made that old habit get worse. Maybe she'd try hypnosis. She'd heard hypnosis could help break bad habits.

Without missing a stride, she dropped from the sidewalk to the street to avoid a low hanging branch and did a sort of sideways hop back on. Traffic that early was almost nonexistent. The air smelled good, full of damp green things, and the scent of flowers.

Her next thought was even more mundane. She had to start thinking about paint colors for the outside of the house. They'd agreed it needed a new coat this year, but did they want to keep the same color of go with something different?

There were library books to be returned. Thinking of things needing to be returned, she needed to get that casserole dish from Grace. She kept meaning to go over; maybe she would stop on the way back from her run.

A pair of Pomeranians sprang against their wire enclosure at the side of a house, yapping their disapproval. She sped up.

There was also the little matter of Nicky's wedding. So much to deal with there. She'd have to think about a wedding shower. Then, there was the wedding gift. She thought she should find something classy and traditional, maybe, but with a twist.

She was still trying to figure it out when she let herself in through the back gate, stopping at the back steps to stretch her calves and tendons before going inside.

When she reached the kitchen, she found everyone up and having breakfast.

"Hi, babe," said Tom. "Kids just wanted cereal this morning."

"Funny how much they like cereal when you're the only one around to serve them breakfast."

"You'd think they don't like my cooking."

"Does anyone?"

"Hey," argued Lindsey. "Dad cooks real good—most times."

"I know, Linds, I was just kidding. Your dad doesn't much like cooking."

"He makes spaghetti, and macaroni and cheese, and cinnamon toast sometimes," Lindsey continued, steadfast in her defense.

Storm marveled at the daughter-and-dad relationship. There were times she could have become jealous, if she allowed herself.

"There, you see, said Tom. "My customers have vindicated me."

"I like cinnamon toast," said Joel, around a mouthful of raisin bran.

"What's vindicated mean?" asked Lindsey.

"It means I'm right. Now, do you want some cereal?" he asked Storm.

"Of course," she said, "Cereal is wonderful. I love cereal." She got a bowl from the cupboard and joined her family.

The weekend passed too quickly. It was unusually warm for so early in the year, and after weeks of gray skies and rain, everyone was eager to be outdoors.

On the Sunday, Storm managed to spend time in the yard, tying rose runners to the fence and scattering fertilizer around the flower beds. Runners and dog walkers moved past the Mackenzies' house all day, most with friendly smiles, some even stopping to chat. Everyone seemed to be happy.

Each time Storm began to analyze how much better it felt not to be spending every spare moment planning a justice killing, researching someone's movements, and basically stalking them, she stopped herself. Overanalyzing every thought and emotion was unhealthy. She needed to live in the moment, enjoy what was going on around her.

She even tried hard not to dwell too much on finding her mother. Perhaps she should have called and talked to her on the phone. When she'd found out her father had been arrested in Brookings, she knew immediately he had either been heading to Crescent City or was on the way back. Logically, this meant he must have known where her mother was staying.

Her first impulse had been to call and warn her mother. But what if her mother had invited him?

She had to think this through very carefully. If her father had been released from jail in Brookings on the 16th, it would have taken him about forty minutes to get to Crescent City. She knew because she'd looked it up. That meant if he meant to kill her, she'd be dead.

If she had invited him and they were together, well, she was in no hurry to know. Both of those outcomes were too painful to consider.

A phone call from her couldn't fix anything, but it could have sent her mother into another guilt-filled panic.

She might have run again and ended up homeless. Her mother was older now, much older, and maybe not even healthy.

Storm realized she was consumed by thoughts of her mother, but there was little she could do to stop it. When she had a moment of tremendous honesty with herself, she knew she didn't want to stop. There was something close to joy in this much hope. It was as addictive as a roll of dice to a gambling addict.

Hope was a bitch.

CHAPTER
TWENTY-NINE

IN HER DREAM, they danced—no—glided across the floor. The fabric of Storm's dress was blue, the kind of blue she imagined a blue rose would be, if there could be such a thing.

It was the dress she'd tried on in a shop that specialized in prom and cruise wear on some crazy whim when she was twenty-three. Well past the age for proms and too poor and young yet for cruises.

They had let her take the dress into the dressing room to try on. It fit as if it had been custom-made for her. The princess neckline showed off her long neck, the hollow of her throat, the creamy perfection of her skin. The color made her eyes sparkle, the luxurious fabric hugged her torso, following each curve, and fell, a vivid-blue waterfall, to her bare feet.

Taking the clips from her hair, she brushed out the dark curls and watched herself in the mirror. Utterly charmed by herself, she had, for the first time in her life, thought she was . . . dare she say it? Beautiful. The word had crossed her thoughts like something forbidden but tantalizing. "Beautiful." she had said, watching her own eyes widen in surprise. She was enchanted by the pink color rising to her cheeks. She was, she realized, just a little bit in love with herself, and in loving herself, she felt love for the entire world.

It was one of the most insanely happy moments of her life and one she still thought of with awe and wonder. Of course, the moment passed. The dress, which she could not afford in any case, had gone back in the window. Life and the reality of her scars, both physical and emotional, remained.

Oh, but that dress. To dance in that dress. So she did, in her dreams now and then. Usually it was Tom who held her, which made sense, since he was her most familiar partner. Sometimes it was a stranger—never a movie star or musician. She often wondered why she didn't dream of celebrities. Her friends certainly did.

The music became strange. A piano and violins joined in a melody that rose and fell in a lovely pattern of sound and emotion. But now it was loud, chaotic, even rude.

The sound, which was not music at all, woke her from the dream. The blue dress faded away. She let it go begrudgingly. It had been such a wonderful dance.

Storm opened her eyes. Tom rolled to his side, turning his back to her as he unconsciously tried to escape the noise. She scrabbled for her cell phone, sitting on the charging station on the table beside her bed. It was the phone's harsh ring which had torn her from the dream. "Hello?" she said.

"Hello, partner," said Howard.

It had been over a week since Storm's ultimatum. The last time she'd given much thought to Howard was when she'd reviewed his file three days earlier and made sure it was in order. He was getting to the end of his probation period, and she wanted to make sure there were no problems and nothing to keep Howard from becoming a bad memory.

"What do you want?" Storm asked. A glance at the clock told her it was one in the morning. Tom was breathing deeply and evenly. She kept her voice down and her tone conversational so as not to wake him.

"What do you think I want?" Howard asked, his tone matching hers.

"Do you know what time it is? Can I speak to you later?"

"You mean when you want?"

"Yes," replied Storm, struggling to keep her temper.

"No."

Storm tightened her grip on the phone. All she wanted was to slip down under the sheets where it was warm, comfortable. But her heart beat like it belonged to a scared bunny. "What do you want?" she finally asked.

"I want you to get it. To actually understand what I am willing to put up with—and what I'm not. I have tried to explain it to you, slowly and clearly. It's as if you refuse to learn. But you know, that's my fault, not yours. It takes a good teacher to make a good student. A good teacher knows that, if you really want to make a lesson stick, you need both a carrot and a stick, a reward and a punishment. You know how I like to punish, huh? But you don't know how I like to reward."

Storm's stomach clenched. Her extremities were suddenly cold. There was something in Howard's voice that was both seductive and darkly sinister.

"Let me tell you your reward. I am going to let you save the little red head from your office. If you want to, that is. Do you want to save the little red head?"

Storm nodded and then realized he couldn't see her. She swallowed and whispered, "Yes, I want to save her."

Imagining Carrie strung from the ceiling of the kill room, poor love-struck Carrie with her freckles and red hair slowly tortured to death for no reason other than working in the same office as Storm, nearly made her sick. Her stomach lurched, the coffee she'd been drinking all day a sea of roiling acid. She got up slowly and carefully. Tom made a low groaning noise but didn't awaken.

Storm closed the bedroom door behind her and took the phone into the living room where she began pacing back and forth.

"What do you want?"

"Oh my, that really is a very good carrot, huh? What I want is for things to go back the way they were. I want us to be equal partners, working together, counting on each other, and doing some good in this fucked-up shit hole of a world." He took a shuddering breath as if he were trying to steady himself, perhaps aware of his escalating anger and afraid of his subsequent loss of control.

"I don't think—" began Storm.

"No one asked you what you think. I was saying that was a good carrot, but there's still the stick to consider. You've been a very bad girl, Stormy. You've been rude and sarcastic and just, well, unkind. That's not the kind of behavior one wants in a partner. But, since you've been a good partner up until this little rebellion of yours, I'm willing to let it go—once you've had your punishment."

"What kind of punishment?" Storm asked.

"I'm going to give the bad girl a little whipping. Nothing extreme," he was quick to explain. "Not the special whip, don't worry. I was thinking maybe just a nice, thick, leather belt, and let's see, how about a count of a hundred? You're a big girl, after all. I bet you can take it, huh? I'll even let you keep count. It'll be like love taps from Daddy.

"After that, your friend goes free, you say you're sorry you were so bad, and we go back to the way we were. Except you'll be a little more respectful. What do you think?"

"I think I don't know if you'll really let her go. How do I know for sure?"

"You don't. But so far she hasn't seen me. No reason for me to get rid of her. Of course, if you don't show up soon, I'll probably start getting impatient, might have to take that pillowcase off. Once that comes off, once she sees me, well I can't be held responsible for my impulses."

There were so many things Storm wanted to say, to shout. She took a calming breath and said softly, "I'll take the punishment, but you have to promise me you'll let her go. If you do that, I'll agree to become your partner again, and we can get back to doing justice killings. But only justice killings, and the targets have to deserve what they get."

She hoped she sounded convincing but was sure her lies sounded as improvised and desperate as they were.

Tom knew Storm had restless nights. He wouldn't question the note she planned to leave telling him she was going out for a run. She crept back to the room and quickly gathered clothes, shoes, and her gun.

CHAPTER

THIRTY

STORM PULLED INTO the parking lot of Traynor Chemical for what she was sure was the last time.

She would take her punishment, as Howard saw fit, and if she survived, she would do her best to kill him as soon as she could find a way. In any case, despite Howard's delusions, the partnership was finished.

It was early morning. The street lamps hummed their constant and erratic tune. Shadows slept in every corner. There was a scent of rain and a fog of marine clouds that would probably burn off as soon as the sun rose.

She ran the mag key across the lock. The light changed from red to green. There was a low click, and she pushed the door open. The metal was cold and wet with condensation.

As she moved down the long hallway toward the kill room, scenes of horror flashed through her mind. What sadistic scene had Howard constructed for her? She didn't want to know, but couldn't stop wondering. Had Howard badly hurt Carrie? God only knew what he might have already done to her.

Breaking into a trot, Storm soon reached the entrance to the shower. She skidded into the room and saw the naked bleeding woman tied to the overhead pipes.

"Oh, hell, no. You son of a bitch."

There was a choke collar around her neck and a knotted rope led from it to the overhead pipes. Her wrists were tied to the rope, allowing her to grasp it and hold herself up to keep from strangling. Storm understood immediately. Howard had perfected his technique.

Storm could barely believe what she saw. Nicky's pink hair was dark with sweat and matted to her head. Black tracks of mascara stained her cheeks. Her eyes were focused on something Storm couldn't see. Her face hadn't been touched. Every other inch of her skin was mottled with blood, both dried and fresh. Blood spatter decorated the concrete around her feet and the nearest walls.

As she drew closer, Storm saw there were hundreds, if not thousands, of small cuts, barely more than scratches, crisscrossing Nicky's skin. What had he done to her? "Nicky!" The scream tore Storm's throat. Slipping in a thin puddle of blood, she almost fell against Nicky, but caught herself. Carefully, she reached up, and her fingers tugged awkwardly at the tight knots.

Paying no heed to the blood soaking into her clothing as she pressed against Nicky's torn body, she struggled to find the end of the rope which, when tugged, would undo the slip knot.

The room stank of cleaner. An empty bottle at her feet nearly tripped her. She fumbled for the correct rope and tugged with trembling hands. The knot was too tight. She got a better grip and took a step back. Howard's forearm slammed into her chest, and she fell backward, feet flying out from under her. She came down hard, the breath knocked out of her.

Howard stood above her and next to Nicky. Idly, he ran his hand down Nicky's side.

She flinched and lost her blind stare. Turning her head she saw Storm. "What? Why are—"

Howard slapped her face, the sudden sound echoing through the space. "You don't talk," Howard told her.

Nicky bit her lower lip. She stared down at Storm but said nothing more.

"You said saving your friend would be a good incentive. Have you changed your mind?" Howard asked.

Storm shook her head, still unable to speak.

Howard reached down, offering Storm his hand. "Sorry about that," he said. "You sort of surprised me. Come on." He wiggled his fingers, an impatient gesture.

She took his hand and let him help her up. She stood in front of him and kept her eyes on his, unwilling to look at Nicky.

"What's wrong? Wasn't this our deal? You look so unhappy, Stormy."

"You won't let her go. She's seen your face."

"Doesn't matter. She'll never turn me in now. Will you sweetheart?" He turned to Nicky. "You may nod or shake your head."

Nicky shook her head, over and over, frantically.

"See. She'll be good. Not so sure about you, Stormy."

His use of Tom's pet name was a mistake. Fury, her old friend, ripped through her veins, tingled through every nerve. A frightened, helpless woman stood there, aware her best friend was tied up, had been tortured, and was probably dying.

A second later, an angry woman, a killer in her own right, looked at him appraisingly and allowed the smallest smile to lift the corner of her lips. "Well played. I have to appreciate the gamesmanship."

"Like chess, huh?" said Howard, nearly purring under her praise. "I didn't know if you'd think it was cheating. Pink. Red. It's sort of, I don't know," he shrugged, a sheepish look on his face.

Storm chanced a quick glance at Nicky, knowing it could destroy her fragile equilibrium. In response to Howard's commands, she had gone silent and remained so. Her lower lip trembled, and fresh tears washed her cheeks. She appeared exhausted, scared, and worst of all, obedient.

"What did you do to her?" Storm asked, keeping her tone conversational as if she were simply asking about the weather. "Something special?"

"Special? I didn't use the whip on her the usual way, if that's what you mean. That makes it go too fast. This time I sort of just dragged it over her, rolled it around some, spanked her a little here and there. The washers made lots of little cuts . . . sort of beautiful, really. I left her face and her hair alone so you would recognize her. Worked good, huh? You were surprised."

"I was."

"You sometimes act like I'm stupid, too dumb to plan anything like this without you."

"Plan something like this?" she asked, her tone still calm but her words cutting. "Like kidnapping an officer of the court? Someone engaged to one of the most powerful and connected men in the area? Yeah, that was smart, all right."

"Fuck you," said Howard. His chin went down, his shoulders back. Storm stepped forward so that her body was pressed lightly against his. She slid her arms around him, and she held him in a tender embrace as she kissed his tight-lipped mouth.

For a second, she could sense his astonishment and felt him stiffen as if he was about to pull away. The next instant, his fists unclenched, his arms wrapped around her, and he pulled her close. As his lips went soft against hers, he moaned. She was sure he was unaware of the sound he made.

"You didn't even know," she chided, her shrill voice dropping to a lower register, husky, and bantering. "See how you need me? Tell me. Tell me you need me."

"Storm," he said. His arms tightened around her. He kissed her again.

Though she didn't believe in God, she prayed he wouldn't slide his hands farther down her back and find her holstered gun.

As she allowed him to kiss her deeply, to slide his tongue between her lips, Storm was filled with repugnance.

He moved his hips against her, grinding slowly. She broke away, but continued to place light, teasing kisses on the corner of his mouth, the edge of his jaw, his neck. He moaned again. She gave him a smile she hoped looked playful and twisted away.

If she could have smashed the heel of her boot into the top of his foot, then spun and hit him in the face or throat with her elbow, she might have been to disable him, if only for a moment. It was a move she'd practiced in defense courses. She needed to break his hold just long enough to get free of his reach and pull her gun.

She began to turn in his arms, forcing herself not to tense up and telegraph her intentions. He pulled her against him with crushing force, then spun her around and slammed her, face first, into the wall.

Her nose broke with a crack that reverberated through her entire body. Her forehead also struck the wall, and pain and tears instantly blurred and darkened her vision. Her legs felt rubbery, and only Howard's muscular arms kept her upright.

When she was able to stand on her own, he loosened his grip, pulled her gun out of its holster and tucked it into the waistband of his jeans.

"Oh Stormy, so predictable. You vibrate like a live wire when you're angry. Did you know that?" She tried to jerk loose but only managed to move them both a step away from the wall. Warm blood from her broken nose gushed over her lips. Her head pounded and she wanted, needed, to break free.

Howard let her turn away and then drew her back against him, his breath hot against the back of her neck.

Keeping his left arm around her waist, his right hand slid clumsily up, found and cupped her breast, and squeezed.

Black and orange points of flame erupted before Storm's eyes. She was there again, trapped in her father's arms, his rough hands grabbing, his strong fingers pulling, twisting and hurting.

With the memory came a bleak and horrifying revelation. A secret she had hidden even from herself.

At the nexus of that memory, immersed in the shock and the pain, hid a dark and lurid ugliness that tore her from time and place and transported her to her childhood home.

She remembered that for a second—no—a mere millisecond of time, but time enough, she had responded to her father's drunken caress.

Her body, pressed against that warm flesh, her nostrils filled with that familiar scent, her body pinned, and breasts bruised and aching, had responded with a throb of intense heat, a hunger so forbidden it couldn't be survived.

The moment had created a schism, a division between the Willow that had been and the Storm that would be.

Was she wife and mother who tried to serve justice and help others to pay for their crimes, or a vicious, unrepentant murderer? She was both. She was Willow and Storm, dark and light.

This, Storm realized, returning to the here and now, was the nexus. This was the truth and the origin of who she was. But the truth did not set her free. It caged her in bars of self-loathing.

CHAPTER
THIRTY-ONE

IT WAS NICKY who brought Storm back to the present. Though she'd gone quiet at Howard's command, the sight of her friend struggling in his grasp reanimated her. Nicky screamed, the sound rising to a shrill note.

Storm did the only thing she could think of. She went completely limp. It caught Howard unaware, and he let her dead weight fall from his arms. She crumpled to the floor, cracking her knees on the hard ground, but she ignored the pain and rolled as fast and as far as she could. As soon as she was free of his reach, she jumped to her feet. He lunged at her, his fingers catching the back of her blouse, but he didn't have enough fabric, and she pulled free easily. Then she did something she was very good at. She ran.

Sprinting across the shower room, she plunged through the doorway, slid around the corner, and ran for the exit.

Behind her, she heard the stomach-dropping snick of a round being fed into a chamber. She was nearly to the door. She tried to remember that the odds of him hitting a moving target were small.

"Handguns are terrible weapons to take someone down," one of her instructors, a SWAT team captain, had told her. "People can be shot with a small caliber round and keep coming at you. If you really want to stop someone, use a rifle."

"I can't fit a rifle in my purse."

"Get a bigger purse," he'd joked.

That such an insanely out-of-place thought should be in her mind at such a time added a bizarre tone to her flight. The doors were close.

"I'll put the first one in her knee!" Howard shouted, pulling her own gun from his waistband.

Storm skidded to a stop. She grasped the door handle as she spun around to face him. She couldn't leave Nicky.

He wound the rope around Storm's throat twice, tied a knot, and tossed one end over one of the pipes that formed a maze in the ceiling. Howard's lips were set in a grim line and didn't speak as he worked. Storm thought she had never seen him so angry.

He pulled on the rope until it was tight around her neck, and then he pulled more so that she had to stand on tiptoe. Even then, the rope cut off her breath. She grasped the rope and managed to pull herself up and steal a gasp of air. Too quickly, her arms grew tired, and the rope slid through her hands. She was certain she was going to die. Her body fought, legs kicking, hands scrambling for a better grip on the rope, no thoughts, only instinct.

"Not yet," Howard said. "We've got way more fun ahead of us."

He let out some of the rope, enough so she could stand flat—breathe. She coughed and took panting breaths through her mouth. Her throat was sore, and the taste of the blood running down the back of her throat from her broken nose made her nauseated.

He grabbed her wrists roughly and pulled them behind her back, turning her in the process so that she faced Nicky. He tied her wrists together with his homemade whip.

"I. Can't. Believe. This," said Howard, emphasizing each word as he tied another knot in the whip. The sharpened edges of the washers sliced her skin, but she didn't make a sound. He moved around to face her.

"I thought we were partners. I thought, maybe even friends."

Storm remained quiet.

"You really piss me off. I'm fucking hurt. You know what it's like to be hurt?"

Storm looked down, afraid her stare might increase his rage.

"Your friend knows. Want to see what hurts her the most, what she really hates?"

Storm shook her head vehemently. "No," she said. No, don't."

"This," he said, ignoring her. He walked the few steps

to Nicky, bent and picked up the bottle of cleaner that Storm had stumbled over earlier. He shook the bottle, which was half full. Nicky whimpered, her eyes rolling wildly.

"No!" screamed Storm. "Not her. Me, Howard. You're mad at me."

Again, he ignored her. He uncapped the bottle and shook the contents over Nicky's ravaged skin. She screamed, a horrible scream that went on and on.

Nicky took deep ragged breaths. Her body shook. Tears ran down her face. "Storm," she heard Nicky whisper hoarsely.

Storm blinked several times to clear her sight. She watched as Howard dumped the rest of the cleaning fluid over his hands and reached between Nicky's legs, brutally inserting his fingers and laughing as she screamed.

"Clean up our messes. That's what we do. Right, Storm? Look at you," he said with a note of surprise. "You're practically vibrating."

It was true. Storm's anger had reached such a pitch that her body could not contain it. It felt as if every cell in her body was trembling.

Howard wiped his fingers on Nicky's back, then left the room.

"I'm sorry, Nicky. I'm so sorry." Storm didn't think Nicky heard her. She stood swaying, her eyes closed, breathing heavily between clenched teeth. Storm was afraid she would faint and hang herself. "Hang on, Nicky. Don't stop fighting."

Howard returned with a cart.

"Let her go," Storm pleaded. "Please let her go. I'll do

anything, Howard. Please, I promise—anything. I'll go away with you. Anywhere you want. Do anything you want."

Howard held the short leather-covered club he sometimes carried when he was in uniform. He put the thicker end of it under Storm's chin and pushed her head up. "Sex, you mean? A blow job maybe? I wouldn't trust you not to bite my dick off," he told her. "Your promises are worthless."

He pulled his arm back. Storm couldn't help herself. She flinched, anticipating the blow. But instead of hitting her, he spun on his heel and slammed the club into Nicky's face.

Storm screamed. She screamed and screamed as Howard, all pretense of control gone, methodically beat Nicky to death.

When it was finally over, the sounds only echoes that would live in her mind forever, Storm let go. The rope tightened around her neck, cutting off her air. Her body struggled, but only feebly, and darkness, a kind and welcome friend, crept from the edges of her vision.

Panting as if he'd run a marathon, Howard dropped the blood- and bone-encrusted club and hurried to tug the slip knot loose and lower Storm to the floor.

He was prepared to provide CPR, but as soon as the rope was drawn from her neck, Storm coughed and took a deep breath.

When Storm reached full consciousness, she found that Howard had tied her ankles together, leaving about a foot of rope between them.

"Uppy, uppy," he said, leaning down to grab her arm and help her stand. "Look at that—you went and pissed yourself."

Storm realized her slacks were soaked with warm liquid. She couldn't have cared less. There were more important things to deal with—like killing Howard.

Howard had different ideas.

"Time to clean up our mess."

Storm staggered to her feet and turned to look at Nicky's body still hanging from the pipe. She heard an anguished howling, realizing the sound had come from her. She wanted tears, tears to wash away her sins, but she couldn't cry. Instead, she threw up, over and over until her stomach was empty and it felt as if she were attempting to rid herself of her soul.

Afterward, he made her clean it up. Not just the vomit but the brutalized remains of Nicky's body. As she helped lower the body into the recycling cart and wheeled it, step by small step to the back of the building, Storm prayed for her friend's salvation and her eternal life in heaven.

They placed Nicky in the oxidizer, and Howard, taking Storm's fingers in a crushing hold, forced her finger tips to press the on button.

They returned to the kill room to finish the cleanup. Howard made Storm put on a pair of protective coveralls. She wouldn't have bothered otherwise. She no longer cared about blood on her clothing, and she had lost the belief that she could control anything. Her face throbbed, especially when she had to bend forward. A lump had formed on her forehead, and it too ached, but the emotional pain made the physical pain seem unimportant, even distant.

She had learned many things about the world that night. One of them was that there were worse things than an angry drunk setting a fire, that there was a different kind of cruelty: cold, sober, organized, and as intentional as a sharpened blade.

CHAPTER

THIRTY-TWO

STORM THOUGHT she was numb to anything more that Howard could have done. There was only one thing she wanted—to kill him. That was the only goal, to get her hands on her gun. She had to concentrate on that.

"Where did you put the things you say you have on me—the gloves, the whip? Where are you keeping them, huh?" Howard asked, his voice rising to be heard over the sound of the water as she rinsed the walls and floors.

"I don't have them," Storm confessed. I never had them. It was a bluff. I just wanted you to leave me alone."

"If it's true—and I'm not sure it is—your bluff sure as hell backfired."

Storm nodded, shut off the water, and hung the shower nozzle in its holder. Her hands were cold, fingertips wrinkled from being in water so long. Damp, untidy strands of hair hung in her face.

"You look like hell," said Howard. "Let's get you stripped out of those coveralls. Toss them in the garbage. Fuck the oxidizer."

Storm looked up at him in a way she hoped seemed fearful, even timid. If he thought she'd lost the will to fight, he would let down his guard. She might still have been able to surprise him.

"Don't worry," he said. "I'm not going to do anything to you, not now. We've got all night for that."

Storm obediently removed the overalls. They were sopping wet to her knees, and she had to struggle to peel them off, but eventually she managed. Howard grabbed them from her hands and stuffed them into a nearby garbage can, never once taking his eyes off of her.

She was afraid he would tie her up again, but he'd burned the whip in the oxidizer. Besides, he had the arrogant attitude of someone who knew he was stronger.

"We're going to leave now," Howard said.

She was surprised. The entire time she'd been erasing any trace of Nicky's murder she'd been awaiting her own death. She'd never expected to leave the kill room or the building alive.

Understanding her puzzled look, Howard reached out and grasped her wrist, grinding the bones together and making her wince at this new pain. "No, it's not over yet. I was mad when you wanted to break up our partnership. I was pissed when you started bossing me around, but when you threatened me . . . well, honey, that was the last straw. I went past get mad to get even. That's a place you probably didn't want me to go, huh?"

Part of her urged compliance. Another part of her however was silently shrieking, and she couldn't completely fight the urge to run. She tried to pull free of his grip.

Howard laughed at her feeble, half-hearted attempt and tugged her along with little effort. "We'll take your car," he said. Your husband won't think twice when he sees it pull in."

"W . . . what?" asked Storm.

"You heard right. We're going to your house. I told you, you shouldn't have threatened me. Besides, you might be lying. You might really have that glove and that piece of the whip, enough evidence to put me away. Can't take the chance, so guess what we're gonna do? We're going to take a ride to your house. I'm going to tie your husband and your kids up. Guess what happens then. Come on, you want to guess, don't you?"

Storm's jaw clenched so hard on the words that she dared not say it made her face ache. A fresh trickle of blood slid over her chin.

"Okay, you don't have to guess. I'll tell you. I'm going to set your house on fire. Won't that be fun?"

Storm slammed her shoulder into Howard's side, trying to bowl him over, knock him off balance. He moved aside easily, shifted his hold so that she was in a wrist lock, her right arm pinned behind her. Slowly, he exerted more pressure, bringing her to her toes.

She whimpered as the pressure increased. Just when

she was sure her wrist would snap, he loosened his hold, though he kept her arm bent behind her back. Feeling defenseless and frustrated to the point of tears, Storm stood mutely as he checked her pockets and found her car keys.

"Let's go. You ready for a ride, huh?" he asked, pushing her ahead of him. After they went through the door, he stopped to make sure it locked behind them. No one would find anything unusual in the morning.

They walked to Storm's car, Storm in front, Howard half a step behind, his hand wrapped around her throbbing wrist.

The night was dark, warm, and breathless. The sound of cars, evidence there was something more than this horror, were few and far between. Up above, a large plane growled its way across the sky, its blinking lights showing its line of descent toward the Hillsboro airport.

Bringing her to a stop against the cool metal trunk of her car, Howard took a moment to lean into Storm, his hips rolling against her. "Soon," he promised. "Here, open the trunk." He handed her the keys then squeezed her wrist, to remind her he was in charge.

She took the keys inexpertly in her left hand and nearly dropped them. Her fingers were cold, stiff, and still trembling. There was enough light from the streetlamps to allow her to see, but the key skittered across the lock, nonetheless. Finally, she got the trunk to pop open.

Howard reached past her, grabbed the edge of the trunk lid, and pushed it all the way up. She knew he was going to make her climb inside. The trunk was spacious and empty but for the red canvas bag she kept there. It was partially unzipped.

Without thinking, Storm slid her left hand into the bag. She felt a familiar shape, but slid her fingers forward to be sure. Yes.

Jerking the screwdriver from the bag handle forward, she drove it back past her left hip and into Howard's thigh.

He bellowed and let her go. She spun right and ran.

Dashing through the parking lot, shards of pain and fresh tears half blinding her, she reached the row of evergreens along the edge of the parking lot. She broke through, branches scratching at her arms, and reached the sidewalk.

More certain of the footing, she ran faster, expecting Howard to be close behind. She heard her car start up and the heavy thump of a car door. She knew she was in trouble. Howard would run her down without hesitation. She needed to flag down a car, but there were so few cars at that time of night. Far in the distance, she saw a set of red taillights. Surely there would be more in time, if she only had time.

Moving away from the four-lane road and the possibilities it offered, she turned into the wide-open field of roughly shorn grass and wildflowers. What had once been a hay field before the onslaught of business that created the Silicon Forest was now a haven. Storm raced across the uneven terrain, hoping to reach a nearby orchard. The rows and rows of trees would protect her.

She reached the trees. Underfoot, years of unharvested hazelnuts crunched with each step. She was in an hazelnut orchard, no doubt soon to be cut down to make way for more industrial buildings.

Storm paused, a stitch in her side burning, her eyes wide as she searched for Howard. The car rolled to the exit of the parking lot. Storm expected it to come barreling across the street. Taking a deep breath, she prepared to run.

The car's left blinker came on, and it turned slowly, even sedately, and drove away. Soon, it was nothing but a blur of red taillights.

"No. No. NO!" The scream was sub-vocal, heard only in Storm's mind. Howard was driving to her house.

CHAPTER

THIRTY-THREE

STORM COULD RUN the distance. Her children and her husband were only six miles away. But she couldn't run fast enough to save them.

A pair of cars were coming toward her on Evergreen, one in each lane, only a car's length apart. Storm ran into the street in front of them. The one in the lead swerved and a horn blared, but it continued on its way.

The second car's brakes locked. It slid to a stop, leaving a smell of burned rubber. A pale face in the driver's side window stared at Storm, took in the blood on her face and her wild eyes.

Storm ran to the driver's window and stood there,

afraid to bang on the window and frighten the driver away. "Can you help me," she pleaded, not having to pretend she was frantic. "There's been an accident."

Though there was no wrecked car in evidence, the young woman rolled down her window. "Do you need a doctor? Should I call 911?"

Knowing she had no time to waste, Storm shoved her forearm against the girl's throat, reached in and unbuckled her seat belt, tore open the door, and dragged her from the car.

The girl tripped and fell, landing on her hands and knees in the street.

"Get up. Get up you idiot," Storm shouted at her. "Get the hell off the road before you get hit."

The girl staggered to her feet. "You can't. You—"

"Go," shouted Storm. Another pair of cars was coming from the opposite direction. Staring at Storm as if she was something unpleasant, a large spider, or venomous snake, the girl backed away and then turned and sprinted for the side of the road.

Storm jumped into the driver's seat, threw the car into gear, and smashed her foot against the accelerator. The Volvo station wagon was old and heavy, but it responded, and soon she was flying down Evergreen Road.

Traynor Chemical was situated on a long straight section, but the road soon became a long 's' curve, lined with homes.

Coming up on NE Jackson School Road sooner than she expected, Storm slammed on the brakes and slid into the turn. The rear of the car fishtailed, and the tires squealed. She straightened it out and accelerated up Jackson School.

The next turn was Roghan. She was forced to slow down to take the corner and realized the sound of the racing engine was going to foolishly telegraph her arrival to Howard. Turning into the parking lot of the New Creation Church, she brought the car to a rocking stop, jumped out, and ran toward her house.

Well before the house was in sight, she slowed and considered the best and quietest way to approach. The sun was rising, an orange glow against the dark roofs in the East.

Deciding the only way to get to her house without being seen was to come up on it from the opposite side, Storm ran around the block.

Two thirds of the way around, a wave of dizziness hit her, and she wove drunkenly sideways, almost running into a mailbox. She stopped, put her hand on it for balance, and took a few deep breaths.

She should have called the police. Surprisingly, her cell phone was still in her pocket. But would a police presence have stopped Howard or just hurried him along?

The only thing on Storm's side was her knowledge of the way Howard liked to kill. How he felt cheated when he didn't get a chance to 'play' with his victims. Control and intimidation through inflicting pain was Howard's need, and that was what would keep her family alive—for a while.

Storm's house and garage faced a paved street with a row of street lights, but behind the house was a dark alley. Storm crept down the alley, trying to stay on the dirt and avoid the patches of crunchy gravel.

She found the neighbor's back gate was unlatched. The

six-foot cedar fence hid her movements as she followed it to the front gate, which she found was also unlatched.

Once she slipped through the gate, she was able to reach the side of her garage, out of sight of the house. Peering around the edge of the garage, she could see her car in the driveway behind Tom's.

A long time ago, getting ready to go shopping, she'd strapped Lindsey into the car seat, then run inside to grab a grocery list she left on the table.

Lindsey had unbuckled herself from the seat and locked the car doors. Frantic, Storm had run to Grace's house and borrowed a phone to call Tom. He dropped everything and raced home with the spare key.

By the time he arrived, Lindsey had unlocked the door, but Storm had vowed she would never go through something like that again. She went out that very day and purchased a magnetic key holder.

Storm wondered if it was still there. Since attaching it to the frame of her car, she'd never once had reason to use it.

Roses grew inside the white picket fence that lined the driveway. Their foliage was thick enough to form a fairly dense hedge. Dropping to her knees, Storm crept between the cars and the fence. She passed Tom's car and made it to hers. When she was just past the rear tire, she rolled onto her back, reached up above the wheel, and felt around in the dark and dusty area.

Almost immediately, her fingers found the little metal box. She used her thumb to press the sliding door open. It slipped aside stiffly, and two keys, an ignition and a trunk key, fell to the concrete driveway with a jangling clatter.

Holding her breath, Storm dared not move. After several long minutes, she rolled onto her stomach and felt around for the keys. She found one, but even though she thought she'd touched and patted every inch of ground, she couldn't find the other. All she could do was hope she'd found the right one.

Again on hands and knees, she crawled to the back of the car, reached up, and felt for the trunk lock. Once she located it, she slid the key inside, then placed her other hand on the trunk so the lid wouldn't spring up. She turned the key and the lock opened. The trunk rose an inch, and when she moved her hand, it stayed there.

With an anxious glance toward the house, Storm rose to a crouch and lifted the trunk a few more inches, just enough to reach inside and feel around for the red bag.

Slipping her hand inside, her fingers found and curled around the canister of mace. It slipped from nerveless fingers and rolled away. "Damn," she hissed under her breath.

Reaching in farther, she found what she'd been looking for: the stun gun. It hadn't been very effective against Helena Smith. Still, it was a weapon and better than nothing. She removed it and slowly lowered the lid of the trunk as far as it would go without actually latching. She couldn't risk the noise and could only hope it would stay in place and not pop up, alerting Howard.

She crawled back toward the garage and the gate, this time along the fence. The sun was beginning to rise, casting a dim glow in the east. It didn't care its timing wasn't good for her. Still, it was dark enough for the lights to be on in both the living room and kitchen. Where was he? More importantly, where was her family?

Crawling between the cars and the fence, she stayed in shadow as much as possible. Finding a spot where she could look through the pickets and an empty area in the tangle of roses, she stared at the windows. She hoped to see a shadow pass. There was nothing. No. There was something.

The curtains in the kitchen window moved a little, stirred as if a breeze had swept in, but the window was closed. Someone must have walked past and brushed them.

They were in the kitchen, or at least someone was in there, moving around. A plan began to form. It was insane, reckless, but it would give her family a better chance than having the police come in, guns blazing. Or so she hoped.

As fast and quietly as she could, she crawled to the far side of the cars and back to the side of the garage.

A wave of dizziness struck as she got to her feet. She leaned back against the garage. Whether it was the blow to her forehead, the loss of blood that continued to drip from her nose, or just fear, she didn't know. But it didn't matter. She had to keep going.

Storm pulled the phone from her pocket and glanced at the time. It was 5:43 a.m., a ridiculous hour to call someone.

She called her neighbor, Grace. The phone rang four times and went to voice mail. She hung up and dialed again. This time, on the end of the third ring, Grace answered. "Yes?" she said, tentatively, her voice soft. Storm could imagine her keeping her voice down so as not to disturb her husband.

"Hi, Grace," said Storm. "Hate to bodder . . . bother you.

It's just, you know that casserole pan you took home with you on Thanksgiving? Well, I really need it this morning."

"Storm, is that you? You sound funny."

"Head code. Losing my voice. That pan, Grace. I need it," she repeated.

"I bring it in little bit." As Storm had noticed on previous occasions, Grace sometimes lost words and gained a slight Germanic accent when stressed. Otherwise, she spoke proper American English.

"No, I need it now," Storm argued. "Right this very minute. And don't use the back door. I just waxed the floor. Hurry it up, please."

"Hurry? I hurry. You see. I . . . I be there very soon."

How long would it take Grace to toss on a robe, find the pan, tell Alex their neighbor was an inconsiderate pain in the ass, and storm over? Not long, if she knew Grace.

Storm made sure the phone was off and then slid it back into her pocket. She moved to the edge of the garage and stared at the kitchen window. The curtain was still. Staying low, she reached the gate to the picket fence, swung it open just enough, and slid inside. It was essential she hurry, be hidden before Grace came down the sidewalk.

Beside the back steps was a trio of hydrangea bushes. Between them and the wall was a natural hiding space. The hydrangeas grew in a bed landscaped with river rock. Grace took one of them, twisted it, and revealed a hidden key to the house.

She grasped the key carefully, she slid between the porch and the shrubbery. The ground was wet. Storm knelt in the mud, waiting. She didn't have to wait long, only about ten minutes, but it seemed like eternity.

She heard the knock clearly: three solid thumps, a pause and three more. Storm slid from behind the bushes, grabbed the porch rail, and used it to help her turn and race up the stairs on tiptoe.

Three steps across the landing and her hand wrapped around the doorknob. It turned easily. No key needed. She pushed the door open a tiny crack and peered through.

The door opened onto the kitchen or, more precisely, to a walkway that skirted the kitchen, and became a hallway to the living room ahead.

Just inside and to the right was a trio of curtained windows, the ones Storm had seen move. To the left was a long breakfast counter, where the family ate their meals, unless there was company.

Along the counter was a row of tall wooden chairs. Her family sat in them now, all in a row. Closest to her was Tom, then Lindsey, and then Joel.

They were facing away from the counter, and for a moment, Storm was afraid they might see her. Then she realized that duct tape covered their eyes. Their hands were tied behind them. Storm could hear Joel, who was whimpering, and Tom, whispering words of encouragement.

Where was Howard? If she were lucky and her plan was working, he would be in the living room, responding to the unexpected knock at the door.

Slipping out of her shoes, she stepped into the kitchen, took a long, shallow breath, and tiptoed silently toward the front of the house.

Grace knocked at the door a third time. Storm moved

more quickly.

Howard stood by the front room, his hand on the doorknob. Was he going to open it or ignore the pounding on the door? It didn't matter. All she needed was for him to be distracted for long enough. She only had one chance.

When she was halfway across the room, there was a sudden silence. She froze, her heart pounding, and her breathing stopped. She tried not to look directly at Howard, afraid he might feel the weight of her gaze.

As soon as a fresh round of knocking began, she ran across the room as if her life depended on it. She held the stun gun high and aimed for the back of Howard's neck.

Just as she reached him, he turned and brought up his hand. She saw the gun, the barrel as large and dark as the pit to hell she carried inside her soul.

Ignoring his gun, she pressed the stun gun against Howard's throat and pulled the trigger. The effect was immediate. His head went back and his knees gave way. As he went down, Storm hit him again, this time holding the gun against his temple.

Howard's eyes rolled blindly, and his finger tightened. The gun went off, and there was a crashing noise of breaking glass.

Storm fell with Howard to the floor. She sat astride him and reached for his wrist, fighting to take the gun from him. Despite his lack of motor controls, his grip was tight.

She wrapped both hands around his wrist and slammed his arm to the ground and then drove her knee into his forearm and ground down. His hand opened and she pried the gun away.

"What's going on? What's happening?" Tom shouted.

"Daddy, Daddy!" Joel shrieked.

Storm stumbled to her feet. Howard was kicking and flailing convulsively. He was completely helpless. She took two steps back, aimed, and fired into his face. Three tightly spaced shots she couldn't miss, just as the front door swung open.

"Storm," said Grace sharply.

Storm was bringing the gun up, but hearing her name brought her attention to the fact that this wasn't another target. She lowered the weapon.

Having grown impatient, Grace had used her own key to the house, the one she used to water the house plants and take in the mail for her good neighbors.

The gun shook in Storm's hand as if it was filled with blood lust and eager to find another victim.

"Help me. They're in the kitchen," Storm said, looking over her shoulder."

"God help us," declared Grace, tearing her eyes from the body at her feet, to the children, and their father huddled in the kitchen.

Clutching the casserole dish, she started toward the kitchen. Halfway there and not slowing her pace, she turned to Storm to say something, to ask something, but Storm wasn't there. She was kneeling beside the dead man, sliding something into his pocket. They locked eyes.

"A bad man," Grace said.

Storm nodded.

Tom, still tied, his eyes covered, was herding the children awkwardly but steadily toward the back door, shielding them with his body.

"Tom," said Grace gently. "It's over."

Storm, her heart breaking at this proof of his courage, called out to him, too. "It's okay, Tom. The kids are safe. We're all safe."

CHAPTER THIRTY-FOUR

"YOU SAID THE PHONE RANG?" the detective asked.

They'd promised the interview would be quick, questions kept to a minimum. The kids were next door with Grace and Alex. They'd decided the best place to talk was Joel's room, a room that hadn't been entered by Howard and one farthest from the scene.

A detective sat in the rocking chair in the corner, and a uniformed officer stood just inside the door. Storm and Tom sat side by side on the bed. His thigh was pressed against hers, and his arm was wrapped around her waist. She knew he was trying to lend her his strength and support. She was grateful, but she wasn't afraid. Maybe the fear had been burned away by her anger, or maybe it would come back later, in the night.

"The phone?" The detective repeated.

Storm turned her attention to him. "Yes, it was my friend, my friend, Nicky. She told me she needed help. Her car died and she wanted a ride home. She sounded funny, out of breath, scared. I didn't know what to make of it."

"She didn't try to call a cab? You didn't think to suggest she do that?"

"Of course not. It was the middle of the night. A woman, alone in a dark parking lot, she isn't going to call a strange man, cab driver or not." He nodded as if he understood, though Storm doubted he did.

"So she called you. What did you tell her?"

"That I'd be there, of course. I asked where she was. She said the parking lot behind REI."

"Weren't they closed?"

"I suppose. I didn't ask. I just went."

"So you spotted her car."

"Like I told you before, I saw a car parked in the back lot. I thought it was hers—it was silver, a sedan. But the street lights are yellow, and they change the way things look. Plus, half the lights were out, I think some sort of energy-saving thing, so it was dark.

"I didn't see anyone, so I got out to check if it really was her car. Maybe she was in the front lot and I'd gotten it mixed up.

"She has a thing that hangs from the rearview, this sort of dried hand she picked up in New Orleans on vacation. Not a lot of those around." Storm tried to smile, but knew it looked more like a grimace.

"That's when he confronted you?"

"That's when he jumped me, yes. He came out of nowhere. Must have been in the darker shadows near the building. He slammed me into the side of my car so hard it knocked the air out of me. I sort of slid toward the ground, but he grabbed me by the front of my shirt and pulled me up and punched me. I tried to pull away from him, but he was too strong."

Storm was so enmeshed in the story, she could almost feel the ground under her hands and knees, smell the hot asphalt and the rubber of the tires.

"His hand slipped and I fell. I tried to crawl away but he dragged me to my feet and punched me again, this time a lot harder. I heard my nose break. It was bad, really horrible, hearing it and then the pain, so sharp. It made my eyes water so I couldn't see much and that made me even more scared."

"Would you like a glass of water?" the officer asked.

Storm took a deep breath and shook her head. "I thought maybe he was on drugs. He was acting so crazy. I didn't even know who he was at first. He said something about how he wasn't going to report to me anymore. That from now on, I was going to report to him. That's when I recognized him. That's when I realized he was the person I'd bought seeds from." Storm squeezed Tom's hand and turned to look at him.

"I must have known, at least subconsciously. So when he came here that time, I knew I had to get you and the kids away. Once we were away and nothing happened, I guess I convinced myself I was making a big deal out of nothing. I told myself I must have bought the seeds from a coworker.

It happens all the time. You buy wrapping paper or whatever to support your coworker's kids."

She addressed Tom but had to explain the story about the seeds to the detective. As she told him, Storm felt as if she were standing at a distance from herself, watching herself carefully craft the lies, smooth over the inconsistencies.

"It sounds like Mr. Kline had been interested in you for some time. He set up a way that allowed him to show up at your house and make it plausible."

"Except he shouldn't have had my address. That's part of the reason I talked myself into believing I bought the seeds from a coworker. A client wouldn't have access to my personal information. We aren't listed in any directory."

"Yet he did manage to find you."

"Yes," Storm answered, rubbing her hands across her eyes. He knew a lot about me—where I lived, who my friends were."

"Nicky?" Tom asked.

Storm nodded, looked at the detective, and said, "I asked where Nicky was, but he wouldn't tell me. He said I had a nice family, sweet kids, but I had picked the wrong man."

Storm let her exhaustion show, slumping in her seat. She looked up, her lower lip trembling. "He told me he'd met my husband, my kids. Told me he'd be a much better dad. He took off in my car. I knew where he was going and I ran. I ran through the parking lot, down Cornell and all the way to Evergreen. I was running in the middle of the street when that woman stopped to help me and I . . . I."

Storm wasn't acting as hot tears slid down her

imperfectly washed cheeks. Rust-red blood stains mottled her skin, and the area at the corner of her eyes was beginning to darken to a twilight blue. She looked every bit as bad as she felt.

"Did you have any issues with this man previous to this?" the detective asked.

Storm took a deep, quavering breath. "No. Nothing. He was an almost-perfect client. Got his sanctions out of the way, paid all his fines. I never would have suspected him. I mean, I did feel something was weird lately. I didn't know who, or why, but I had this feeling someone was following me. I even told Big Ed . . . I mean Ed Lofton, my boss."

"I know Big Ed," said the detective.

"Good, then you can ask him. He'll tell you."

"Excuse me," the detective said. The officer at the door was gesturing to him. He got up and left the room.

Storm turned to Tom and whispered, "I'm so glad you're all right, that the kids are all right."

"Are we?" Tom asked.

The detective re-entered the room and sat back down. He had a small plastic bag in his hands. He held it up and asked. "Do you recognize this?"

"Sure," said Storm. That's me and the kids. It's a picture of us at the fair. It used to sit on my desk until it disappeared . . . oh," she said, as if the wind had been knocked out of her. "Do you think he stole it? It went missing weeks, maybe even months ago. Tom's missing and the kids. He cut them out of the picture."

She stared up at the officer, horror and shock making her eyes widen, her fingers tremble as she touched the edge of the plastic bag.

Storm had used scissors from her desk at work to cut Tom and the children from the picture. She had placed those pieces in the office shredder knowing they'd be safely hauled away and destroyed and no one would ever see them.

She had intended to plant the photo on Howard. Slip it into the pocket of his jacket or tuck it into his car. Then she'd call the police. Tell them about her stalker and about her concern that one of her clients had stolen the picture. She'd give them a short list of suspects and, with luck, they'd find the picture.

The idea had come to her the day Howard admired the photo in her office. It was supposed to be another small insurance policy in case he got too far out of line. She never thought she'd be planting it on his dead body.

"I suspect the guy was obsessed with you, was stalking you," the detective said.

"I knew it. I knew someone was following me. I told my boss. You'll ask Big Ed, right? He'll back me up."

"I doubt it," he said. Then he explained: "We have no reason to pursue this further. We aren't questioning what you did, and you don't have to explain or defend yourself. You aren't in trouble here. At least, not as far as our office is concerned.

"Of course. there is the matter of you taking that car. I don't know if the owner will press charges. We sent someone to take her to the lot where her car's been towed. They'll explain the situation. My guess? I don't think she'll pursue it either."

Storm managed a small smile of gratitude. She hadn't expected such kindness and still wasn't sure she trusted it.

He must have read her thoughts.

"Look, there will probably be a small investigation. There was a shooting, but it won't be you we're looking at. This guy broke into your home, held your family hostage. You did what you had to do.

"Now, we need to let you go, and you need to see a doctor. You want us to call an ambulance?"

"No ambulance," she said. I'll go to my own doctor and I'll go under my own power."

The officer nodded. He didn't say it, but Storm sensed his approval. It went a long way in stilling her sense of panic.

After getting his permission to wash the blood off her face and put on a clean blouse, she walked down the familiar hallway to the bathroom. It looked the same, but everything felt strange, a little off, as if she'd stepped into a parallel dimension where everything was just a few inches to the left.

In the bathroom, she stared at her darkening bruises and the dried blood on her face and realized just how scary she must have seemed to the kids. The darkening bruises were worse, and pain crackled across her nerve endings. She dabbed away most of the blood.

Her nose was so swollen and misshapen, it didn't look like hers. But the doctor could wait a bit longer. She grabbed a bottle of ibuprofen from the medicine cabinet and gently slid four onto her tongue, filled her cupped palms with water from the tap, and swallowed them gratefully.

They found Alex and Joel playing with a set of dominos, moving them around the living room carpet as if they were cars on a race track. Joel seemed unfazed by it all. Storm envied his ignorance of the danger they'd been in and was hopeful there'd be no lasting affect on him.

Lindsey, who had cried for a while clinging to her father and refusing to look at her mother before finally allowing Grace to lead her away, could be a different story. If she hadn't hated Howard before, Storm would have hated him now.

Lindsey was in the kitchen with Grace.

"The child is a natural baker," Grace informed them. "She helps me by decorating the räderkuchen. Look, we have enough to send with you." Grace held up a plate of oddly shaped donuts that had been dusted with cinnamon and powdered sugar.

"I put the sugar on," said Lindsey.

"And just the right amount, too." Grace patted Lindsey's shoulder, and she beamed at the woman.

"I think Lindsey's adopted you," said Tom. "Can I call you Granny?"

"Lindsey can call me Granny. You, not so much." Grace wagged her finger at Tom but couldn't hide her smile. "This has been a bad time for you, but it is over, you are safe. Your whole family is safe. Lindsey understands this. We have talked. Right?" Grace asked Lindsey.

Lindsey nodded solemnly.

"Good, so now I will wrap some of these for you while you gather your things, and by things, I also mean your brother."

Lindsey smiled broadly and skipped out of the kitchen.

"Guess I'll go help," offered Tom.

"Yes, and help that old man of mine off the floor, too."

Tom promised and left the room.

As soon as they were alone, Storm turned to Grace. "A very bad man," she whispered.

"We do what we must," said Grace.

* * *

They buckled the kids in Tom's car and then stood next to each other at the driver-side door, reluctant to part.

The sun had risen fully. Birds sang in the trees. The family of robins that came back each year hopped around the lawn searching for worms.

If not for the police cars lined along the road and the occasional squawk of a radio, it would have seemed like any other day.

"I'm going to take the kids to the same hotel as last time," said Tom. "We'll order breakfast from room service. I'd leave them with someone and go with you to the doctors, but—"

"You don't need to tell me. Take them. Get them out of here. I'll be there soon."

"Good. I have some questions."

Fear rose in Storm, a rolling cloud as black as doom. "Questions?" she asked.

Tom nodded. "Can you stand to live here after this? Will the kids need to see someone?"

Her eyes must have reflected her fear. She thought he was going to call her out about all the late nights, the lies.

"Don't think about it now. We'll work it out later." Tom reached, as if to caress her cheek and stopped himself. "I don't think I can touch you without hurting you,"

Storm smiled, even though that did hurt. "Stand still."

She kissed him gently, softly.

"Call me when you get to the doctors. I want to know what he has to say," Tom asked.

"He'll say I have a broken node."

"Nose," said Lindsey, who'd been listening through the open back window. Storm's smile grew even larger. She winced.

She waved as Tom and the kids pulled away and walked to her car. She pressed down on the trunk and heard the latch catch.

As she climbed into the driver's seat, Storm wished she could just sit and think. There was a lot to think about, so many secrets and lies, stories that had to remain consistent, but not too consistent.

As much as she wanted it all to be over, she knew it was too soon to relax. Despite what the detective said, she was sure there would be those who would want to know more about what had happened.

One thing was certain. She was done with delivering justice. There was too much danger in being judge, jury, and executioner. Her family had to come first.

She opened her purse and dug out her keys. In addition to keys to her car, home, and office, there was a card-sized, white, plastic mag key attached. It was the mag key that granted her access to Traynor Chemical and the kill room.

Her key ring was threaded through a hole at the top of the mag key. Using her thumb nail, she spread the ring, and bit by bit, slid the mag key free.

She started the car, backed out past the two remaining police cars parked on the street, and drove in the direction of her doctor's office.

* * *

The sun shone hard and bright. Not a cloud in the sky. Her headache was still there, but in the background. Her nose throbbed, but the pain was more dull than sharp. Everything was going to be all right.

Storm clutched the mag key in her right hand. She had decided when she reached the bridge over Beaverton Creek, she'd slow down long enough to fling it into the water. Then she'd drive off, leaving the key behind her, along with all the horror and death. There had been so much death.

Jeffrey Franklin Malino, who used dogs to discipline his children; Gavin Lester Everett, who used cigarettes on his son; Helena Smith, who left her child on a sodden mattress beneath a car; Angela Ruiz, who hurt her children by dating bad men.

To the list, she now added Howard Kline, who had killed an innocent prostitute and her best friend, Nicky. He had also gone after her husband and her children.

Just as she reached the bridge over Beaverton Creek, Storm was gripped by the thought of the children, of all the children, even the one that she had been—a long time ago.

She reached for her purse on the passenger seat, slid open the zipper, and dropped the mag key inside.

ABOUT THE AUTHOR

Pam Cowan writes mystery and suspense thrillers. Her short fiction has been published in magazines and anthologies, and read on radio. Cowan has worked as an audio producer, a magazine editor, and in the probation and parole side of criminal justice.

She lives with her husband and a number of four-legged roommates in Oregon, where she is currently working on her fourth novel, *Cold Kill*, the second mystery/thriller in the Eulalona County series.

Please visit the author's website: pamelacowan.com

Also by P.J. Cowan - A Mystery/Thriller

SOMETHING IN THE DARK

"A tense, convincing and powerful psychological thriller." ~Beshon, UK Reviewer

"Psychological thrill seekers should find this novel one big roller-coaster of unexpected twists, turns, and loops." ~Hodge Podge, Amazon Reviewer

"Well written and crafted with enough scare factor to keep the pages turning . . ." ~Karen Doering, Little Black Book of Parenting

"Fantastic story. Full of suspense. Kept me guessing whodunit clear to the end – and I was wrong. ~Jamie McCracken, Charlie McCready Series, Secrets

"Something in the Dark will quickly pull you in and keep you guessing. Plenty of twists and turns to keep the reader entertained. ~Jackson Cooper, Amazon Reviewer

"P.J. Cowan's mystery-suspense grabbed me from the start! It was an up and down roller-coaster ride that alternately had me chuckling and guessing whodunit all the way through the many twists and turns. The writer has an easy to read style and a blunt honesty.." ~Anna Brentwood, The Songbird with Sapphire Eyes

"This one will keep you guessing—and you'll probably be wrong! ~Mike Chinakos, Dead Town, Hollywood Cowboys.

READ EXCERPT
SOMETHING IN THE DARK

And God saw the light, that it was good,
and God divided the light from the darkness.
Genesis 1:4

PROLOGUE
Building No. 246, US Army Family Housing,
Pattonville, West Germany

"I don't want to play," Austin said.

"Sure you do," her brother, Muncie, insisted. "Come on. All you have to do is sit inside, right here in this spot," he patted the ground inside the doorway, obliterating the tic-tac-toe game she'd drawn in the dirt earlier. "We'll shut the door and the lights will come on. You just have to look around and see what's in there. After we count to ten, we'll open the door and let you out and you'll tell us what you saw."

"You promise you'll open it right back up?" she asked.

"We promise," said Muncie and his friend Brian, both solemnly crossing the area above their hearts.

"And you promise you'll play hopscotch?" she asked doubtfully.

"We promise," said the boys.

"Well, okay," she agreed reluctantly, glaring at them to let them know they'd better.

She let them half-lift, half-push her through the doorway. The dirt floor was soft and powdery. It made her sneeze.

While the boys went back to work unwinding the wire that held the door open, Austin began clearing away the bits of rubbish around her, tossing empty soda bottles and crumpled bits of newspaper deeper into the impenetrable maw of the hole in the wall.

The place was really creepy and dirty. Maybe she should tell them she'd changed her mind and that they didn't have to bother untwisting the rest of the wire.

It was too late. The weight of the huge, metal door finished the job for them. The strands sprang apart with a hissing sound, one sharp end slicing Brian's cheek. The door slammed shut with a sound like thunder that echoed down the long hallway.

Austin gasped, shocked by the noise and the sudden darkness. Immediately she began to count. "One, two, three." She couldn't hear anything.

Were they there? "Four, five, six." She didn't hear them moving, or counting, or anything. "Seven, eight, nine, ten." Well, maybe she was counting too fast. She counted again—then again.

She started to get angry. Creeps. Boys were creeps. They liked to push you down, and break your things, and tell lies about you. She wouldn't ever play with them again. They probably weren't even really going to play hopscotch. They only said that so she'd sit in this dark, dirty hole. There weren't any lights. There wasn't any secret room. It was all a big fat lie. If they lied about that–maybe they lied about letting her out too.

She blinked her eyes. Were her eyes open? She thought they were, but it was so dark they must be closed. Putting her hands to her face she felt her eyelids quiver.

Open or closed the dark was just the same. She felt the dampness at the corners of her eyes. They were tears, but she wasn't ready to cry, at least not just yet. She was a big girl, after all. She counted again.

"One, two." What if they didn't come back? Her mom would be mad. Her dad would be mad too. They would ask her brother where she was. But what if her brother was afraid to say? What if he thought he'd get in trouble if he told them she was in the hole-in-the-wall? What if he never told anybody?

She cried a little bit. It made her feel better. Then a new thought struck.

Maybe her mom and dad would think she was strangulated, like that girl on the television that she heard her daddy say got kidnapped, and strangulated, and dead. That girl was six years old. Horrible things happened to children nowadays. That's what her mom and dad said. Horrible things like getting put in holes.

Crouched, shivering in the dark, she knocked on the heavy, iron door until her knuckles ached and she had to stop. At least the pain was a distraction, a reassurance that there was something other than darkness, even if she was too young to put those feelings into words.

After a while, not knowing what else to do, she knocked on the door again, first rapping with her knuckles, then with her balled fists, and finally, with the palms of her hands. Smack, smack went her hands. Just like patty cake. Slap, slap, slap.

She pressed her face against the door. It was icy cold against her flushed, tear-streaked face. "Mommy. Mommy," she called. "I'm in here. I'm right in here."

No one heard. Minutes, that seemed like hours later, her throat was sore, her voice a raw rasping whisper. She was exhausted–with a deep, ragged breath she sank to the floor. She pressed herself against the door, as close to outside as she could get. Without thought her thumb slipped into her mouth, a habit she had outgrown by the time she was three. She closed her eyes and did the only thing left; she waited.

After awhile, once her heart had slowed and her sobs had subsided to an occasional hiccup, she began to hear— something. It was a very small noise. She only seemed able to catch it in between breaths. She held her breath to see if she could hear it. Yes, there it was. It sounded like—like someone breathing.

Her eyes flew wide with alarm. She took a long but shallow breath and held it. She heard it again. Someone was breathing. Someone–or something–was in here with her. Maybe it had always been here, hiding in the shadows where the light couldn't reach. Maybe it was a man, the man who made that girl dead. Maybe it was a big rat. Her brother had a fake, rubber rat. It was creepy, with its long naked, whippy tail and its fat pointy teeth. He was always throwing it on her lap so she would jump up and yell.

"Rats will eat your face off," he had told her. "Bite off your nose and eat your eyeballs."

She put her hands over her face. From her small strained throat came tiny, broken whimpers.

"No they won't", her mom had told her. "Your brother

is teasing you." But moms lied. Moms told you shots didn't hurt, and if you're nice to him your brother won't pick on you, and your dad will be home in time to tell you a bedtime story. Still, she would give anything if her mom would come soon.

But her mom didn't.

16336614R00180

Made in the USA
San Bernardino, CA
29 October 2014